The Art of Loving Libby Green

The Art of Loving Libby Green

BELLEBIRD JAMES

FOR THE ONES WHO ARE AFRAID
TO CHASE THEIR DREAMS — YOU GOT THIS.
AND FOR MAT,
WHO NEVER LET ME FORGET MINE.

One

A security guard leans against the open door of the corner shop. Resting my bike against the lamp post, the light flickers above; the bulb's about to blow. Still visible in the shop window are the photos of me and Dad beneath the words:

THE FOLLOWING PEOPLE ARE BANNED FROM ENTERING.

"You grab, I'll watch," I whisper to Dad.

He stops and lights a ciggie. His hands shake – the first sign his tank is on E. It's more than Dad's freaking turn.

"For shit's sake, boy, already told ya. You grab, I'll watch."

He's never been one to take turns. It's the same cussing from Dad, *every time.*

"I'm sick of hauling shit for you." My voice rises, along with my insides. I'm like a chameleon changing colour – red, right now, because this dude is pissing me off. I'd give him grief about what a lazy arse he is, but the security guard looks right at us.

"You're better at it," Dad whispers.

"Because I'm always doing it."

Dad pulls a roll-your-own packet from his back pocket and evenly distributes weed leaves amongst the tobacco. He's ignoring me on purpose; doesn't show any emotion. It's his tactic. He knows I hate not being onto it and having a plan before we haul.

Dad looks at me, smiles at the guard, and back to me. Loitering amps up your nerves, makes you panic and more likely to mess up. Even with a tight plan – Dad always changes it at critical moments, and we get caught.

"I don't even drink. You want booze, you freaking do it."

Dad leans close. "Come on, boy." And I know what he's gonna say.

"Don't you even –" His cheesy-arse grin; that alone pisses me off. And then he says it.

"Like the good people at Nike say, just do it."

He rolls off the words like he's relaxed, unfazed. I grit my teeth. What he means is, he wants someone else to do it.

"Stellar fatherly advice." And I push him towards the shop. I'm raging-hot-lava red. "I told you, I'm not hauling shit for you anymore, apart from food."

Smoke billows from Dad's mouth as he leans in close, his breath reeks of weed. The guard watches. We look tragic and obvious, because we are.

"Obvious, much."

"We need food ... aaand dog food."

He's right, and a cunning son of a bitch. That line gets me every time. He's useless as shit at hauling, never gets what we need, only booze. And it's like he read my stomach. My tummy growls. He's a skilled manipulator, and it's seriously the only thing he excels at – oh, and being the world's worst dad. I picture Bear, back at the flat, nudging her empty bowl into the kitchen wall, looking around for me – someone to give a shit she's hungry and alone.

"For fuck's sake," I mutter.

Dad holds his cigarette in his lips; his hands shake as he leans into the flame. The guard glares at us as our faces light up. Dad leans against the lamp post, the bulb above broken and buzzing. "And while ya there, get me a bottle, whatever's easy."

The Mitsi's parked right there, door open.

I'd yell in his face, stamp my freaking foot like a five-year-old, if my stomach wasn't irate with hunger. Bear's must be too.

Isn't he the one that's supposed to make the sensible decisions?

As we cross the road, police sirens wail – background music in these parts.

I edge towards the shop. *Be cool. Don't act dodgy and things will be sweet.* My plans have turned to shit already, and my nerves are flustered. My stomach groans – it's enough to straighten my focus, like a spoon banging an empty tin.

The shop door buzzer announces my arrival.

"Evening," the guard says.

"Hey." I don't make eye contact; my focus flicks around the shop for the location of dog food. They don't keep booze at the front anymore, too convenient for those *grab and run* situations.

The guy at the counter watches my every move as I beeline for the back of the shop, passing fake cheese and pita bread, a bag of cat biscuits in a box labelled *Expired Stock*; I make a mental note of their location. The dog food is too far away, the bag too big to carry. Cat food will do – Bear loves it anyway. This is what bad planning does; your nerves are wrecked, you overthink. You gotta get in and out – second-guess one decision, and hesitation will get you caught. I've got three seconds to grab like I have all the intention to pay, and one second to run.

Along the back wall I spot the biggest bottle of whiskey, the only one in a plastic bottle, but before I grab, I check behind for the safest exit route.

As long as the security guard is outside and Dad has the car started, my door open, ready and waiting, we are all good. I grab one large bottle of spirits, turn around, sprint out of the shop, and randomly grab packets on my way past from the expired box.

"Come back! Get him!"

I burst out of the shop. My insides twist, my heart hammers, like it's trying to escape through my ears.

The Mitsi's not there. Dad's not there. He's bailed – of course he has. He's a selfish a-hole. At least he left my bike parked where the Mitsi was.

The security guard's huffing right behind. I bolt across the main road to where Dad should be waiting by my bike. The least Dad could do is not suck at being watcher, just once! My throat tightens; it's hard to breathe properly, the guard is a few metres away.

The stuff won't all fit in my bag. The spray cans from last night's haul are carefully stacked inside, in every colour I've ever wanted. I push everything in and try to force the zip as the guard crosses the road. I throw the booze; it rolls along the pavement. The guard reaches out for my bag, but the zip is now shut; I swing my leg over my bike and pedal like crazy, fuming too much to care who's yelling behind me. I don't even drink, yet I'm the idiot hauling it, risking my arse. Knowing Dad, he got a better offer.

Cutting the lights through Main Street, a truck beeps its horn and its brakes screech as it comes to an abrupt stop.

Mum would be gutted – me and Dad are vandals and thieves with little to no prospects. Mostly, she'd be disappointed I've not kept my promise to look after Dad, make him better. I've failed; he's messed up as hell. The trajectory of my life is towards a prison cell with the world's most annoying cellmate.

I jump the bike up the footpath and enter the alleyway that cuts through the city. I pedal towards the light at the end, hop off my bike. The Red

Gallery Café behind me overlooks the end of the alley and the main road that separates it from Central Garden Square.

Using the torch on my phone, I hold the light up against the wall, which is painted a patchwork of different shades of white, covering the street art that was there yesterday.

Message from Dad: *Bring the booze to the flat, get the baggy from Marv's on ya way – tell em I'll pay him later. Scored us a keg.*

I don't reply. There's no sorry, no lame reason why he ditched me when I needed him.

I open my bag and admire the colours of the spray-can lids. The entire rainbow and a few extras: metallics, gold, silver and bronze. Rare finds worth the cuts on my hands from the glass window I had to climb through to steal them.

If my mood were a colour, it would be the black at the bottom of a deep, cavernous hole. I pull out the black spray, admire the rainbow, like a secret, forbidden treasure – something to be savoured for the perfect art piece worthy of the best spray a person can steal. I've painted in black for so long I can't remember being in the mood to colour. Knowing they're there is a secret power, waiting for a mood that screams for technicolour.

It's Sunday night, about to be Monday morning. I've got school in a few hours, and time to kill. The alley is both safety – it's black, quiet, and a refuge for vandals and thieves – and terrifying, for the same reasons.

I set my phone on the ground to light the wall. The fumes of freshly laid white paint remind me of helping Mum paint the walls in her art studio. The same white that covered the ugly brown walls of the shitty garage she called her happy space.

Using the entire height of the wall, I spray the outline of Mayor Tim Hope's face. Slender nose, sunken eyes, fake smile – the perfect villain features. There's nothing hopeful about him, considering his quote in the local news: *Homelessness is a choice.* It was one of his campaign slogans for cleaning up the city.

I go over all his features, blackening and darkening. The smell of fresh spray fills the air. The *pssst* of the can would usually evoke calmness, but not today. Underneath, I spray *AN INHUMAN MASTER.*

A police siren and a rush of voices, echoing in the night. Torchlight flickers at the end of the alley; I zip my bag, pick up my bike and lift it over the wall and into the back of the Red Gallery Café. The security light flicks on, and as I wait, frozen on the other side, footsteps – two, maybe three people – run past. For someone who spends an incredible amount of time in the night, on the streets alone, it never gets less scary. You can't trust anyone.

Looking up at the back of the gallery, I realise I've trapped myself. One more move and the security lights on the other side of the building will flick on; that's enough to set off warning beeps in some security systems. The windows in the flat above are still black. In that apartment is Libby Green's bedroom. She's Beachlands High's head girl, queen of the anti-bullying and environment council; she's *that* kind of annoying, moralistic overachiever. She's also slightly distracting – I'm not blind. If she were a colour, she'd be turquoise. Perfect on its own, but garish when combined with the wrong yellow. Colour has a way of hiding what's underneath.

My mind drifts. And without thinking, I lean against the wall, and the other security light flicks on, illuminating the back wall of the café ... and me. And the sign *GRAFFITI IS A CRIME.*

I can't ignore it. It's legit screaming at me for help. I can for real hear its cries.

A white sign with thick black letters, right where people would park their cars, for all to see. My hands sweat; I should leave it. The Red Gallery Café is the second-best place in town to see art that doesn't suck. But I swear the sign is crying at me, *save me*, practically grabbing me, pushing me towards it, to help it unleash the truth. You wouldn't see this kinda sign at SOFA, the School of Fine Arts. This is the best place in town to see art that will blow your mind.

My phone vibrates in my pocket. Message from Dad: *Where are you? Got the stuff?*

Just seeing his name in my inbox ignites a twisted, burning pain in my neck. I don't answer, my passive-aggressive way of saying, *stuff you*. It's pointless, anyway; he's immune to the meaning of subtle hints that I'm pissed at him, or he's nailed the art of not giving a crap about anyone other than himself. I drop my bag in front of the *GRAFFITI IS A CRIME* sign.

I wait a few seconds; the windows in Libby's apartment remain dark. Then, in black, I spray an X through *A CRIME* and write *ART*.

GRAFFITI IS ART

And now I can breathe, and order is restored. For this sign, at least. My heart wants to write *Art is the only thing that makes sense*.

I know Mum would agree. She painted a canvas with that line, thick black letters; we spent hours detailing the flowers that filled the hollow of each letter. Now she's gone; it's just the hollow that remains.

I spray *Xavier* in the corner – not my real name, my street name. Lucky for me, no one knows that Dylan Marshall, who is practically invisible at Beachlands High, is the wanted vandal spraying controversial portraits around town.

Under *GRAFFITI IS ART*, I outline in black a dude: floppy hair that needs a cut, hoody, too-baggy skinny jeans, Chucks, and his arm raised spraying the sign *GRAFFITI IS ART*.

I drop the empty can in the bin by the back door. There's a noticeboard with two posters: one says *Art Lessons This Way*, with an arrow pointing into the café; the other one is advertising the School of Fine Arts scholarship competition. As I take a closer look, a light flicks on in the apartment above.

7

I pull my hoody down, slip my bag on, lift my bike back over the fence into the alley, and ride into Central Garden Square. As I look through the trees into Libby's room, a silhouette strides past her window, and the lower floor of the café is now lit.

A police car drives past slowly. My cue to leave.

I ride through town to the train station and follow the tracks parallel with the coastline out of town. I speed past the paths down to the beach, and the peeps that rough-sleep there; they're outcasts, even by the city's homeless standards, too dangerous, too notorious, banned from the city. They sleep in makeshift tents in the dunes. They're opportunists – I get it, it's survival, it's how it is out these parts. This time of night, they'll take everything you've got and leave you bloodied and broken if you don't do what they say. Or, in Dad's case, if you rip them off, they'll beat you to within an inch of your life.

I know this for sure because I'm the one who breaks into a pharmacy to get painkillers. On the streets, Dad would be dead if I wasn't around to look after his impossible, useless self. I promised Mum. I might be a vandal, thief, and low-life degenerate with little to no life prospects and a future of who the fuck knows, but I am one to keep a promise.

The first-of-the-morning commuter trains barrel past, transporting people with jobs into town. As the track heads inland, the light of the city fades, and I leave the beach behind. Not much later, I reach the ten-foot concrete wall, the council's answer to improving the view for the train occupants, tagged apartments on the other side.

I jump my bike up a stack of rusted train tracks, onto a ramp made by yours truly from pulled-apart pallets, and drop my bike over the fence into my backyard. Technically not mine – shared with the others that live in the apartment block. At the back door, Bear whimpers and scratches from the other side of the glass. I tug on the door, but it doesn't budge. I head around the front, a line of faded brown doors, and stuck to the front of ours is a notice, black letters: *EVICTED*. I pull the message from the door and scrunch it tight. The paint on my fingers cracks. I swallow hard, breathe deep. It's not the first notice. It won't be the last. My palms sweat; I pull my arm back and smash my fist through the plasterboard covering the last hole in the door. Pain radiates through my already cut fingers and up my arm into my shoulder. The pain distributes the pent-up fury over the dickhead that can't be bothered to pay rent.

We alternate between sleeping on the street and this – not on the street, but close. And even though none of this is a surprise, every time it happens, Dad gets more feral and harder to tame, and hiding it from people at school is an ever-present worry. School counsellors have a way of interfering, thinking they're helping but making things worse. Without me, Dad would last a week on his own, tops, before he was dead in a ditch. And that's why my night-time street-art gig has to remain a secret. If I'm caught, the peeps at social services will interfere, and Dad will be left alone. Now I'm eighteen, anything on a police record will stop any chance of doing something with my life, if being practically homeless wasn't enough. No one can know I'm Xavier, and no one at school can find out I'm homeless.

I open the front door, and the reek of stale booze slams into me. I'm ready to yell it out with Dad, but he lays motionless on the couch, and the rage is immediately replaced with worry he's dead. His head is slumped back, his feet rest on a keg. Dodging empty booze bottles on the floor, I lean my ear into his chest. He snorts a breath in; he's alive. Sometimes it's hard to tell, and then I call an ambulance, but most of the time he's fine, alive, existing. That's my life; we live to exist, to survive. To hope for anything more would be extravagant and wishful thinking.

I pull the eviction notice from my pocket and chuck it hard at his shoulder. The ball hits his chest and falls onto his lap, does nothing to wake him. Out cold like a stone.

I rest my bag on the kitchen bench and take out the packet of fake cheese, the pita bread and salami, and drop them on Dad's lap. He lurches forward, opening his eyes, looks down at dinner or breakfast; it can be whatever he wants it to be.

"Eat."

Dad picks up each item and inspects it. "Where's my beer?"

"Back where you didn't meet me. Couldn't carry it home, bags full."

He groans and sinks further into the couch, like he's the kid.

Isn't he supposed to be telling me my moral compass is pointed in the wrong direction? And the rage returns – hidden, of course – I push it down, think of the rainbow in my backpack. Having it out with him is pointless. I've never known Dad to be anything other than a useless alcoholic. No amount of anything has helped or will help him change. Doesn't stop me from trying occasionally, only to end up wishing I'd never wasted my time. Like the drug and alcohol counselling, which he never shows up to. Even the threats of me being taken away by social services haven't changed a stupid thing about him. His comment, "You're eighteen soon, boy," was his way of dealing with it.

I suppose it's better than last time I raged at him about drinking and his general sucking-at-parenting-ness; his solution was to disappear on a ten-day bender. I had no idea where he was.

He rips the packets open, tears off a hunk of bread, and stuffs it with salami and cheese. He continues, consuming every last bite of food. My stomach grumbles. But I don't complain. It's good he's eating, a change from his usual liquid diet.

Bear weaves between my legs. I tear the top off a tin of Fancy Feast cat food and tip it into her bowl. She jumps and licks my face, her moustache tickling my cheek. "We'll hang later, okay, girl?" I ruffle the fur on her head as she gets stuck into her food.

In my room, I drag my mattress from under Dad's bed and unroll my sleeping bag. I lay there listening to the commuter trains, one passing every few minutes, unsure why I'm trying to sleep; school starts in two hours. I can't handle another all-nighter, can't handle falling into a deep sleep either, the hallucinations about the old house, with Mum, the old life. Which was still shit, but hands down infinitely better because Mum wasn't dead.

I'm not sure if this will be the last night we sleep here, or where me and Dad will end up ... we never know. That's how it is with the surviving-to-exist thing – expect the unexpected. The only constant is the hustle to stay alive, and sucking it up no matter how hard you wish it was different. Unless you've got a pot of magic beans, there's no way out. If there was, me and Dad wouldn't be here. We'd have a permanent roof, eat at the table, with food from all food groups, and I would have a plan for the future. I'd know how to become somebody. For now, it's survival, each day having to figure out where we're going to sleep safe for that night.

Bear curls up on the pillow next to my face, her breath cat-food flavour. Stealing to feed her, to feed us – what choice do I have? There is no escape and only one option – survive or die.

Two

The school bell rings as I jam my tyre into the bike rack under the droopy oak tree. I prefer to arrive on or just after the bell to avoid unnecessary waiting in gossipy corridors. The school bus stops out front, and streams of uniforms walk the steps into the grey brick administration building. With our uniforms all the same, unless someone looks close enough, I blend in.

Holes dot the undersides of my shoes. Luckily, this is my last year of school, because next year my shorts will be well above my knees, my shirt a crop top. In this school, anything sideways of average and you're the weird kid.

I wait by the bike racks for the stream of people to go. I've done well to blend in at this place; I'm a nothing. Not the loser who is picked on. No one knows my name or where I come from, and it has to stay that way.

I walk the steps into the admin block and head down the hall towards form meeting. Up ahead, Miss Reed's door swings open. Bad timing. I speed up. She got me the scholarship into this place, and I owe her, but I can't deal with her today. She asks too many questions, and it's hard to maintain lies about Dad's job status, our address, topics that always come up. I've been lying for so long, it's a complicated, tangled web of deceit, and it's only a matter of time before she discovers I'm full of it.

"Dylan," she shouts from up the hall. "We need to catch up."

Any other teacher, and I'd pretend not to hear. It's a legit excuse; lockers slam, a group of juniors shout to friends at the opposite end of the corridor. I don't want to talk to her, especially after another eviction letter. Lying takes energy, and with less than two hours of sleep and nothing to eat, I only have enough energy to muster for art. Art is the only reason I want to be here; the other subjects' grades allow me to be in Mr Campbell's honours art programme.

Miss Reed taps me on the shoulder and repeats, "We need to catch up."

She has black hair today. She wears blue skinny jeans and a black biker jacket, which is misleading because she rides the teeniest, banana-yellow nifty fifty. She and Mr Campbell sometimes ride to school on it together. I don't know how they are together. As far as school counsellors go, she's the least irritating I've come across. He's a talented artist, blah in personality.

"You're not getting out of meeting up, my friend." She crosses her arms, pretends to be annoyed. She's not; she does think she's funny, though.

I smile, hold the shoulder straps of my bag, and hope she doesn't ask questions that require going through my bag, as there's nothing but my art book, spray cans and a pen in there. Then I remember I was supposed to meet with her yesterday afternoon to talk about university scholarships, or the lack of, for next year. I loosen the grip around my shoulder straps, relieved she's not going to interrogate me about Dad and his work.

It's Saturday tomorrow. A sly grin escapes, but just for a moment. "We could meet tomorrow?"

Miss Reed laughs as she looks down the hall. "I'm not that silly. I'll check my diary and send you a message. But it's important; we *will* catch up."

Her attention diverts as a red-faced junior meanders our way, wiping her eyes with a wad of toilet paper.

I take my chance to leave as Miss Reed rushes over to the girl.

The downside to not meeting with Miss Reed is no free muffins or a loan of her sweet art books, which probably come from Mr Campbell's art supply shop in town.

The second bell rings and I edge towards art. Down the corridor, people disappear into their classes. Up ahead, I spot Libby. She removes a biology book from her locker and drops it in her bag. My stomach rolls like when I steal something and know a shop person has watched my every move. I avoid making eye contact; any conversation will give her an opportunity to ask if I know anything about the art on the back of her café, or worse, she'll tell me she saw me do it.

The hallway crowd thins till I'm directly behind her. I'm shoved from behind as Luka pushes past and swings his arm around Libby's shoulders.

They're as corny as their names sound when they're said together: Luka and Libby. He's deputy head boy, a bruised ego no doubt, outshone by his head-girl girlfriend. They're predictably boring, predictably beautiful.

He's the only guy who wears his school shirt fitted and, to be fair, he's got visible muscles. If he was green and twisted at the waist, he'd be an acceptable Hulk.

Libby holds the art-room door open. Her strawberry-blonde hair is wound into a bun held together by a coloured pencil jammed through the middle. Ignoring her, I walk into class, and my insides sink as I feel her watching me take my seat in the back corner by the window. I pretend to look through my bag and avoid eye contact as she sits down next to Luka in the front row.

Mr Campbell stands at the front of the class as the last members drip in.

14

"Learn the art of punctuality, would you!" He turns and writes on the whiteboard, the last teacher on the planet not to use the smartboard. Tan lines peek from under the short sleeves of his blue shirt dotted with waves. He picks up a stack of posters from his desk and dumps the pile in front of Libby. "Hand these out."

Libby says nothing and begins handing out posters, starting with the front row.

I'm not a fan of Mr Campbell's condescending tone, or that he thought I faked my art grades to get into his class. According to him, an A in art at my old school was equivalent to his C. If it hadn't been for Miss Reed, I don't reckon he would have accepted me in.

Libby begins the next row, handing each person a poster, the coloured pencil in her hair etched with the word *Artistry*. The girl knows her top-end art brands.

Libby looks at me. I divert my attention to Mr Campbell, who's writing *scholarships and assessments* on the whiteboard, his jet-black hair making the stray white strands pop.

"Hey." Libby stands in front of me and holds out a poster, the same one I saw last night pinned to the back door of her parents' shop. The words *SOFA Scholarship Competition* bombed in technicolour, each letter resting on top of a black building, each recognisable from Beachlands city.

"Sweet, thanks." I take the poster, pretend to read the terms and conditions on the back. My heart is popping like candy.

Libby pulls a folded piece of paper from her pocket – a note – and slides it in front of me.

"Also, for you." I look up, and for a split second we make eye contact, long enough for me to see her eyes are green, and she has dimples when she smiles ... before I remember that eye contact is not a good idea, and I divert my attention out the window.

Libby moves to the next row.

On the top of the note, *Dylan* is written in curly handwriting. I didn't think she knew my name. I slip the letter into my pocket, imagining what could be written or drawn on it, the possibilities etching into my leg like a tattoo – comic-book styles, her saying, *I know it was you* and a picture of me being carted away by police, while Dad rots alone somewhere. Maybe I'm dramatic? What is it she couldn't say to my face?

Libby has one person to go when Katie bursts through the art-room door, to be met with a sigh from Mr Campbell and the same *Learn the art of punctuality* speech. Katie carries a guitar case and takes Libby's seat at the front, next to Luka.

"Sorry, my music exam went over." Katie's the odd mix of perfect adherence to the uniform regulations mixed with black boots and black fingernails.

Libby glances around and slides into the only available seat – right next to me. Like she had any other choice. I inhale a whiff of her perfume ... vanilla, or something else sweet, toxic, but in a good way.

"Katie stole my seat," she whispers.

I glance at her. "It's cool." I rub the palms of my hands on my school shorts. I've never realised how much my hands sweat.

She pushes her "used to be blonde but now borders on light pink" hair from her face, the colour totally going against school rules. Freckles dot her nose, and that smile looks harmless, probably fake. The fake goes soul deep with everyone in the group she hangs with.

Mr Campbell huffs something about how the class needs to focus. I try to concentrate on him, not on the few centimetres that separate me from Libby, or that I'm frozen, worried the way I sit is awkward. But I am awkward, and I'm almost angry at Katie for stealing Libby's seat.

Libby pulls a Chapstick from her pocket and smears it over her lips like there wasn't enough there already. I try to distract myself with details; the reflection on the lino, the seven different colours of pins stuck to the wall where a picture was. My mind drifts to the note and what's possibly written on it. Maybe it's an invite to one of Libby's lame groups; she's always trying to recruit people to join, like she thinks she and her friends will have any effect on people not littering, or will be happy to donate food to the starving. But people just aren't that nice. Although it's easy to donate money when you have truckloads of cash at your disposal. She's hard outta luck if it's money she wants; I have six bucks to my name, and that's for emergencies. And I come to the conclusion that whatever's on that note, it's gonna be irritating.

I snap back to reality when Mr Campbell reads out the terms and conditions for the SOFA scholarship competition. "The most exclusive private art school in the country; the only way to get in is to win your way in or pay their fees," he says.

And to do that, you'll need a pot of gold, out of reach even for regular people, let alone the non-regular.

If you want to be somebody in the art world, that school will get you there. It's not only the best art school in the country, but part of the course involves setting up a business to sell and market your work. I can't imagine being paid to bomb walls – it would be living the dream, a massively unrealistic, unattainable dream. It's hard to get into SOFA, even for those who have the money and are semi-talented – they admit only thirty percent of people who apply. A fact Mr Campbell has repeated twice in the space of one minute.

He stands at the front of the class and holds up the poster. "If you're smart, the portfolio you create to pass my art class could be the portfolio you submit for the SOFA competition. To gain entry into SOFA, you must" – he holds up a finger – "receive an A in art" – the second finger pops up – "ace the portfolio" – his third finger rises – "have a referee write you a glowing referral" – four fingers wiggle – "and attend an interview."

At least half the class sighs.

I grab my art book from my bag and push my bag shut, so no spray cans escape. Libby's bag lies open, old-school chemistry and physics textbooks jammed inside. Doesn't she know you can get stuff online? I place my art book on the table; *Bear* is bombed on the front.

Mr Campbell continues. "You need ten pieces for the portfolio that fit the theme, 'art and society'. The winner receives a full scholarship and one year at the halls of residence."

I'm assuming that doesn't include those with juvenile police records or a tag-along alcoholic pain in the ass.

Libby leans in, cranes her head to get a better look at the bomb on my cover. "It's amazing."

The butterflies return; she's too close. It's unnerving. I open the book and flick to a random page in the hope it's empty and she won't be reminded of my work. Nope. The page opens on *Xavier* in fat gold letters across two pages. The more I flick, the worse it gets; her eyes grow large, her gaze never leaving my work. I close the book and turn the cover face down.

"I mean it – the detail in those portraits, crazy detailed for spray work." Crazy because she now has proof it was me last night? Or crazy, as in she likes my work? Not sure street art is her scene.

Heat floods my face, and I jam my book back into my bag. When I sit up, Libby looks straight at me. "Sorry, I shouldn't be nosey. What I meant was, your work is clever." And she smiles. It feels genuine; I shift on my seat. Something about compliments make me uneasy, untrusting, like they can inflate your ego and make you blind, especially if the person is lying. She's the first to say anything positive about my work. I'm not about to get ahead of myself.

"Thanks."

Mr Campbell booms from the front, "Would you two stop talking!"

Libby retrieves a notepad from her pencil case. There's a bee on the front with *Bee Kind* written in curly handwriting. She flicks through the pages, writes something, rips the paper off, folds it in half, and slides the note in front of me. I can't look at her. I don't want another note, I don't like surprises or unexpected things; they're never good, and I've now got two of those burning a hole in my pocket. I fight the urge to roll my eyes, bashing my mind with what's written on the stupid things.

I'd read both now, but Mr Campbell stares at us, and he'd read them out in front of the class given a chance – he's done it before. He directs us to start our portfolios, and Libby leaves to work in the resource room with Katie. My shoulders relax; sweat stops emptying from my hands, and for the first time since I made it into class, I take a breath using the total capacity of my lungs. I'm relieved; at least I can concentrate on art with her gone.

I work on a portrait I've been struggling with for ages.

The bell rings. As the class packs up, Mr Campbell yells, "New stock of computers and graphics tablets in my shop, two percent off; we have payment plans available."

Mr Campbell's art shop is the lamest, saddest excuse for an art shop. Ever since the SOFA was rebuilt – including a beautiful art supply shop, its outside covered with regularly changing art I'm so envious of – Mr Campbell's shop has looked like a dreary monotone oil painting.

Ha, payment plans. With prestigious art schools, the gear isn't optional. I can't pull off dinner with all the food groups, let alone new tech; but if I *could* acquire the gear, I'd already have a better shot.

Libby picks up her bag, swings the strap over her shoulder. "Bye, Dylan."

She beams a luminous smile that I'm not sure is fake or genuine niceness. How do you come back from that?

I muster a "see ya." By the time the words fall out, Libby is distracted by Luka. He drapes his arm around her shoulders. "Missed ya, let's go. I need to check on Sam."

Luka might be head douchebag, but credit has to be given that he stands up for his little brother. I've seen him take a punch setting things straight when people call Sam dumb or slow; we agree on one thing – ya always have ya family's back.

When they're out of sight, I tug the notes from my pocket and open the first one.

I know it was you last night.

Fuck!

I open the second.

Love your art, Xavier. Will you enter the SOFA comp? Promise I won't nark; yall help with the ball art, aye?

She knows I'm Xavier! It's like I've been turned inside out, raw and exposed, and I can't flip back to normal. The one thing I never wanted anyone to find out is now known by the most socially busy, get-stuck-in-people's-business person at school. Who's she told? She can't tell *anyone*.

I look around the empty class, paranoid someone else is here; the walls of the room are closing in. I re-read her note, hoping I've misunderstood. The way it's worded, I can't tell if the *promise I won't nark* bit is an ultimatum, like if I don't agree to ball art duties, she'll tell ... who? Or is it not an ultimatum and more a *PS hey, side note, thought I'd mention ...* kind of thing. Either way, she knows.

And hell no, I'm not doing the ball art. She's mad-crazy to think my art style would work for the school ball, or that I'd let her suck me into a dodgy deal, ultimatum, or whatever it is she's getting at.

For the rest of the day, I avoid Libby. I'm irritated that I can't get the ball ultimatum note out of my mind. What if she narks? I can't have anything else added to my police record; SOFA wouldn't be open to anyone with criminal convictions, even well-intentioned art-related ones. No art school would accept me, even the shit ones. And if the police get involved, they'll ask for my address, and when they find out I'm officially homeless, social services will be notified. The last time that happened, Dad disappeared and I got sent to a foster family, till they couldn't handle me and gave up trying.

Libby's got me by the art school balls. And what's the social protocol to reply? Another note written on cutesy paper? *Please don't tell anyone I'm Xavier, especially the police, especially Miss Reed.*

To her, it's nothing; her life is perfectly mapped out. To me, it could ruin everything. At least she doesn't know I'm homeless – that secret would spread like free music downloads, and no one, *no one* at school can know, most of all Libby Green. That kind of info in the hands of someone who wrongly thinks they can change the world can only end in shame, the soul-sucking kind.

After school I bike home, pounding the pedals, pissed I got caught, pissed I'm gonna have to do ball art for the most annoying girl on the planet. I pause outside, hesitant to open the door and see what state Dad is in. But I hear nothing. Just the squeaky belt from the air-conditioning unit a few doors down. Meaning Dad's passed out, or dead.

I push open the door, grab my phone from my pocket, ready to call emergency services. I creep through the front room; Dad isn't on the couch. I wish I could hit *Pause*, stop the images flicking through my mind of all the ways I've found him, all the possibilities. It's not over yet; I creep into our bedroom, forcing myself with every step to face what might be there, as if picturing the reality before I find it might soften the blow. I glance into our room; Dad's bed is unmade, the room empty. He's not home. I forgot about that option; it gets me every time. And like a flood gate has opened, the worry floats away, replaced with anger.

On the kitchen bench, another eviction notice. The gist is, we've got till tomorrow to be out of here – that, or the police will escort us. The word *EVICTION* never gets easier to read.

It's official: we're homeless, again. At least I wasn't stupid enough to believe Dad's promise, that this time would be the last. I've been so distracted with the Libby ultimatum that I've buried the eviction stuff in a deep, dark corner of my mind, temporarily ignored, paused because it's the only way to not fall apart. There's no one to help pick up the pieces.

I swallow hard. I want to lay blame – it's Dad's fault Mum is gone, if he hadn't … but I push those thoughts down hard. It wasn't just him; if I'd stopped her getting in the car, accepted her offer to pick me up, she might be here.

I slump on the couch, the eviction notice in my hand. Crying won't help either; it won't bring Mum back.

On the back of the eviction notice, in block letters, I write *EVICTED FROM LIFE* and in the empty spaces within the letters draw intricate flowers the way Mum would have, though she'd have used popping watercolours and the last of her art supplies are long gone. I make do with a black pen. I picture her in her studio at her desk. As the years go by, it's harder to remember her face; it's been three years and six days.

I run out of light before I can finish; it's too dark to see now. The downside to living with Dad – he doesn't discriminate when choosing which bill to pay, he just pays none of them.

No matter how many jobs I've applied for, when you tick the *yes* box to having a criminal record, you're guaranteed an emailed rejection letter with a thanks but no thanks. I've tried lying, but they must run checks because those emails have always been more along the lines of *you lied, never apply for a job here again.* Eventually, I stopped applying, stopped hoping someone would give me a chance.

I grab my phone and art book out of my bag, but my phone's out of juice. I throw my art book across the room and sit in silence, wishing one of Dad's parties was raging; at least someone would be here. He'd be here to be pissed at, a distraction from missing Mum's pie hot out of the oven. At least nutting off at him about a party on a school night would make it easier to bury memories, and guilt at being unsure I can ever forgive what Dad did, even though it wasn't on purpose. My eyes sting, and I'm relieved when the rattle of a commuter train barrelling past lights up the room and snaps me back to reality.

I trudge to the other side of the room, stare down at my sketchbook, lying open, a portrait of Mum staring at me with accusing eyes. And then I see it. I know where me and Dad can crash. At least, until I figure out a better place.

I bike to the public library on autopilot, cut through the empty car park and follow the path around to the back, which is secluded in trees, the other half being in open view of the men's night shelter and high-rise apartment blocks. The security light flicks on. I lean my bike against the brick wall next to the fire escape ladder that leads to the roof of the library. The wall where my last bomb was, a portrait of Mum, is now a bright white square, layers of portraits underneath. They never last. Most of my work is lucky to last overnight; most is painted over hours later. The city council has a zero-tolerance policy for street art.

I take the stencil from my bag, hold it against the wall, and spray black; the outline of a kid sitting on his mum's lap reading an X-Men comic appears with *Miss Mum* written as the comic's title. I spray *Xavier* in black in the corner. I'm not sure what bothers me more: how quick the last bomb of Mum was sprayed over, or hearing the familiar rumble of the security van out front.

I load my sprays into my bag, ram my bike into the bushes, and climb the fire escape to the second storey. The bald head of the guard stops below me. I freeze. He knows I'm here; he's just not sure where, yet. If this dude finds me, I've got nowhere to go but up. And that leads him right where I don't want him. He can't find out what's on the roof.

The guard holds his torch over my graff, wet paint glistening in the light. He wipes a finger across the face of the lady, the paint now smeared on his finger. Bastard! The guard takes a picture. He coulda done that before he ruined Mum's face.

He skims his torch along the fence, through the bushes where my bike is, retrieves his walkie-talkie. "Library to base, that Xavier guy's back."

I move up the next rung, my bag slips back, and two spray cans fall out. *Fuuuck!*

"Oi!" the guard yells and points his torch at me.

I sprint up the ladder, across the library roof bombed in an explosion of my technicolour graffiti, and gap it towards the rooftop stairwell.

"Stop," the guard shouts, still hauling himself up the fire escape.

I race inside the stairwell, shut the door, and crouch under a portrait of Bear bombed on the back door. I remove the padlock from my bag, hook it through the holes in the lock, and click it closed. Sitting against the door, I'm barely able to make out the steep metal stairs down to the library.

Footsteps edge closer on the roof. The guard pushes the door open, and a crack of light ignites the stairwell. The guard shoves the door, lurching me forward; the padlock stops the door from opening wider. My heart races. Torchlight peeks through the cracked window paint, casting a shadow of my face on the wall behind. The stairs that lead into the library are now lit; the door at the bottom is always locked.

I huddle behind the door as one hand extends through the gap. A grunt rises as the guard tries to squeeze through. I hold in a laugh. Dude's dreaming of his thin days.

When he gives up, footsteps clomp around the roof. The door's still ajar; every part of me wants to slam it shut, but instead I peek through paint cracks on the window. The guard takes a picture of the rooftop portraits. Politicians, Mum, Dad, my life. He photographs my tarp, collapsible chair, plastic storage box of spray. My emergency place, the closest thing to home, my canvas, my peace and safety in the city – discovered. Once your spots are found, they're relentlessly patrolled.

I knew they'd figure out what's up here eventually, making the option to stay here off the cards. The guard snaps a picture of my box of spray cans, more photos for the Beachlands Police Station collection.

I'm tempted to open the door, beg him not to nark to the police. If he knew it's the only non-risky place me and Dad can crash, maybe he'd take pity on us. Then again, who wants pity? If the police get involved, it's too risky.

I peer through the window, and the guard climbs down the fire escape. But relief doesn't follow. He'll be back.

I grab my keys from my bag and slip one into the padlock. Outside on the roof, my stuff is laid out like they're ready for a crime scene examination. I pack my bag with as much spray from my stash as I can fit in. With a lump in my throat, I avoid looking at the portraits. No time to get sentimental; they'll be painted over by tomorrow.

I climb down the fire escape and jerk my bike from the bushes. Flinging my hoody over my head, I speed around the front of the library and past the parked security guard. I should have waited longer, a rookie mistake. I jump the lights at the intersection, bike up Main Street and down the alleyway, and pause at the concrete wall – the back of the Red Gallery Café.

I lean my bike against the concrete fence and stand on it, hoisting myself up. My bomb from last night is partially blocked by a van, but it's still there.

A guy opens the back door and slides a tray of food into the back of the van. I concentrate on the apartment window above. It takes a second to click; it's the guy who delivers food to the homeless. The food is epic, but I only eat it if it's not Libby or someone from school there, collecting extra school credits.

I realise the guy is staring. "You alright, bud?" The same face shape as Libby, his hair more unruly.

"Sorry." I jump back in the alleyway and lean against the wall, nowhere to go, nowhere to be, the alley silent, no one to be seen, although how would I know? It's too black to see. The smell of food makes my stomach roar; for a second, I'm tempted to follow the van. I haven't eaten since yesterday morning, but the thought of Libby seeing me eat food from that van tames my hunger. The last thing she needs is a whiff of me being homeless; that girl knows enough, too much. The food is for the homeless. I hate the word *homeless*, can't say it, can barely think it without wanting to ignite the word and blow it to smithereens.

The security lights from the café click on, and Libby's voice says, "Ready, Dad." The van door slides shut, and the engine roars, its lights igniting the alley.

I grab the two notes from Libby from my pocket.

I know it was you last night.

Love your art, Xavier. Will you enter the SOFA comp? Promise I won't nark; yall help with the ball art, aye?

On the wall, I spray a massive black heart and inside write *Yes to art* in thick loopy handwriting like Libby's. I sign *Xavier* in the corner in gold. Even with practically zero chance of getting into SOFA, art is the only thing that makes sense, even if it means agreeing to Libby's ball ultimatum. And what have I got to lose entering that SOFA comp? Things can't get worse.

Three

I convince the real estate lady to give us five days to move, on the promise Dad finds the money for missed rent. The lady knows we're full of shit, but by law she has to grant us an extension. She makes sure to be a pain in the arse though, with multiple requests to meet at her office, and daily calls and visits. It gives us extra nights with a roof, but means I miss art all week.

I sit on our couch, the flat dark, the only light second hand from next door. My phone rings. I recognise the real estate agent's number.

"Hello."

No introduction.

"It's not your fault, you've done all you can, but I need to warn you, police will be escorting you to jail if you're not out by tomorrow. I've left a message with your dad, as he won't answer my calls."

The door opens in the flat above. I walk out front and look up. Marv stands on the balcony, gives me a heads up to say hi as he lights his ciggie. His dreads hang down the shoulders of his blue t-shirt, uniform for Mr

Antoni's Souvlaki. Marv blows a stream of smoke. I realise the real estate lady is still there.

"Can you hear me?" she snaps.

In front of our flat, where the Mitsi usually parks, sits Marv's ute, one light held in place with masking tape.

"Yes, police will escort us to jail if we're not out by tomorrow." I slip my phone into my pocket. It's not until that moment that it really sinks in. I no longer have the convenience of being able to crash at the same spot every night with a guaranteed roof, and a door that locks.

Marv works two jobs to help feed his four sisters: the souvlaki shop, and as a street sweeper. His mum is like Dad; Marv gets it.

"The real estate lady went septic at your dad, bro, till he took off in the Mitsi."

I eyeball Marv's ute.

"Mind helping me move?" It's not like I can count on Dad.

Marv pulls a ciggie from his mouth, and smoke billows into the sky. "Sure, bro, I got an hour till I gotta be back at work."

Marv and me stand in the doorway of the sparsely furnished flat.

"Couch, TV and beds stay, they were here when we arrived. Everything else, boxit or bagit."

"Gotcha."

Marv packs the kitchen stuff into a box while I bag clothes. In no time, everything Dad and me own is in three rubbish bags and two boxes stacked by the front door. All my spray, stencils, and dog food – the important stuff – in my school bag. Marv carries the boxes outside and lifts them onto the back of the truck. Marv and Bear follow me out the back door. The tropical garden oasis bombed on the back wall separates us from the train tracks.

Marv inspects the wall. "You gonna paint over it?"

"Nope. I don't have enough spray, and it improves this shithole anyway."

"'Nough said." Marv lights another ciggie.

I lock the back door and pace in and out of the rooms, double and triple check we haven't left anything behind – we haven't. I don't want to leave. I check one last time, my pace faster, trying to calm the weight in my chest that's threatening to escape. I've lost count of how many times we've been evicted and made homeless.

Marv waits in his truck; I'm relieved he's not asking any more questions about which stuff stays or goes. Right now, I'm not sure I could speak without my voice quivering. I'm not sure when or if we will have a roof with an address again. On the side of a cardboard box, I write a note to Dad: *Meet me outside the library*. And I leave it on the kitchen bench with the key. It's weird how you don't think much about something until it's taken away. I'd do anything to call this shithole home. I close the door for the last time.

Marv backs his ute and creeps down the street. "Where to?" The car edges past rows of flats as shitty as the one we left. I lean back in my seat and adjust Bear sitting on my lap. I knew that question would come; I thought I'd know what to do, where to go.

"Town library."

Marv gives me his *really, bro?* face. "Ain't you been evicted from there, in and out?"

"I know." I don't tell him it's the only place that's weirdly homely, familiar, that's closest to Mum. And despite being evicted from there, too, it's a place I understand. I focus out the window. Marv gets the hint I don't want to talk, or more like I can't, and he doesn't say anything more till we hit town, the library in view. I had hoped – stupidly assumed – I'd know what to do to get us a place, but that's the problem with hope. It's a guarantee for disappointment.

"You can stay at mine, bro. Till you get on your feet."

I'd love to take his offer, but his two-room flat has four girls in the only bedroom and him and his mum in the lounge. Add the substances his mum deals with – no thanks. Dad needs no new habits.

"Thanks, man. It's cool. I'll figure something out."

"Y'all always do, man." His tone is less light-hearted and upbeat than usual; he knows exactly what we are up against, that there's nowhere to go, nowhere for people like me and Dad other than the streets.

Marv pulls up outside the library entrance, the glass doors concealed with a pulldown metal gate, padlocked shut to keep the good in and the unwanted out. We unload the banana boxes and bags on the bench seat by the main doors; I lean my bike against the library wall. Bear jumps out of the ute and investigates some plants.

A car drives into the car park. Leaving the engine running, an older lady lifts a stack of books off the back seat and feeds them one by one through the after-hours book return. She looks me and my stuff over and says nothing, ignoring us.

Marv rests the last box on the ground by the bench seat. "Gotta head off, man, it's nearly six." Once he's gone, I'll officially be alone. I scramble for an excuse big enough to make him stay; my face must say it all. Marv stares at me for a split second; it doesn't help that he looks worried.

"You'll get through this."

There's nothing to say or anything left holding me together; I don't know how I did this before and all the times before that. This time feels more brutal, like I'm lost in an angry ocean storm, furiously treading water to keep my head up so I can breathe, knowing there's no help in sight.

Marv leans in and bro-hugs me, and tops it off with the fist pump that he always does. I muster a half-hearted wave as he drives away, his truck headed into town.

The library is dark, the car park deserted. I watch each car that passes intently to see if it's the Mitsi, which is a waste of time for two reasons: our car is loud as hell, thanks to a muffler that's never been fixed, and there's no guarantee Dad will show.

I sit next to Bear and stare at the front door, flashing back to when Mum worked here. Things were better then – still shit, but perfect compared to now. We had a home, a tiny shitty flat that was technically a garage split in the middle with heavy blankets strung from the ceiling to make two rooms. There was always warm food and the same bed to sleep in, and an art project me and Mum had on the go. We had plans to sell our work at the markets, set up our own stall, her stuff on one side, mine on the other.

No matter how many jobs she had, Dad drank the money before bills were paid, and yet she never gave up on him changing. She had an epic sense of family loyalty to her *two boys*, and you felt it hard. She always believed in my art, always had my back, and I always knew she would. No matter how much of an arse Dad is, I have to keep my promise to Mum that I'll look after him. It's what she wanted, what she'd expect. And I know it's the right thing to do, even if he is the most aggravating person known to man.

Me and Bear sit on the bench and wait. I look back at the library entrance. I'd do anything to go back to the days I could guarantee Mum would be inside. She'd have an art book picked out, biscuits and a cup of tea she'd steal from the staff room. Wherever Mum was, it felt like home.

No amount of swallowing calms the sting in my throat. Better toughen up; there's no place for that on the streets.

The wind picks up and whips my cheeks. Autumn is on the out, and soon the snow will be here. I grab a blanket from the bag and lay it over me and Bear, pulling it up to my chest. I'd use this time to sketch, but there's not enough light, and my phone is dead.

A familiar voice comes from around the back of the library.

Jack appears, eyes to the sky, hands clasped together as he rocks back and forth.

"Dylan, Dylan, Dylan. Food truck will be here soon," he repeats till I pat his shoulder. I'd give him a hug – it's been ages since I've seen him – but hugs aren't Jack's thing. We go way back, since we were in the same class in primary school, when I'd push away the dickhead kids that would try to touch him just to get a rise. We've been buds since.

"Hey, man." I jump to my feet, grab two boxes and ferry them around to the side of the library. Me and that stuff have to be outta here before the food truck arrives.

Jack's still chatting like I'm still there and all ears. Usually, I would be.

"Sit, sit, sit." He swings his arm out, trying to grab me as I stack another load.

"I'll move this stuff," I say, "then I'll sit, just for a bit though, bud. I gotta be somewhere in a sec, okay?"

I hate being rude to him; he's been roughing it at the men's shelter behind the library for as long as I can remember – even when Mum was still working here. We go way back, hanging out at all the free community art workshops Mum would sneak us into. He's got mad talent as a comic-book artist.

As I pick up the last stack of stuff, Jack grips my bag and pulls me down onto the seat. I fall back; all that free food has kept him a healthier weight than me.

"Sit, sit, sit." He takes his art book from his bag, flicks to a page of his hand-drawn comic, and points. A superhero flies over a city, the streets jammed with cars. The speech bubble from his mouth reads *Global warming is an abomination.*

Jack watches the road. His head moves in time with a car until it passes the library, then he moves on to a taxi. The great thing about Jack is his eagle-eye attention to detail; the second he sees that food truck, we'll know about it.

When the food truck service started, me and Dad were living behind a recycling centre, and the food saved us. Until volunteers I knew from school, like Libby, started helping. Then we stopped showing up and got used to baggier jeans. The last thing I wanted was word getting around school that me and Dad were homeless. News like that makes you freakishly neon, the weird kid with everyone up in your business for all the wrong reasons. If shame wasn't enough to keep me away from free food, keeping word I'm homeless off Miss Reed's radar is paramount.

That food should be for people who are actually roughing it on the streets, doing it hard, like Jack. It's not like he can haul from the supermarket.

I help Jack push his trolley of homeless essentials up the ramp to the library's front door. His way-too-big jeans hang around his gumboots. The seagull picture on his t-shirt looks like it used to glow in the dark.

We sit on the ground, backs against the library's main doors, my focus on the road.

He's waiting for food.

I'm waiting for my life to start.

As I try to stand, Jack grabs the strap of my backpack and holds on; the spray cans inside clank together.

"Aerosols are an abomination; climate change will kill us." He holds up his free hand as if he's talking to the moon and does his rocking thing, backwards and forwards. Every time I see him, he gives me grief about my graff. But mostly, he rants about how environmentally unfriendly spray cans are. That, or how polluting plastic is. Get him started and he'll get fixated on how turtles wash up on the beach dead after mistaking plastic for food.

A bunch of Jack's buddies crowd around us at the spot where the food will be unloaded. Even before Jack does, I recognise the roar of the food truck. I bolt up, and Jack in his excitement yanks hard, pinning me down.

THE ART OF LOVING LIBBY GREEN

And before I know it, the van with *The Red Gallery Café Food Truck* plastered on its side is parked right in front of me.

"Let go!" I say, harsher than I intend, which is lost on Jack; he just yanks harder. As I try again to stand, his force pulls me back, and our combined momentum means I face plant on the ground. Bear licks my face. As I scramble to my feet, ready to beeline around the back of the library, I'm met by Libby as she steps out of the van carrying a stack of food trays. I legit feel naked, exposed; I glance around for a quick exit, but that damn dog of mine, in all her cuteness, paws at Libby's legs.

Libby faces me, does this double take, and I spot the exact second that she recognises me. I want to sink like a boulder pushed off a cliff into the ocean.

"Hey!" She sounds upbeat, surprised. Because up until now, I was relatively normal. Now Libby's got reason to suspect I'm homeless. Why else would I be waiting with a crowd of homeless people at a location known to have regular free food?

"How adorable. Is it your dog?"

Bear weaves in and out of Libby's legs as she pushes her way through the crowd and rests the tray by the library entry. I follow, and scoop up Bear with one hand. She'll be all over that food, and I can picture her tripping up Libby and Libby falling headfirst into the glass door of the library.

"Yep, she's mine. Sorry, she will jump on that tray."

Libby giggles, and I can't help but smile; the image of my teeny dog scoffing back the food in a mad rush before the waiting mass *is* pretty funny. I take my chance to leave, but my crazy dog wriggles out of my grip and races back to Libby, now steadying two stacked trays. And like I predicted, Libby missteps to avoid Bear, squeals and trips. I grab her arm before she faceplants cream-filled buns.

"Thanks. What are you doing here?" My heart steps up a gear. Libby brushes herself off as I let go of her arm while Jack digs into the food.

"Making sure Jack doesn't miss out."

A smile spreads across her face. "Aww, that's so sweet of you." I don't know her well enough to read her smile; it's killing me that I can't tell if she believes me.

Libby laughs. "That was close; I would have had a face full of cream if it wasn't for you."

"Haha, that would have been funny."

Her grin at my comment makes her dimples pop. But I'm done talking; the longer I'm here, the more time it gives her to contemplate *why* I'm here.

I'm relieved when she's distracted by her dad, who's balancing more trays. He looks directly at me, wobbling as he moves the heavy weight from the van.

I grab two trays from the top and place them with the rest.

My stomach grumbles as the sugary-sweet aroma of iced buns and fresh fruit hits me. I can't remember the last time I ate.

Libby's dad wipes his hands on his apron. "Thanks, heaps. Plenty for everyone."

I avoid eye contact. What if he recognises me from the other night, when I was mid-climb over the Red Gallery wall?

The crowd swarms. Jack hovers at the back of the pack, glances back at me, and makes whining noises. I roll my eyes; I can't not help him. Through the vultures, I grab one of everything and shove my way out. I'm met by Libby – and Luka, as if he's come from out of nowhere. They are each carrying a plastic bag filled with mini bottles of shampoo, conditioner, and body wash.

I thrust the food at Jack and glance at Libby, who's busy handing out care bags. I'm warmed that she knows everybody by name.

Jack calls me, holding his half-eaten cream bun to the sky. "Dylan," he repeats. "It's terrific tasting." Bun crumbs fly like confetti from his mouth.

"Libby, Libby, mmm terrific, terrific." Jack uses *terrific* for anything good. He sits on the ground in front of the bench. One hand stuffs bun into his mouth, the other lines up the bottles from Libby's care package. He carefully checks each one is the same distance apart from the other.

Libby sits next to Jack. "So glad you like it; it's good to see you, buddy."

I don't mean to stare. Most people avoid Jack, but she's lining up bottles, following his detailed instructions on how they must be precisely the same distance apart.

"Like this?" Libby asks Jack as she rearranges bottles.

Jack beams, and she seems genuinely pleased to have helped him.

Luka stands next to me. "What are you doing here?" Like he's caught Father Christmas at Easter.

I'm basically sucking at life.

Libby turns her focus to me. Jack interrupts, and I've never loved him more for it.

"Plastic's un-biodegradable, turtles will die, don't you know." Jack's focused on the plastic bags Luka's carrying.

I ignore Luka's question.

Libby pulls out one of the shampoo bottles. "They're all made from recycled plastic or plant-based materials, I made sure." She speaks to him like he's no different.

Jack takes the bottle from Libby.

"See, it says it here." She points to the spot on the back.

Jack rocks back and forth. "Terrific, terrific, terrific."

Libby hands Jack the plastic bags filled with mini self-care products. He tips the contents onto the ground, and one by one lines up the bottles in a row, like dominoes.

Libby hands one of the bags to me. I glance at my feet. I can't look at her. "Oh, I'm not homeless; I don't need those. Thanks, though."

"This stuff is good; I can personally recommend it." She hands me an orange shampoo bottle.

"I'm good, thanks, not homeless." Why did I say that? I turn my attention to helping Jack with the bottles. To ride off now would be super obvious.

"No probs."

Jack pushes a pile of bottles towards me, and I help add to his line of dominoes.

"What's all this?" Luka says as he stands over the three of us and Jack's bottle dominoes.

Libby laughs. "Um, dominoes, obviously." And there's this smirk between us, a shared inside joke, almost. For a split second.

Luka's attached to his phone, smiling each time it beeps. "We finished yet?"

A face pops out of the van, a younger version of Luka – his brother, who goes to the special ed unit at school. Luka slides his phone in his pocket and turns to Libby. "I gotta get Sam home before he loses it."

Sam screams, "Go. Now."

Luka sits in the van, his arm around Sam, talking to him softly. At school, Luka's arrogant, aware everyone knows he's good at everything, including dating all of the hot senior girls. Come to think of it, he's been with Libby the longest. Seeing him around Sam, gentle and calm – I haven't seen this side of him before.

Jack stuffs the last of a bun in his mouth. "Flat," he says. He points at my bike's tyre. Which *is* flat, and my bike pump is in the Mitsi.

Libby walks back to the van and returns with a pump and a repair kit. "Should do the job."

"Nice, thanks." What am I saying? I never say *nice*. As I fix the tyre, Jack squeals as the line of shampoo dominoes fall one after another. At the same time, Libby and I let out, "Terrific!" And there's a shared smile between us – not gonna lie, it feels good.

Her dad packs the empty trays into the van.

Libby inspects the paint job on my bike, running her finger along one of the bars.

"Beautiful work; I've never seen a bike with artwork like it."

I concentrate on my tyre, don't want to sound up myself, but she won't find a bike like it anywhere else because I custom painted it.

"You did this?" she asks.

"Yep," I say, trying to sound casual, pumped she sees something in me that isn't tragic.

The familiar roar of the Mitsi groans down the street. I'm stoked Dad's showed, but his timing sucks. Dad misses the library entrance and drives over the curb; the bumper scrapes the concrete on its descent. Everyone watches as the Mitsi lurches forward and stops next to Libby's van. For the first time, I wish he hadn't shown up. If I could ride off now, I would, but my tyre won't inflate.

I can't look at Libby. No doubt she'll realise I'm with him.

Jack yells, "Dylan, Dylan, Dylan, you don't have to hide your things." And he points around to the back of the library. "You can put them in your car."

Thanks, Jack. Thanks for nothing. I make zero eye contact with Libby; every part of me wants to bolt.

Dad pokes his head out the window and yells, "We're free, my boy," waving the beer in his hand.

Jack stands and waves. "That's Gary, Dylan's dad."

I'd take being invisible right now, or the ability to go back in time and not to have come here.

Libby and Luka load the last trays in the van and jump in the back; her dad hollers out the window, "Have a great night, guys. See you next time." I know it's rude to ignore them, but I have to. I can't face her expression, or the thought of how much she and Luka have pieced together. It's highly likely she's seen enough to know I have no home.

I watch Dad stumble out of the car, and push him back in before he can make more of an arse of himself, although the damage is done. I have nothing to say to him; my silence hints that I'm pissed off. If I get started ranting on how he's cringeworthy as fuck, and how life sucks because of him, it always ends with me frustrated as hell, then a wall and bloodied fists. He never gets it; and ranting doesn't tame the pressure in my chest that's got nowhere to go, that gets swallowed down. He'll never change.

On the passenger seat floor, two bottles of wine, a bottle of whiskey, and a dozen of beer. And that tips me over the edge. The lid's off – that bottle's about to explode.

"You can buy booze, but you couldn't pay the rent! Could you be any more embarrassing?"

The words shoot out of my mouth. So much for holding that shit in. I know I'm yelling, on the verge of losing control.

"Why do you have to mess shit up every time?"

It's like he's unaffected by my outburst. "It's all good, ma boy. We're free." And the moron raises his beer as if expecting me to grab a beer and join in.

"You're humiliating."

Those lingering, still eating free food, stare. I'm making a scene; I don't care.

"I'm going for a whizz," he says, and he takes his beer to the closest tree.

I swallow hard. I want to run after him, yell that life would be better, easier, without him, that maybe I'd have a shot at being somebody if it wasn't for him. But I suck it down, I swallow it all. It's pointless – having it out with him feels worse than keeping the pent-up rage suffocated within, buried.

40

The crowd at the library disperses. I inflate my tyre using Libby's bike pump and load my stuff into the boot while Dad listens to the radio and sips a beer. "Come on, boy, let's celebrate."

I slam the boot and flop onto the passenger seat. Dad extends a beer towards me.

"You know I don't drink." I stare straight ahead, my arms folded at my chest.

Dad's eyes crinkle at the sides, half-closed. "All the more for me, then."

Even though he's only seventeen years older than me, he appears to be seventy. Booze has a way of weathering a person – weathering my dad. He's the poster child for why you shouldn't drink. I can see the tagline: *Alcoholism: guaranteed to ruin your life and everyone who has to put up with your crap*, and a picture of his dried-up face. Easy poster to picture ... it's my actual fucking life. This guy's the reason we're homeless, and he doesn't give a crap. No one does. The only person who would, is dead.

Dad and I sit there for ages; he gets more drunk while I fume. A security van parks next to us. The guard taps on Dad's window.

"Geeze, talk about give an old man a fright," he says. But the fright sounds more like fight, as if he's asked if the guard wants a fight. I sink into the seat and stare out the window, my bike in view against the library wall. Dad rolls down his window as the guard I recognise from the other night shines his torch into the car.

"You know you can't sleep or drink here; your car will be towed if it's here in the morning."

Before Dad can say anything stupid, I jump in. "We're waiting for someone; we'll leave soon."

The guard shines his torch into the bushes, and leaves, following the path around the back of the library. I wait for him to finish his rounds and then for his van to be out of sight. I look up onto the roof of the library. Camping on the library roof is not an option.

Dad's mouth hangs open, and loud snores fill the small cab. I push his arm. He falls into the door but doesn't wake.

I grab my bag of sprays from the back seat and creep around the side of the library, freshly painted white. I outline the food truck in black, title the number plate *Food4homeless*. On the van's side in print font, I spray *EMPATHY FOR THE WIN*. Around the truck, I outline faces: Jack, the crowd of hungry homeless stuffing their happy faces. I colour Libby's mad mass of strawberry-blonde hair and add a red pencil through the bun. Instead of *Artistry* etched at one end, I write *beekind*, like it says on the cutesy paper she used for her ball ultimatum note. I dread school tomorrow and the ball stuff. School was my hideout where no one noticed me; now I'll hide in the toilet coz I can't deal with how much of a loser I feel like compared to them, with their lives neatly together. Mine falling apart in front of everyone.

I move to the library's back wall and peer through the slits in the fence to the men's night shelter on the other side, the porch lit twenty-four seven. There's always room, but it's risky; you're more likely to get bashed or have shit stolen there than on the street.

In the middle of the wall, on the ramp up to double doors, I spray a life-sized weathered man sleeping, wisps of dog fur peeking out from under his jacket.

It's Dad now, future me.

Gold spray drips from the corner to the ground as I spray *Xavier*. With my phone, I take pictures of both – my only way to document my work for my portfolio.

Me and Dad wake in the Mitsi, still parked outside the library. Condensation beads down the windscreen. Across the road, Central Garden Square is packed with the Farmers Market. Every Sunday, if there was spare cash, me and Mum would buy curly potato fries smothered in tomato sauce, check out the art and get ideas for our stall. I didn't realise it then, but she ditched art school to work; gave up on her dream to care for me and Dad.

A library lady follows a woman carrying a bag of vegetables in one hand and a takeaway coffee in the other, kids lagging after her. The librarian taps the woman on the shoulder. "Excuse me, this car park is for library patrons only."

As they pass, I notice under the Mitsi wiper blade a parking notice. I grab the ticket – to sum up, a message from the library slash council, move the Mitsi, or they'll tow it. A one-thousand-dollar fine to get your car released from the car prison.

I open the boot and grab a towel. Curled up on the back seat, Dad yells, "Shut the bloody boot; it's freezing."

The librarian huffs towards me. "It'll be towed, mark my word." On her shirt a white name badge reads *HEAD LIBRARIAN*. She's crazy, but we can't lose the Mitsi; it's our home, what keeps us in and the street out. We're lucky; most homeless have nothing – a box, a bush, or a street corner to choose from.

I follow the librarian into the library. She turns and snaps, "Excuse me, you must move your car!"

I'm busting for the toilet. "We will, in five, promise." I continue past the children's section to the disabled toilet with a shower. As soon as I shut the door, three sharp knocks boom from the other side. "Excuse me, you don't belong here."

Don't I know it.

She continues, "This toilet is for patrons of the children's section. It's not a community shower, as you people seem to think it is."

What does she mean, *you people*? Like we're made up of something different.

I fake groan. "Arrrrgh, got it really bad, wouldn't come in if I was you."
I run the tap and throw handfuls of water into the toilet.

"For goodness' sake. I'll be waiting with security."

Four

Since library security guards operate on a skeleton crew over the weekends, I figure I've got time. I plug in my phone; it won't have time to charge much, but it's better than nothing. I've been two days without a shower, and I can smell me, which means everyone else can, too. Plus, I need to figure out if this can become a regular thing; I can't go to school smelling homeless. And I don't want to get caught using the school showers every morning like I have been. Now Libby and Luka know, I'm not taking any more risks.

The warm water cascades down my back. I use the hand soap to clean my body and wash my hair, which reminds me of Libby and her shampoo bottle dominoes.

A bang on the door makes me jump. "The security guard is here, and we have the key for this shower."

Safe to say, this won't be my regular shower spot. I reek of hospital-grade hand soap; at least I don't smell like my life is going nowhere – it only looks that way.

I slip on my jeans, hoody, and faded Chucks. Using the mirror, I rake my fingers through my hair to tame the mass. If I'd taken the bag of stuff from Libby, I'd have a comb, possibly hair gel.

Outside the bathroom, I scan for the librarian. In the children's section, kids rifle through alphabetised boxes of books. I reckon Dad would have read most of those to me while waiting for Mum to finish work.

That was then.

In the central part of the library, I pass two policemen at the lending desk, helped by the parking warden slash librarian. I quicken my pace; my first thought is *What's Dad done?* My second, *The Mitsi*. I break into a run, and when I'm outside, see that the spot where the Mitsi was parked is empty. My heart goes full death metal as I scan the car park in case Dad moved spots, then I see the Mitsi on the back of a tow truck being driven out of the car park. Jack sits on the bench seat, Bear on his lap.

I race to my bike and pound the pedals hard after the tow truck as I shout, "Look after Bear!"

Jack screams, "Your dad didn't use gentle hands; policeman took him away." And he adds something else, which I miss; my heart's too busy trying to escape through my ears as I pump the pedals furiously hard and fast.

The tow truck stops at the lights, sandwiched between two lanes of traffic. Cars toot for me to get out of the way.

I bang my fist frantically on the cab door. "Where are you taking my car?"

Country music booms from the cab, and the driver doesn't notice me. The lights change, and the truck speeds ahead. I weave between traffic, my focus not leaving the truck. My lungs sting, my thighs burn; I'm not sure how long I can keep up, but there's no time to slow down. If I lose sight of the truck, we've lost our only safe place to sleep.

The truck slows as we pass a petrol station, and indicates the turn into the industrial subdivision. I hang back and watch as it glides into a gated compound, other impounded cars in neat rows. The truckie backs the Mitsi inside the compound before parking his truck on the road.

Leave the gate open.

But it's as if he reads my mind. He ambles up to the gate and swings it shut, securing it with a padlock, then goes inside the building. Through the window, I watch as he sits at a table.

All the essential stuff is in the Mitsi: my art book, spray, dog food. Without the Mitsi, bed options are a park bench or under a bush; neither guarantees sleep. At least the Misti doors lock, and it's slightly less polar than sleeping outside.

I climb the side of the truck, hidden from view. Reaching through the window, I snatch the keys from the ignition and drop them in my pocket.

What I'm about to do next is crazy, especially in daylight. If I'm caught, trapped behind that gate, there's no escaping. I survey the compound fences, ten feet high at least with barbed wire looped around the top. My palms clam up, coating my handlebar grips in sweat while I contemplate whether saving the Mitsi is worth the risk of getting caught, whether stealing my own car without paying the fines is considered a big enough criminal offence to go on a police record, or would be viewed by SOFA as a definite *hell no* to being accepted. The last time the Mitsi was out of action, Dad would go missing for days, choosing to sleep in friends' cars – and it's that thought that makes me decide. The Mitsi is what will keep Dad close and Mum a teeny bit closer; it was her car.

I pedal down the street to the petrol station and stash my bike around the back. The only cars around are those driving in and out of the car wash. I head back to the Mitsi.

Back at the tow truck I inspect the keys and narrow it down to three that could open the compound. The guys are still in the building, eating. I duck low along the side of the office window and run towards the gate. If one of the men looks up, I'm snapped. I push the first key into the lock and twist. The keys jangle against the gate – wrong key. As I slip in the next key, there's a bang on the window, followed by rushed footsteps on gravel.

"Oi, mate!" One truckie runs towards me, the other to the gate.

I jam in the last key; the lock releases and I swing the gate open and gap it into the Mitsi. The two truck drivers stand in front, blocking my way out. I rev the engine and floor it towards them; both dive out of the way when they realise I ain't gonna stop.

I screech down the main road and into the petrol station, detach the front wheel from my bike and shove it in the car, then sit in the front and catch my breath. Dad's nearly had us evicted twice in twenty-four hours.

My phone beeps; a text from Dad. *Beer, cask wine, smokes and drop off here*, and there's an address.

Did he see the car get towed? My shoulders tense. I drop my phone in my bag and grab my sketchbook, flicking through for a blank page; there are none. The SOFA art poster falls on my lap: *the winner of the best portfolio receives a full scholarship and one-year halls of residence.* For a split second, my mind drifts to what it might feel like to win; I'd be living my dream, proud I'd be somebody going places. Free halls of residence, a safe, secure place to call home for a year – but it would mean ditching Dad and not keeping my promise to Mum. And I snap back to reality.

I punch my fist into the steering wheel; it lets out an unsatisfying beep that fades to a broken, repeated clicking.

Art is what I do; it's like oxygen – I can't be me without it.

I also can't make a portfolio without more supplies. Spray is not included in the free supplies school provides. I'm the only person in art that doesn't have a tablet; they're a must-have to compete with the quality of applications that SOFA gets, especially from rich kids with limitless budgets to buy whatever art supplies they want.

I drive the backstreets into town and park in front of Steve's Art Supply Shop. Why Mr Campbell named his art shop after himself, I'll never understand. Seems like anti-marketing. In the window is a red banner: *5% off everything.* I don't know why I'm here; he's never going to let me pay off a graphics tablet – a pad of paper, maybe.

A buzzer beeps as I walk inside and down a narrow aisle tightly packed with dust-clad art supplies. Mr Campbell is at the counter, talking with a woman. I wait behind them; a graphics tablet rests on a nearby seat with a half-unpacked box of sketchpads, waiting to be priced and put away. The graph tab is just sitting there, unattended. My hands tingle, that start of the hand sweats and the first indication I'm about to do something real dumb.

Mr Campbell gives the woman the stink eye. "It declined again. Unless you can find the last six dollars, you can't take it home."

Katie appears beside her mother and says to Mr Campbell, "No worries." Then she yanks her mum's arm. "Let's go."

Katie glances at me and steps back into an aisle, out of sight.

I get it. My card was declined so much I don't bother using it.

"Come on! It's fine; I'll figure something out." Katie's voice is a shouted whisper.

If she wants a shot at SOFA, she's gotta have the gear – a graphics tablet, minimum.

I turn my attention from Katie and pretend to check out the stack of sketchbooks. No one wants attention in that situation.

Katie's mum pleads with Mr Campbell. "Please, can I bring you the six dollars on payday?" She sounds desperate now. "It's essential for her to get in."

"Let's go. Now, Mum," Katie snaps.

Mr Campbell stands his ground. "It's not shop policy, no."

I dig into my bag, unzip the side pocket, and pick out the last coins to my name, totalling six bucks. I reach past Katie's mum and drop the cash on the counter. At least someone will have a graphics tablet and an *actual* shot at SOFA.

"Six dollars." I wait by the graphics tablet on the chair.

"Thank you! How can I repay you?" Katie's mum looks over at me.

"Really, don't mention it." It's more awkward for them than for me.

Katie pulls her sunglasses over her eyes. I'd always assumed her family was rich. Guess I judged wrong.

"Well then," Mr Campbell says. "Here's your new graphics tablet." And he passes Katie a box.

Mr Campbell's graphics tablet is right there on the seat next to me. He's distracted, talking at Katie about his strict no-returns policy. While I watch them, I pick up the tablet, shove it in my bag, and walk out of the shop. The buzzer beeps as I exit.

It's not until I'm outside that I realise I didn't check for cameras, and panic sets in. I unlock the Mitsi, hide the graph tab in my bag, start the engine and begin reversing. I narrowly miss running over Katie, who's tapping on the passenger window. Now's not the time to for thankyous, I need to get gone. I keep edging back, hoping she gets the message. She doesn't, continuing to tap the window, pacing back with the car. I lurch to a stop, focused on Mr Campbell, who's standing in the shop doorway. I wind the window down, expecting him to run after me any second.

"Hey." She holds up the graph-tab box. "Thanks – I'll pay you back when I can." She looks around and leans into the window. "Would you mind not telling anyone what happened in there?"

Her mum comes out of the shop and unlocks the Mercedes in the car park.

"Sure." I edge the Mitsi backwards again.

Katie whispers, "Anything I can do to repay you?"

"No, thanks."

Katie gets in her car as I reverse the Mitsi, but then I drive back into the car park. I'm not sure what's come over me. Maybe because I've got a graph tab, I can now plan some dope art for my portfolio and the ball. Show Libby not everything about me is tragic. Come to think of it, why is Libby not asking Luka to help? No doubt he'll have all the gear.

I draw alongside the Mercedes and Katie winds down her window.

"Is Luka doing the ball stuff with Libby? I'm … asking for a friend."

"Riiiiight … You promise not to say what you saw?"

"Promise."

"Ha." She laughs as she rolls her eyes. "You can tell your friend, it changes weekly, like their relationship status."

And her window closes.

I glance at my bag; I got tech support. But I'm doomed if Mr Campbell saw me.

The SOFA game is on.

I park the Mitsi under the trees that line Central Garden Square, in the furthest spot from Libby's apartment, the café, and her room above, which is lit. I call Dad, but he doesn't pick up or answer my texts. Where is he?

For the rest of the night, I sketch on the graphics tablet till the battery dies.

Five

I'm awakened by my phone ringing and a motor humming outside the car – an obnoxious sound at four in the morning. By the time I locate my phone, which has slipped under the seat, I miss the call. I pull back the newspaper taped to the windscreen – my attempt at insulation – and a guy with straight hair, not dreads, drives a street sweeper along the gutter. Sucks that it's not Marv.

My phone beeps. A missed call from Dad. And a text.

Meet me outside the police station!

I turn the Mitsi key and notice the petrol gauge on E. I risk running out of gas, or I cycle. I start the engine; I dunno what state he's in, and he's the worst person to dub on the back of a bike, flopping around side to side. I start the Mitsi and speed through town; the front entrance of the police station is lit, but Dad's not here. I park out the front and wait, and then wait some more. I text him. He texted me earlier, so he's not dead; it's when Dad goes silent you know he's in trouble.

Where are you?

After an hour, I go into the police reception and press the buzzer. It sends a harsh *zzzzz* out back.

A policeman strolls up.

"I've come to pick up Gary Marshall."

He taps at his computer. "No one's come in by that name."

I nearly ask him to double-check, but Dad's a manipulative waste of space, and this is not the first time he's used a message like *pick me up outside the* [insert place that will get my attention] because his arse is too lazy to walk the three blocks back to the Mitsi.

I text him again: *Better come soon, or you're walking.* I know I'm full of it; I wouldn't ditch him, coz what if he genuinely *does* need help? The familiar tightness in my throat returns, sitting heavy. He's pissing me around, and I'm the idiot wasting my time running around after him, waiting for my life to start. He waits for nothing and no one, like he's got his shit sorted, happy just existing. And every time I'm sucked in by his shit, I know I can't do this anymore, that there's got to be more than this – but here I am, *again*.

There's a bomb I've been dreaming of painting on the police station – a risky and stupid move, since there's an actual person who's paid to watch their security cameras twenty-four seven.

I wait another half an hour, till I can't sit like a loser being had anymore.

The police station is the only place in town where you can do all the wrong things and they'll take you into a tropical cell and feed you. I sneak around the back to the double doors of the service entry. Two security cameras point to each door. Using a chair from the courtyard, I spray the camera faces black, careful to not get my face in view.

The textured lumpy concrete wall is the worst to bomb. As I lay out my sprays, a police siren wails, and I automatically roll my eyes; it better have nothing to do with Dad. On the double doors, I spray in black the outline of an open door, an inmate sneaking a line of homeless people inside, and from the inmate's mouth a speech bubble: *Welcome, it's warm, and there's free food.* In the bottom corner, *Xavier*. SOFA wants portfolios that reflect art in society – that's my jam. I take a photo, push all my spray into my bag and head around the front.

Dad sits on the footpath, his back against a power box, a beer in hand.

"Howsy, son."

"You weren't inside the station, were you?"

Dad shakes his head as he takes a sip of his beer.

"You know I got better things to do than be your taxi. I was legit worried."

He's wasted, his face weathered, eyes drooping, his clothes hanging off his frame more than they used to. He opens his bag and shows me the bottles of rum. It reminds me of the hospital, the worst night of my life, the nurse giving me a box with everything from the car that survived the crash, the same brand of rum Dad is drinking now. How could glass bottles make it unbroken, not a chip, and yet Mum died?

"No – you can walk." I'm surprised how calm I say it, numb; he's literally sucked all the life from me.

He tries to stand, swaying as he rises. I catch him before he falls, and I'm reminded why I'm here, that catching him when he falls is the promise I made to Mum, and now I'm pissed at her, too.

"Dons bees mad, son, josh a lit-tle party, promset, it'll be the last."

Who's he kidding? Does he think this is my first time? Never trust Dad's promise – he's full of it, the words have no meaning.

I walk Dad to the Mitsi, where we sit and wait till it's time to drive to school. I give him the silent treatment, but he doesn't get the hint. The more he sips from that rum bottle and hammers on about his parties and friends, the things that mean something to him, the closer I get to yelling, *Shut the hell up, get out of my life!* and legit shoving him out the door. I could tell him about the SOFA comp and Libby, but I'm not that stupid; it'd be wasted words.

At each intersection, on the way to school, I'm worried the car will stall and not start again, hungry for more gas. Dad goes on about how he'll pick up gas on his way back to town. I zone out; he's full of crap. A static wall of empty promises makes for irritating background noise. He won't get gas; we'll push the car to the nearest petrol station that we haven't been banned from, fill up the tank and drive off without paying, like we always do. He mutters something about it being my turn, that he did it last time. I can't even. He's not followed through once.

Outside the school entrance, I open the boot. "I know you get the family assistance payment today; put gas in the f-ing car." And I slam the boot.

I bet he drives straight to his friends via the booze shop.

I pop my head into the passenger window; Dad's hands shake as he grips the steering wheel. What happens when *his* tank is on E?

"Get gas, and while ya at it, food."

He avoids eye contact, looks in the opposite direction. "Sure, sure."

"Don't forget dog food."

But he drives off mid-sentence.

I lock my bike at the back of the teachers' car park. I keep my focus on the ground – after what Libby and Luka now know about me, I'm paranoid everyone knows, that everyone is looking, talking about me. As a pack of guys ride up, one slides his bike next to mine.

"I've seen your bike around. Sweet paint job."

"Thanks." My focus is firmly on clicking my bike lock, and panic sets in; what does he know? He's parked his bike next to mine for months, and we've never spoken a word. I feel like the spotlight is on me in a crowded arena as the group check out my bike. It's all too much, I could leave and never come back, but I need to sort this ball deal with Libby.

A brown station wagon drives up, Libby in the front. I fumble with the lock, biding my time, digging for the courage to ask about the ball ultimatum in a way that doesn't come across as desperate or that it's a big deal. Irritation sweeps through me; what does she care if everybody on the planet knows I'm Xavier, the homeless street artist? Why would she nark about my work on the back of her gallery? Any more criminal convictions could ruin what little hope I have of getting into SOFA, while her life is perfectly mapped out with multiple good options.

The front passenger door opens, and a wall of arguing explodes out.

"I can't believe you're leaving us for her!" Libby's voice is sharp, with none of its usual easy-going tone. "Leave, then." Her voice quivers as if on the edge of tears, that point where the lump in your throat is so fat you've gotta let the tears out to release the pressure. That, or implode.

Libby flies out of the car and slams the door, her face red, tears streaming. I force myself to focus on rolling the numbers on my bike lock, fight the urge to ask if she's okay. It's a stupid question; clearly, she's not. What can I say that doesn't sound (1) creepy and (2) states the obvious? Libby glances my way, the usual Libby vibe gone, her face blank. I smile and then regret it. Who smiles at someone when they're sad? Doesn't that make it worse?

She opens the boot, lifts out her shoulder bag and a sleeping bag, and sets them on the ground.

"Good luck with your new life," she yells into the car, then slams the boot shut.

Her dad pops his head out the driver's window. "Libs, we'll talk later!"

"No! We won't."

Selfish me sets aside the ball ultimatum; for now, that girl looks broken. I shouldn't help her, I shouldn't care, and I don't. But you just can't kick someone when they're already down on the ground.

Why is her dad not helping with her stuff, or caring? She's crying; looks like she's got a monumental pain in the arse as a dad, too.

She stuffs three takeaway bags stamped *Red Gallery Café* into her backpack and swings it over her shoulder, picks up a pile of books and sleeping bag, and steadies herself before the line of stairs to the administration block.

Her dad drives off, just like that, no checking to see if she's okay. I feel my own eye roll, and for a split second she looks up at me, and I swear we're talking without words, that she knows I understand how soul-crushing a useless dad can be.

She turns away, and it's like her hollow vibe is contagious. I feel for her; I know what it's like when you realise the person who should be there for you has let you down so often you go numb, and give up trying to let them in.

Libby walks the steps towards the school's entrance. The food slips out of the takeaway bags, and as she leans down to pick it up, the contents of her bag spill down the steps. She collapses in a heap, her gear everywhere, and wipes tears with the sleeve of her school jersey.

I put the keys to my bike lock in the front pocket of my bag. I'm stalling, not sure what I'm waiting for. Would she want help from me? A group of students step over her stuff, and walk up the steps like she's invisible.

I run over, pick up the food, and pack as much as possible into the takeaway bags.

Libby looks up at me. "Sorry, I'm in your way."

"You're not."

She looks at me with the fake smile of someone desperate to keep it together to save what little dignity they have left; her downcast eyes say it all: she's broken.

As we lean down at the same time to collect the books, our heads crash together, and I narrowly miss being stabbed by the red graphite pencil jammed through the middle of her bun.

I try to search her eyes, but they're focused on the ground. "You okay?"

"Sorry," she says again, rubbing her forehead.

"I'll carry these for you." I gather her things, load them into her school bag and sling the bag over my shoulder. I hold out my hand. "Help up?"

I hoist her to her feet. She lets go of my hand, and we stand there facing each other, her hair wild and unruly. She looks past me as a stream of seniors pass. Two look back, and one whispers to the other.

I'm snapped back to reality, to the fear of what she knows or has said. Remembering that I should keep my distance from her, from everyone. I don't mean to blurt it out; it's inappropriate timing, but the words fall out: "Mind not telling anyone about seeing me at the library or that I'm ..." I look around to make sure no one is in earshot. "Xavier?"

Her focus changes, becomes more serious. "Um, sure ... I was going to talk to you about that. You have no reason to be embarrassed about being homeless."

I cast my eyes down; the ground is about to give way, and I'm about to freefall. And there's that word again that I want to blow to smithereens. She's confirmed my worst fears – she one hundred percent knows I'm Xavier *and* that I'm homeless.

My shoulders tense, I still can't look at her. I focus on Katie, who's heading this way. "I'm not embarrassed." I'm full of shit. "No one can know." My words sound harsh; it's not how I intended them to come out, I'm just mad as hell at myself for being stupid enough to get caught.

Katie reaches us. "Tense conversation, much?" Her face is caked in makeup, like she's about to hit the pubs.

"Take this." I pass Katie Libby's bag, and they walk the steps up the main entrance. I'm left without an answer, or confirmation that she won't tell anyone. The conversation is unfinished, the ball ultimatum still up in the air. Is our deal still on? I need to know – if I do the ball art, will she keep quiet?

I head into the administration block and walk towards art. The bell rings; I hang behind a mass of seniors deep in gossip, paranoid my homelessness is one of their topics.

Mr Campbell and Miss Reed push through the staff room door into the corridor and walk in the same direction. I duck behind a guy carrying a giant canvas, who I recognise from art class.

"See you at mine later," Mr Campbell says to Miss Reed.

"Look forward to it." Miss Reed disappears into her office, closing the door. As much as guidance counsellors think they're always the first to know school gossip, they're not. The whole school will know I'm homeless once Miss Reed finds out about it; I'll do what I'm good at and avoid her. The last thing I need is her contacting child services and them getting all up in my grill and causing drama.

From behind, I hear the boom of Luka's voice and his groupies. A junior opens her locker, and I legit contemplate jumping in, but Luka catches up, matches my pace. I brace myself for a snarky comment about being homeless or eating free food; I'm tempted to ask him not to say anything about the food truck, but he's the kind of guy who, if you asked him not to do something, would do the opposite and mock you relentlessly – a joke to him, not to anyone else. I keep my mouth shut.

Luka, low key and casual, not his standard vibe: "How was your weekend?"

Can't he ignore me like he usually does? I glance at him briefly; what's he getting at? I've seen his other side with his brother Sam, but his friends are here, and he almost sounds genuine.

We reach the art-room door, and his buddies carry on down the hall. He pushes me to the side of the corridor, and he almost looks awkward, nervous. "Um, so, your friend Jack."

He better tread carefully – Jack's like a brother to me.

"Err, yeah – what about him?"

"My brother Sam kinda knows him, and he wants to learn how to make a comic book like Jack did. There was a community class or something." He pauses and looks down either side of the hall to check no one is in earshot. "For special ed kids – think you could get me the contact deets for whoever runs it?"

I'm tempted to bargain with him. If I get the number, he tells no one about the food truck situation. But I don't trust him; I've seen too much of his other side to know he's loyal to no one, especially his word. Except for his brother, that is. And it feels wrong to use Jack and Sam as a bargaining tool.

"Yeah, I can get it." I pull out my phone, search under H and hold up the number; he takes a picture.

"And don't get any ideas about Libby. I see the way you look at her. Anyways, you two … are too different."

And there's the Luka I know. His tone is condescending, like he thinks I'm too stupid to get the subtext of his text; the way he gazes down at me with his stupid smirk says it all – that he doesn't just think he's better than me, he reckons he knows it.

My neck stiffens, my shoulders tense; if he mentioned the word homeless, I'd push him into the lockers. But if I touched him, the spotlight would be on us and he'd yell what he knows to everyone.

"What? No. I don't look at her … not like that." I'm tripping over my words, which only makes me sound guilty. I mean, she's nice, but mostly irritating, and I guess she's not hard to look at – I'm not blind. And she's super chill with Jack. My mind stumbles. The ball ultimatum thing, she's irritating. *Irritating.* I say it to myself twice to make sure it was clear the first time.

"Well, good." And Luka beams a fake-as-hell, I'm-better-than-you smile.

I wait for Luka to go into class and hide in the hall.

I'd temporarily forgotten that the graph tab I stole from Mr Campbell is in my backpack, and that, combined with worry I'm the new topic of gossip, has meant my legs have stalled. They refuse to go in – until I hear Miss Reed patrolling late students into class, and I open the art-room door.

Mr Campbell is at the whiteboard, back turned. I grip the shoulder straps of my bag, his graph tab stashed inside, my focus firmly on my seat at the back by the window.

"Dylan, I'd like to speak to you after class, please."

He's turned to face me; I don't shift my focus. "Sure." I continue to my seat. I figure if he knew I took it, he'd have yanked me into the principal's office by now.

I open my bag, allowing just enough room to slide out my artwork book, and place my bag directly under my seat. Mr Campbell turns again from the whiteboard, his focus directed at me; my chest muscles tighten, threatening to cut off my air as I wait for the inevitable, for him to call me out. I divert my attention out the window. Katie and Libby are walking through the courtyard towards class. I shouldn't have come to school; I'm surrounded.

Katie waves; I wave back before realising she's waving at Mr Campbell, who opens the back door of art class.

"Hiiiii, Mr Campbell," Katie says, as Libby follows her into the room.

My stomach flips, the dodgy-burrito-grind kind.

Mr Campbell smiles like he means it.

Luka picks up the bag that belongs to the guy next to him. "Mind moving? Libby's sitting here."

"Settle down, girlfriend," Katie says. "There's seats up the back."

Luka pulls an imaginary dagger from his chest. "Heart ... broken." He gasps for breath. Maybe he should rethink med school for acting, though I'm not sure his ego could cope when he discovers he sucks at something.

Libby sits next to me; my stomach is engulfed with irritated butterflies. I'm unsure where to look. I owe her an apology for snapping earlier, and I need to know if the ball ultimatum is still on. *Act cool, act cool.* Pretty sure actual cool guys don't say that, but before I gather the courage to force the words out, Libby leans close and whispers, eyes focused on Mr Campbell, "Thanks, for before, for helping." Her jacket brushes my arm, sending static tingles through my body. I can't remember the last time I was that close to anyone, let alone a girl.

Before my courage balloon deflates, I force the words out, in a whisper. "Sorry for before, about the ball ..."

Mr Campbell clears his throat. "Gossip on your own time."

He launches into instructions for compiling the end-of-year portfolio and reminds us how strict the entry requirements are for SOFA.

I switch between not knowing how to sit normally and smelling brief whiffs of perfume. I glance at Libby, her hair out of her bun and cascading down her shoulders; it's big and unruly – imperfect. Her fringe is held with one gold hairpin. Her eyes are no longer rimmed red, but perfectly green.

She glances my way. "Thank you again, for earlier. I'm really embarrassed – sorry you had to see that," she whispers.

"No worries." Heat engulfs my face.

Her attention diverts to the front of class when Mr Campbell begins a lecture on Frida Kahlo, a Mexican artist known for self-portraits and paintings of nature. How she was deemed an oddity then, but is revered today. I just wish artists didn't have to die to get the *revered* bit. Frida explored questions of identity, class, and race. In this class, I'm the oddity.

We're given a Frida Kahlo painting to decode. My mind is fuzzy, preoccupied. I want to ask Libby what the deal is with the ball ultimatum, if our deal is still on – if I do the art, she won't tell anyone what she knows about me. But Libby and Katie are busy chatting, something about making plans for their combined birthday party, and there are no quiet spots for me to ask the question.

Frida incorporated reality with surrealistic elements, and all I can think about is how it's surreal sitting here right now, next to Libby, not knowing what Mr Campbell knows.

Mr Campbell looks over our way. "Dylan," he booms. My heart rocks a drumbeat. "Would you stop with the whispering up the back?"

Libby and Katie glance at each other and go silent.

I can barely hear him with the drumming that's now taking over my ear space. "Sorry, sir." And he goes back to his lecture.

Libby mouths, *Thank you.*

I pretend I'm focused on what Mr Campbell is saying. For a head girl, she's surprisingly un-head-girl-like. I'm happy to take the rap for their whispering; it's better than how I thought the conversation would go.

Libby: "He's a homeless vandal."

Mr Campbell: "He stole my graph tab."

Katie: "I saw him steal it."

Luka: "He's a nothing."

We're given time to work on our portfolios, and I transition to the art computer in the resource room off the side of art class. It's for student use, and because everyone else has their own devices, I've always used the school computer in there. No one usually comes in, which I prefer. I stay there till the bell goes. I figure too many people know too much about me, and it's best to lay low.

When class ends, I gap it out the side door onto the courtyard.

"Dylan," Mr Campbell says, following me.

My heart drums.

"You were in my shop this weekend." He pauses, waits for a response.

"Err, yes." I can't deny he saw me; I gave him my last six dollars – well, technically, I gave it to Katie.

"My shop graphics tablet has gone missing. I don't suppose you saw it when you were in?" He glares at me. Gossiping students sit at the bench seats behind. Seagulls gather. I turn, pretending to be distracted by them, mostly to give me a few seconds to think of a response.

A gull charges at another gull, chasing a piece of fallen sandwich.

"No, didn't see it," I say, looking at Mr Campbell directly. I tighten my grip around the handles on my bag. The bag that has his graph tab inside.

"Right." Mr Campbell pats his beard with one hand, glances at my bag, and walks off in the other direction.

My stomach drops. If they look at the security camera footage, I'm screwed.

At lunch, I avoid the courtyard, where gossipers hang, and instead cut through the back fence, behind towering trees that separate the school from the beach track.

My feet hit the sand, and a surge of relief pours over me. I'm alone. Black marshmallow clouds crowd the sky. I reach the beach car park. Continuing, I pass the toilet block – black, with a surfer riding a wave painted on the back. The peeling paint shows layers of yellow, blue, green and brown. I take the path behind the toilet block, and veer off down a track hidden behind a bush, pushing my way through the plants. The path rises steeply up a dune to a picnic table and a not-too-shabby view. The tide is way out; an old couple walk their black Lab, navy umbrella up, turquoise scarves wound around their necks. The clouds swirl and roll, pushed by a cool breeze.

Arguing voices rise from below, and I peek down the sand dune through the bushes and see Libby and her dad. They're standing on the shore and looking out to sea. I lean back into the bush.

"How could you cheat on Mum?" Libby yells, facing her dad, her voice shaky.

"I didn't mean for this to happen. Your mum and me ... we've been struggling for a long time." He digs his hands in his jacket pockets and pushes the sand with one foot.

"So now what?" Libby pulls a tissue from her jacket pocket and wipes her eyes.

"Annie and I are going to move in together for a fresh start."

"I can't believe you'd do this to Mum, and me," Libby yells, and huffs up the track towards me. Her dad follows and reaches out to grab her arm.

"Leave. Me. Alone." She pushes him away. He seems to get the hint but still trails behind her.

Libby passes me with only a bush between us. I'm frozen but wait a few minutes until the misty rain turns to masses of fat raindrops that speckle the sand, and then I run down the track into the car park.

An elderly guy opens his car. His black Lab jumps in. The car pulls out of the car park, revealing the Red Gallery Café van parked next to it. Libby's dad sits in the front. No Libby. The rain hammers down. I run around to the back of the sheltered toilet block and find Libby sitting against the wall, arms wrapped around her knees, earphones in, staring out to sea. She jumps when she sees me.

"Sorry, I didn't mean to give you a fright."

She takes the earphones out, and a depressing R&B song blares from her earphones.

"It's okay." Her eyes are puffy and red, crumpled tissue in her hand.

I turn to walk away and give her some space.

"Dylan. Do you have a light?"

When I turn back, she's holding up a pack of smokes. The black wall behind her makes her pink-blonde hair and green eyes pop. She's fiercely beautiful.

I didn't pick her as the smoking type, but shitty situations make people do dumb stuff.

"Light?" she repeats.

"Yip!" I rest my bag on the ground and search for the lighter, careful not to clang the spray cans together – or let the graph tab be seen. Libby opens the packet of smokes and slides one into her mouth. I flick the lighter, and the flame rises. She leans in and takes a breath, igniting the cigarette; she coughs, waving the smoke away from her face.

"Want one?" She offers me the packet; there's no beaming smile, just sad eyes.

"Sure." I take a smoke and light it, inhale a deep drag and blow a stream of smoke into the rain.

Libby pats the ground, ushering me to sit next to her. We sit side by side, a spray-can length apart, and watch the black clouds swirl. Rain hammers, flows off the roof in mini waterfalls. I blow another stream of smoke into the sky.. I'm not sure where to look, what to say. We're alone. For a while we sit in silence, listening to the rain. She draws a short drag on her cigarette; smoke floats out her mouth. She coughs, waves the smoke from her face.

"You know your dad is parked behind us, right?" I say, taking another drag and blowing the smoke towards a bunch of parked cars.

"Yip!" she says, her eyes filled with tears. "My dad's an idiot."

Turns out idiot dads are universal.

She hugs her knees into her chest, rubbing the goosebumps on her arms, staring out towards the ocean. There's probably a lump in her throat the size of Africa. If I was her, I'd want to be alone, to swallow the loss of having a dad who reeks of disappointment.

I take my hoody off.

"Here," I say, handing her my top. She holds out her smoke; her fingers glide over mine during the transfer. Electricity sparks through me, every cell in my body lit up like fireworks.

"Thanks. You're sweet." She slips on my hoody; it suits her, the green the same colour as her eyes.

I pass back her smoke.

She takes a big drag and coughs, which turns into a gasped wheeze.

"You okay? Do I need to pat your back?" I try not to laugh.

"First time smoking. Is it that obvious?" Her smirk turns to a laugh. I did that; I made her feel better. Not gonna lie, it feels good.

"They're shit for your health anyway," I say, laughing. I butt out my cigarette on the ground and hold out my hand to take Libby's. She stubs it out and drops it in my hand. I stick them in the rubbish bin and sit back down in the exact same spot.

The rain hammers down on the roof. A car pulls up in the car park behind us and parks in the furthest corner, half-hidden by a tree and thick bush.

Libby touches my arm, freeing the butterflies, and points. "Isn't that Mr Campbell's car? Jeepers! He's going to suck her face off," she says as the two people in the car get it on. The rain's almost torrential now so it's hard to see, but there are two people kissing, and it does look like Mr Campbell's white station wagon. Though minus roof racks to carry his surfboard, which I assumed he'd have.

Libby laughs. "He's giving her mouth to mouth. It'll be Miss Reed with him. Gross – teachers making out."

The man in the car looks in the rear-vision mirror, ducks down out of view. I catch a glimpse of dark hair and crane my neck to get a better look, but it's hard to see through foggy windows. I really wouldn't have picked

Miss Reed and Mr Campbell as the types to ditch school to make out at the beach, so close to school.

Libby's hand slaps my leg. "Holy shit. Mr Campbell and Miss Reed are freaky," she says, moving her head from side to side to get a better look, which cracks me up.

Miss Reed gets out of the car and places a bag in the rubbish bin ... but it's not Miss Reed. It's Katie. She gets back in the car.

Libby gasps and a violent shiver rocks her body. "Is that Katie?" Her voice is high, serious; her hand flies over her mouth. She leans forward, grabs her phone from her bag and snaps pics as lightning strikes, and a garbage truck pulls up, blocking our view. By the time the guy has collected the three rubbish bins in the car park, stuck each one individually on the hoist and tipped the contents in the back, Mr Campbell's car of horrors has left. I knew Mr Campbell could be a douche, but this is low, way low.

"Oh my god." Libby repeats it till I lose count.

Miss Reed has always been so good to me. A nervous knot twists in my chest; sadness for Miss Reed and Katie. "This can't end well for Katie," I say, and both of us sit there, still staring at where the car was, then back at each other.

"This is dodgy – Mr Campbell can't mess with Katie like that; it's more than wrong."

Libby shows me the blurry photo; it could be anyone in a blurry white car.

"Was that her? It was her, right?" She looks at me, her eyes pleading for an answer.

"I think so – it's hard to tell."

She slides her hands in my hoody pocket, pulling out a spray nozzle. "It's gross; what the hell is she thinking?" Libby shivers again. "She falls deep for guys and thinks her life is over when they break it off with her." She scrolls through her phone. "Jesus, I can't decide if I should tell her I know." Libby holds up her messenger conversation with Katie.

"We have to tell Mr Anderson; Mr Campbell is a ..." Libby searches for the word.

"Predator," I say, and she nods in agreement.

What does she mean, *we* have to tell Mr Anderson? No one's going to take anything I say seriously. It's gotta be done to protect Katie, but selfish me knows going against the teacher responsible for passing me in art is not an intelligent thing to do. I'm more selfish – more like Dad – than I thought.

Miss Reed has so got the sweets for him, too. This is gonna break her. Going by the hardcore collection of romance books on her shelf, she's a believer in the Prince Charming trope. What if Katie believes in it too?

I realise Libby's staring at me, waiting for me to answer.

"We gotta do something; it's the right thing to do," I say, looking directly at Libby with all the pretend confidence I can muster.

Libby stands. "We better get back to school. Dad can give us a lift." She waves at me to follow her towards her dad's van. As I stand, I lift one handle of my bag, and the top flips open. Mr Campbell's graph tab slides out; the sticker on the back reads *PROPERTY OF MR CAMPBELL'S ART SUPPLIES.*

Libby's eyes go wide. "Is that Mr Campbell's?"

I flick my eyes to the left. "The sticker is; the graphics pad is mine." Lame – she's too onto it to believe that.

"Oh, of course."

I can't look at her. Her tone says she believes me, but does she really? She watches me slide the graph tab back in the bag, and I manage to keep the spray cans from sliding out.

We run towards the white van, Libby a few steps ahead, dodging puddles. It's the same van that dropped food off at the library. Libby slides the door open and climbs in. For a second, I hesitate; what's her dad going to think about his daughter hanging out with me?

It starts to pour again, and raindrops bounce off the van. "Come in." Libby pats the seat next to her.

"Can you please drop us back to school?"

"Sure." Her dad looks me up and down.

I extend my hand. "Dylan. Nice to meet you, sir."

He shakes my hand firmly, eyes red and glazed, like he's got hay fever.

"Dan," he says, focused on my hoody that Libby is wearing.

The van engine starts. Libby's leg bumps mine as we go over a pothole. The window wipers go nuts; Dan leans forward, wipes fog from the inside of the window. At least the rain hammering on the roof drowns out the awkward silence.

Within a few minutes, Dan parks next to the bus shelter outside school.

"Thanks for the ride." I slide the door open and run under the bus shelter, Libby right behind me, stepping around puddles.

"Thanks for the loan of your hoody," Libby says. She pulls her arm out of one sleeve.

"Keep it till I see you next."

"Awww, thanks so much." She glides her arm back through the sleeve as the bell rings.

"What's your number?" she asks. "I'll text you; we can sort out a plan with Mr Anderson."

As I read out my number, Libby types it into her phone.

Luka runs up to Libby, holds his umbrella above her head. "My lady."

A few seconds later, my phone beeps, an unknown number. A message: *This is Libby, thanks so much!*

"Got it."

"Yay." Libby smiles, Luka glares.

I change the unknown number to Libby, not believing she gave it to me. And under D in her contacts will be my name; I don't point out to Luka that D comes before L as far as contact lists go. A lame thought; it's the only thing I've got over him.

"Get to class, you lot," Libby's dad shouts from the van window.

"I better get to bio, but I'll see you in art tomorrow," she says, turning to leave.

"Yeah. Sweet. Bye." I walk up the steps towards the main building. I turn around to look at Libby.

Luka holds the science tower door open for her, and they disappear inside.

Inside I head to my locker; I pass Miss Reed's office and the door is open. Bad mistake.

"Dylan." She paces after me. "I need to see you – come with me." Her tone is direct. She ushers me into her office and shuts the door. I stay standing, clutching the straps of my bag and hoping the busted zip isn't revealing what's concealed inside. I glance at her shelf of neatly organised romance books, and I want to blurt out the Mr Campbell thing, to protect her and Katie. I'm not sure what's stopping me – the awkwardness of the situation, the potential of seeing someone that's always been your rock break down?

"Mr Campbell's laptop has been stolen from his shop." I want to correct her – it was a graphics tablet – but I keep my mouth shut.

She sits in her comfy seat. "Sit." She points to the couch with a billion cushions.

I take a seat. I can't put my bag down; the top might flop open.

"Do you know anything about it?" She's doing that thing where she knows I know. Out of everyone, Miss Reed has had my back the most. But since Mr Campbell and her got together, the lines of loyalty are different. She's jibber-jabbering about the stolen computer, and all I can think about is what we saw. I want to yell, "He's a predator, run!" Warn her he's going to break her heart.

"Do you know anything?"

"No. Sorry." I don't feel guilty about lying to her face, like I usually do; there's a way bigger lie she needs to know.

She smiles, drops her shoulders as she lets out her breath. She told me once she'd do anything she could to help me get into art school. But stealing Mr Campbell's graphics tablet ... I'm not sure what repercussions that would have. And her loyalty would be to him, not me. Love is stupid and blind, and she might be too loved up to believe it if I told her, especially coming from me.

"Technically they're school property and shouldn't be off school grounds. Mr Campbell is incredibly stressed about it."

"Has Mr Campbell been selling school computers?"

Miss Reed avoids the question.

"If you hear anything or come across any information that may help, let us know."

I don't answer. The bell rings for the end of school, and I grab my bag and rush out. Outside I pause, unsure where to go; I have no home or any clue where Dad is. But with so many bars on one side of Garden Square, I have a good idea of where to start looking.

I head into town and search for the Mitsi at the usual places. This would be so much easier if Dad answered his phone. After the sixth call, I give up. I don't know what to do. As night falls, and after I've exhausted all the bars and possible places the Mitsi could be parked, I settle on sleeping in Central Garden Square. At least its perimeter is lit; it's unsafe as hell, but compared to a stairwell or shop doorway, it's the best place to sleep out of view and the least soul-crushing, embarrassing option.

Behind the toilet block, I push through tightly packed bushes, sit down on the ground and lean up against a tree. The soil's too wet to sleep on. The crisp night air stings my cheeks and fingers. I pull my knees up to my chest and bury my face and hands in my lap. The hum of the city is deafening. A group of people pass me on a shortcut to the movie theatre; their laughter ricochets through me like I'm only the drawn outline of a body.

Six

I'm not sure how much I slept – dozed, maybe. Starlings chant an uncoordinated song as I watch the sunrise. Shades of pink, orange, and yellow glow behind the Red Gallery Café, the café and the apartment above lit. I check my phone. No message from Libby.

A message from Dad though: *I'm parked up at Central Garden Square, don't call I'm going to sleep.*

When I find the Mitsi, Dad's crashed out on the back seat. I push my bag into the footwell of the front seat and feel around for the graph tab, attach the charger and plug it into the car's old-school cigarette lighter, laying my jacket over top. I wouldn't put it past Dad to take it, sell it for more booze and weed.

The only bad thing about parking in Central Garden Square is when the sun rises or sets, the starlings congregate, and thousands of birds parked above the car means it gets bombed in sticky bird poo. The only poop-free parks are around the other side of the square, but they're too close to Libby's apartment.

I start the engine and edge backwards, blinded by the sun, when there's a bang as something strikes the Mitsi. I glance over my shoulder and spot two guys in running shorts.

"Watch it, mate," one of them yells, but as I brake, the car lurches forward and Dad falls off the back seat, knocking into the driver's seat. I swing the door open and come face to face with Luka and an older version of Luka, looking like Hulk fitness dolls decked out in running singlets, shorts, and shoes. Their combined muscle mass outweighs our car.

Luka's dad rubs his leg.

"Sorry, you alright?"

Luka's dad snaps, "You should be sorry – you nearly ran us over. You could have broken my leg. I could sue for that, you know."

It was a tap, at most. It seems Luka's dad is a fan of playing it up.

Luka snickers. "No point suing, you'd get nothing out of them." He continues to laugh. And he's not wrong.

"There's newspaper curtains on their car – or is it a house?"

Luka's practically in hysterics. The cap has popped, and I'm rumbling, ready to blow. It's bad enough he knows what he knows, but to mock me for it ...

I grit my jaw. I don't want to draw any more attention our way, and his dad's a lawyer so it would be a lost battle if I knocked Luka to the ground. And then I remember why he's doing this, acting like such a monumental douche – it's not about me being homeless. Libby gave me her number, and it's killing him. And my rage turns to smugness; a grin sweeps my face. It feels pretty good – I could get used to this.

Dad wakes and pokes his head out the window. "What's this all about?" He falls out of the car, zip flying low, unshaven, and smelling like a pub.

Luka shakes his head.

Luka's dad starts jogging again. "You're right, Luka," he yells back. "Not worth it. Those kinds of cases are a waste of time in court."

Luka looks Dad up and down, and it's no longer mocking. It's worse – pity followed up with disgust.

Luka steps towards me. I don't budge.

He leans his face into mine. "Don't think you'll get anywhere with Libby; I know what you're up to. You know she called you a homeless nothing." And he jogs off in the direction of Libby's apartment.

It's not her style to call someone a nothing; anyway, she has zero interest in me. I get that girls like her don't end up with homeless guys, but she's not the nasty type.

I watch as Luka and his dad run towards Libby's, and there she is, in running shorts, heading this way. And the air is sucked from me. The last thing I want her to see is our newspaper curtains. I can't do it, see her pity face; she's the kind of girl who would feel embarrassed for me, and I have enough of that to fill the universe.

"Dad, get in the car; we're leaving NOW." I start backing out while Dad dives into the passenger seat.

I take off and speed down Main Street.

"What was all that about, then?" Dad says, as he noses through my bag.

"Nothing, forget it." I reach one arm and swipe Dad away from my bag. "Get out, nothing in there for you."

"Argh, my boy, got any money for ya old man?"

"No," I snap.

He shivers an all-over shake. "What's got you all techy?"

"Where do I begin, Dad?" I snatch the bag off him and throw it on the back seat.

76

"Don't you start with the lectures." Dad leans back in the seat and resumes his unconscious position.

In the rear-vision mirror, I can just make out the three runners edging closer; I have no doubt Luka has filled Libby in with the details, including our newspaper curtains, and I'm sure he's added dramatic effects to enhance the story to his liking.

At the end of Main Street, we sit and wait for the lights to change. From here onwards, the road turns into the state highway that follows the beach out of the city. I think I know of a place we can go – never an option before, but running, soul-sucking Hulks have a way of making me rethink our options. Dad's not gonna like it, nor do I, but we are out of alternatives.

"Drop me in town," Dad grumps.

"We *are* in town. I'm taking us somewhere we can park up permanently."

He points to a liquor store. "What's wrong with there?"

"Everything is wrong with there."

I lean over Dad, open the glove box, take the wad of parking infringement notices and throw them on his lap.

"You wanna get the Mitsi towed again? Where would we sleep?"

The downside to parking under the safety of the lights around Garden Square – fines, and the ever-real risk of being towed. I fail to mention the shame if Libby witnesses the Mitsi house and its curtains.

Dad wouldn't get it; he doesn't even look at the stash of fines, the thousands of dollars we owe the city council. He winds down his window and lets the notices go; they get caught in the wind and float behind us.

"Problem solved." His focus is on the last liquor store this side of town.

I turn onto the beach highway and glance at Dad; his eyes are closed now. Snores erupt.

We leave town behind. The beach is on our left, forest-covered hills on our right. A sign says *Beachlands Cemetery and Sports Fields 200m next right.*

I turn right down a road lined with oak trees. Behind are rows of graves dotted with flowers. I ignore Mum's willow. I know it's there; its exact spot. I don't need reminding. I push thoughts of Mum out, suffocating them by wondering where in the car the tent is hiding.

We reach the end of the road – an abandoned sports field with overgrown grass, surrounded by the falling-down grandstand Dad would sit in when I was a kid and he'd come to watch me play footy. It was our thing, back when he was a normalish dad. Now, a tape covers the access to the stand, marking the space – with its rotten weathered wood, exposed nails, and peeling paint – as dangerous. A bit like Dad – the good parts of him lost in memories.

I park next to a white concrete building with *Toilets* written above a rusted iron gate. Behind, dense forest covers a steep hill. Before the new sports multiplex was built in town, we'd park in this spot on game days. The cheers from the sidelines still ring in my ears; I remember the BBQs in summer, Mum painting as many different varieties of plants as she could, the same tent. We didn't have much, but we were together, and for the most part a typical family – Dad drunk, but in the jolly way people drink at Christmas, not in a soul-and life-sucking way, like now.

Dad continues to snore, his head flopped down. Bear is curled up on his lap, and Dad's breath blows Bear's fur.

I let Bear out and follow her into the bush behind the toilets. The sticks and leaves crunch and crack under my feet. Birds call and sparrows dance along with the leaf litter. Light streams have found a clear path through the trees. There's a weight to being here; Mum would love this. I swallow hard, lock away the memories. It's too much.

The wind bends the tops of the trees and drowns the hum of the highway. Through the branches, I can make out the beach. Between two towering pines is a space just flat enough for the tent.

I unload my bike and gear from the boot and carry the tent to the spot between the trees. I move some large rocks and sticks out of the way, then lay the tent out on a bed of yellow, gold, and brown leaves, hammering the pegs in with a stone.

I drape the waterproof fly over the tent and close the zip. I look over at the Mitsi in the car park next to the bare white wall of the toilet block, the sports ground beyond. The tent is home, at least for now, till I can figure something out. Back at the car, I grab the keys from the ignition and shove them in my pocket.

I grab my bag from the back seat and lay it down in front of the white toilet block wall.

I spray a black outline of a tent, surrounded by a picket fence, add streams of sunlight that reach the ground, overlapping the trees in greens, golds, and browns. At the top in the sky I spray, *Home is not a place; it's a feeling.* It's what Mum used to say. I'm not sure I'm feeling it, but it's the safest spot we've got. I try to remember her voice, her smile; I like to think I can remember, but I know I'm filling in details. I spray *Xavier* – the name Mum gave me because of my mad obsession with X-Men as a kid – in the corner, and I take a picture using the graph tab.

As I pack away my spray, my phone beeps.

I near on drop my phone when I see Libby's name.

I've tried everything. Katie refuses to admit we saw them at the beach. I emailed Mr Anderson. My plan: tell him what we saw, don't name names.

Libby might be one of the smartest and nicest girls I've met, but this is a stupid plan. There's no way Mr Anderson isn't going to pursue this further and demand details, meet with Mr Campbell to get his side of things – and everybody's, including mine.

I'm about to reply to tell her that's a stupid idea, that there's got to be a way to make Katie and Miss Reed see what they've got themselves into, when my phone beeps again.

Mr Anderson replied. Meeting after school today. Come with?

I type *Noooooo*, but my finger hovers over the send button. Fuck.

I delete the message and type: *OK. C U then*, and add a scared-face emoji

My stomach rolls. I lie in the tent, unable to focus. I want to go, do the right thing; I hate the thought of Miss Reed thinking she's loved up only to find out her hopeless romantic story ends with more of a horror vibe. And Katie's being taken advantage of, blinded. I'm torn; I wouldn't usually question standing up for that kind of thing, just not when I stand to lose the only thing that could set me free, my one chance at getting into SOFA. When all this turns to a shit storm – and there's no doubt it will – it's me Mr Campbell will blame, not Libby. It will blow any chance I've got. But if I *don't* turn up to that meeting, Libby will think the worst of me. And right now, despite her seeing all the bad stuff, she knows more of the real me than anyone else, even if she's slightly annoying and that ball note situation is irritating as hell.

My phone beeps: Libby. And there's a GIF of a dog dressed in a Superman costume strutting as he walks towards the camera. The caption: *It's gonna be fine, Superman is here.* It's hilarious.

I reply with a GIF of a dog driving a lawnmower. The title says *What can go wrong*, and we go back and forward with GIFs all day. Her last GIF is a girl falling on her bed, out cold asleep, and *I'll catch ya tomorrow, night you.*

I lie back on the makeshift bed, cardboard underneath and a sleeping bag on top, and re-read her messages. I reply with a GIF, a puppy rolling itself in a blanket and the caption *nighty night*. I slide my phone in my pocket, and when it beeps, a smile sweeps across my ridiculous face; she's got great timing. But it's not her name and the happy buzz fades. Instead, it's a message from the phone company: *You're out of data.*

And that's where it stops.

There isn't a lot of sleep to be had in the cold tent; it's the closest to freezing to death that I've come. And it doesn't help that I can't take my mind off wondering whether I should go to the meeting at school or not. Katie and Miss Reed need help; I *should* go. I re-read Libby's messages; that gal loves her GIFs. I suppose they are pretty funny. No new messages or GIFs to laugh at though, not that I was expecting her to message again, but it was fun while it lasted.

I wind down the school drive and push my bike into the rack.

Inside, I spot Miss Reed near her office, and she sees me before I can escape.

"You remembered." Her voice is upbeat. I swallow the guilt.

Dammit. I didn't remember, it's just bad timing. I'm reminded of all the nice stuff she's done for me: she fought hard to get me into Mr Campbell's art programme; it was she who I called when Mum died, and I barely knew her then. I'm overcome with a need to spit it out, rip the plaster off so she can get over Mr Campbell and move on and find an actual Prince Charming. The existence of such a man is debatable, but at least she wouldn't be living a lie. For all the times she's had my back, I owe it to her to have hers.

Miss Reed opens the door for me as I walk into her office. "I was just about to wait outside your first-period class."

The only times she does that is when she's digging for information, usually about Dad's lack of parenting skills. But something's got me thinking that today's meeting has nothing to do with Dad.

I make room on her couch, push a thousand plush cushions to one side and sit on the edge, my leg jiggling. Mr Campbell's graphics tablet is *still* in my bag.

Miss Reed sits opposite me. On top of her desk is a wedding magazine and a box labelled *student prizes* filled with candy and a stack of mobile phone top-up cards.

And then I see it, on Miss Reed's finger – a rock the size of Texas. And I want to yell, *Mr Campbell is getting it on with a student!* The words are right there, but they won't budge. It's as if I've forgotten how to speak.

Miss Reed peers at me; I glance at the ring. What an a-hole. And for the first time, I know what it feels like to pity someone other than Dad.

"Yes, Mr Campbell proposed a few days ago." She smiles like actual sunbeams. She believes he's great.

"Don't do it," I whisper. It's all I can force out.

And then she turns all condescending. "I know your family has had their ups and downs with relationships, but …"

And then her mood shifts. Mine too. Even if I told her, she's too loved up to believe me.

She shakes her head. "But that's not why you're here." She leans in closer, and says in a whisper, "As you know, Mr Campbell's laptop got stolen from his shop. I wanted to check in to see if you know anything about it now?"

My heart shifts up a beat. And I realise that at this moment, Miss Reed's loyalty to Mr Campbell is stronger than ever before. Nothing I say will convince her otherwise. When shit goes down at the meeting with Mr Anderson, she'll have Mr Campbell's back, not mine. I've officially lost my only cheerleader. I regret all the times I said I'd show up to meet her and didn't, those times I lied to her face. How can I expect her to be loyal to me, to believe anything I say, when I've never come through for her?

"No, I don't know anything."

She knows me well enough to know I'm lying. I can't look at her, and my eyes get stuck on the fat diamond on her finger.

"I'd like to give the person a chance to return it, make it right before Mr Campbell takes it any further and the police get involved." She stares at me intently; we both know they're not going to the police – Mr Campbell was selling school computers to make some cash. She knows it, I know it, and I'm not loving that she's threatening police; it's low. I didn't think she had it in her.

"Cool," I say, my attention focused on the phone cards behind her. I can't give up the graph tab; I just can't. And now I'm convinced they won't involve the police because it will catch out Mr Campbell and he could lose his job, his shop. The graph tab is safe in my bag.

"Mr Campbell told me you've shown an interest in the SOFA comp."

My shoulders tense; she's manipulating me. And just like that, the trust I had for her is shattered.

"Please, do the right thing – you don't want anything to ruin your chance at SOFA," she says. "You'll need a character reference from Mr Campbell."

Miss Reed spends the rest of the session trying to get details of my SOFA portfolio, my plan, the meaning behind my works, the next location, where I've bombed. Her attempt to use SOFA and Mr Campbell's reference as leverage for me to come clean.

"I'm undecided about SOFA." A big fat lie – I'm more motivated than ever.

There's a knock on Miss Reed's door, and Mr Anderson pops his head in. "Sorry to interrupt. It's urgent."

As they leave, Miss Reed turns to me. "Wait here."

Alone in her office, I grab the stack of phone cards and slip them in my pocket and escape into the corridor whereMr Campbell appears next to me.

I take giant strides and continue down the empty, quiet hall.

He matches my pace. "Just wanted to make it clear that I will be marking your end-of-year portfolio that you intend to submit to SOFA."

"Yes, sir." I know that. I'm speeding up, the end of the hall in sight, my study class through the doors on the other side.

"I'll also be your referee, which is a SOFA requirement to enter."

Where's he going with this? "Yes, thank you."

"We wouldn't want to do anything ..." He pauses for a second, pulls on the sleeve of my shirt and tugs me into an empty class, shutting the door behind him. "You wouldn't want to do anything that would jeopardise your chance of getting into SOFA, would you?"

It's like the conversation with Miss Reed is repeating itself.

He's worried I'll nark about the stolen computers; he should be more concerned about the Katie thing. I get it – he could lose his job, his precious reputation, his fake engagement. He could also ruin any chance I have to do something with my life other than living on the streets. He's not wrong. I need his stupid class and him to be a referee.

I sense his impatience as I stand there, clutching the straps of my bag, his graph tab in my backpack.

He sounds desperate, looks defeated. He glances around, his voice still in a whisper. "I understand you organised a meeting with Mr Anderson for this afternoon."

"I didn't organise anything."

He doesn't look convinced. "Mr Anderson said Dylan Marshall and another student, who doesn't want to be named, have set up a meeting to discuss allegations against me. I borrowed some tablets from school as stock for my shop, so if you cancel the meeting with Mr Anderson, I can make the referee happen."

He's more worried about Mr Anderson finding out about stolen technology than the Katie thing.

"Make that meeting not happen. There are private data files on that graphics tablet."

I bet there are; bet he's made a tidy profit too.

He looks desperate now, part begging. "I'll lose the shop if Mr Anderson finds out about the computers. I shouldn't have told you, but money has been tight. Miss Reed said you'd understand." And there's real sadness and worry in his eyes. He's worried I'm narking on him about stolen computers. I don't get why he's not worried about the Katie thing. Isn't that a more serious allegation? It could cost him more than his stupid reputation, shop and job. He'd never get another job teaching art, and he'd possibly even end up in jail.

The door swings open, and it's only then I realise that the class is empty, but there are open laptops on most of the desks, and school bags line the side wall. Streams of juniors float in. I squeeze past the horde, leaving Mr Campbell there, blocked by a ton of students.

I race down the hall to my study class.

The bell for the end of school rings, and I still haven't made up my mind about going to meet with Libby or not.

I walk past the admin office and look down the corridor to Mr Anderson's door. Libby sits outside, waiting for me, head down, looking through a chemistry study guide. I hate the thought of letting her down. Her hair is out today and a tad wild. I'm not sure why I like it like that; it's imperfect, a surprising detail about her. She crosses her legs on the seat and chews on the end of her pen. I'm such a weirdo right now, torn between desperate need to run away, and fighting the urge to send her a GIF that reflects this situation – a guy standing on the edge of a crumbling clifftop feels oddly appropriate.

I hide behind the administration wall and watch as Libby takes her phone out of her pocket.

Mrs Saxton, the admin lady, stops tapping on her computer behind me.

"What are you doing? Shouldn't you be in that meeting? Libby's already there."

I don't say anything. My phone beeps. A message from Libby.

I'm here. Mr Anderson is running late. You coming?

I'm torn. If I don't go, she'll never talk to me again. If I go, I lose my reference for SOFA.

Mrs Saxton gets out of her chair. "This is ridiculous," she says to me. "Just walk down the hall, there's nothing to fear from Mr Anderson. You of all people should know that."

Libby looks up at Mrs Saxton. I'm still hidden behind the wall so Libby can't see me.

"Suit yourself." She faces Libby and points at the wall I'm hiding behind. "He's hiding, scared; you might need to drag him into that meeting."

I bolt into the hallway, where neither of them can see, but I'm still in earshot.

I wish I had the guts to send a message: *Can we ditch the meeting and hang anyway?* Why is it that the girl who could ruin everything makes me beam technicolour, and why do I have to figure that out now – the worst possible timing?

Mr Anderson's door opens. "Libby, we ready? Where's Dylan?"

"He's supposed to be here; I think he's running late." And the office door shuts.

I lean back against the wall, and Mrs Saxton peeks around the corner. "Is it Libby or Mr Anderson you're worried about seeing?"

I say nothing, like a coward. I picture Libby waiting. By now, she'll have lost hope that I'll show. The thought makes me want to run right in there.

It's fifteen minutes past our meeting time, and I'm still outside in the hall. I check the time on my phone, tell myself I'll go into the meeting in the next minute, but when the minute passes, I can't bring myself to do it. The truth is, I've made up my mind. After my no-show, Libby will believe I have zero morals, and she'd be right. I lost my morals when I started stealing to live. SOFA is me surviving and supersedes all moral judgement.

My phone beeps; Dad sends me a list of things he wants me to lift from the supermarket. No *Hey, how's your day* – just *beer, lighter, cigarettes*. I slip my phone in my pocket, regret heavy on my chest, not because I've put SOFA first, but because I've lost Libby as a friend, if you could even call us that.

I ride the beach track towards home. My phone beeps. I pull over on the side of the way, the beach bright and blue. My stomach rolls seeing her name on my screen. *Mr Anderson would like your side of the story. I wouldn't have told him you were with me if I'd known you wouldn't show. Thought you of all people would be keen to stand up for what's morally right.*

I hit *Reply*, type a long-winded text about I need SOFA to change my life, to be someone, and that I can't go against Mr Campbell. But I delete it and settle on *Sorry.* I hit *Send.*

I should feel pumped, excited. I've stuck up for myself. I am, but it's smothered by thoughts of Libby, and no matter how much I remind myself that this is the best decision, I can't force her out of my mind, like a really catchy annoying song.

Seven

I lie in the tent and listen to Dad and his buddies outside, off their faces. I feel for my phone at the bottom of my sleeping bag. Two emails, one each from Mr Anderson and Mr Campbell. I swallow hard; this is not going to be pretty.

I click on the email from Mr Anderson. It's a meeting request for tomorrow and a reminder to bring a support person. Ha, that's funny. If they're cool with a drunk, then that's their choice.

And then I get to the email from Mr Campbell.

I see you met with Mr Anderson and told many lies; he is standing me down from teaching – effective immediately. Our deal is off.

I pull back my hand and drive my fist through my washing box, leaving the most unsatisfying dent as the box smashes into the tent wall. I get changed and storm to my emergency stash of spray cans hidden under a gap in the toilet block. It's dark, the white brick wall illuminated by moonlight. I swing my fist back and drive it into the wall; blood drips. The pain radiating through my fingers and up into my shoulder does nothing to simmer me down. My palms sweat, my throat's thick; I pull the cans from underground, shake each one – most are empty or close to. I have a surprise for Mr Campbell, and it's loud and stupid, and I don't care because I have nothing to lose.

Dad leans against the bonnet of the Mitsi. "What's all that about? Girl trouble?" There's a beer in one hand, and an assortment of booze bottles sitting on the car bonnet. Opposite Dad, a dude leans against a beat-up technicolour Datsun. His potbelly, ginger beard, and especially the halo of weed smoke send me a dodgy Santa vibe.

Dad raises his beer. "Joit us?"

Dodgy Santa laughs.

I ignore them and turn on the tap outside of the toilet block, filling Bear's water bowl. She winds around my feet until I stick the bowl on the ground, then she sniffs the water and pushes her bowl at my feet. "I know, girl," I say, ruffling her head. I'm just as hangry as she is.

I turn to Dad. "Get any dog food while out buying booze?" I know the answer. I don't know why I'm asking.

"Next trip to town, promise."

"You? Keep a promise? That's a joke."

Using a torch, I search through the Mitsi for anything that can pass as dog food or human food, but come up empty. I dig the car for my emergency stash while gathering stuff I need for Mr Campbell's surprise.

Dad pulls a bourbon and cola from the twelve-pack on the bonnet. "Tough night, boy? Take a load off, tell me what's troubling ya?"

I'm not stupid, and even if I wanted to, the lump in my throat makes speaking difficult. I find a tin of dog food for Bear, open the can and empty it into her bowl.

From the Mitsi, I pull apart the cardboard from the bourbon and cola boxes. I tape the pieces together to form one sheet on the concrete floor, and Dad and his buddy continue drinking as if I'm not there. I cut out a stencil, the outline of Katie, a dinosaur, and the word *predator*. Dad and his buddy down booze and smoke a bag of weed as I cut the shapes. Once I'm done, I grab my bike, strap the torch to my handlebars using masking tape, and cycle down the road with the stencils secured under my arm, heading towards Mr Campbell's shop.

Down Main Street, the streetlights are still lit. Before-dawn commuter buses pass; I stop outside Mr Campbell's art shop, the front windows dark. My heart pounds. I'm an idiot. It's upper Main Street, the poshest, hippest part of town, and I'm about to do what I'm about to do at 5.17 a.m., with the sun rising and traffic already starting to build.

I ride around the back, lean my bike against the shop, line up a rubbish bin under the toilet window and slip through into a bathroom below. I scan the room for red flashes of security lights. From what I can tell, there's an alarm in the office with the door closed; I assume that's where all the expensive stuff is kept, like the laptops and graph tabs that Mr Campbell has been hoarding from school.

Better to know if there's an alarm now than mid-haul. I climb over unpacked boxes and shimmy sideways around high piles of merchandise. The skinny isles are so crammed that I might as well be running an obstacle course.

The spray paint is in no order you'd expect, the colours and different brands mixed up in a bunch of boxes. I wade through to find the colours I need, drop the cans into my open bag. I empty a bin with random packets of modelling clay and fill the box; I've got a big space to cover. The mix of brands will create colour variation, but it's going to have to do. Now's not the time to worry about perfect colour matches.

I navigate the aisle and carry the box carefully in smooth movements so as not to drop any sprays out of my busted bag.

In the bathroom, I poke holes into the sides of the box, thread a towel on either side to make a handle so I can lower the box to the ground. I push and squeeze; there's no way to get the box out the window without tipping the spray cans over the concrete.

The sky is no longer pitch black but lit with indigo; I'm losing time.

I dump my bag and box by the back door and search for a fire extinguisher or hammer. Scanning the utility cupboard, I find a hammer and smash the crap out of the lock on the door till it's mangled enough for me to push the door open.

I carry the stuff around to the front of the shop and drop it by the entrance window. I'm insane. Maybe people passing will think I'm being paid to do this, but I doubt it.

I tape the stencil pieces on the window, taking up the full height, and block in the green for the dinosaur, spray Katie's black hair with her head jammed in the dinosaur's mouth dripping with blood, and fill in blue for her uniform.

From Katie's mouth, I draw a speech bubble with the word *predator* inside. This time I don't spray *Xavier* in the corner.

There's something about using Mr Campbell's spray to graffiti his own shop. It's cheap revenge, but it's all I got.

I fill my bag with the remaining cans.

I ride along the beach path, traffic building, the sun rising above the horizon. Teachers usually start arriving at school at seven thirty, and it's ten past now.

I reach the back of the school's sports field and cut across the grass to the front of the administration block. There are no cars in the school car park, but there will be soon. I bike around to the triple-storey stacks of school classes centred around a courtyard and lean my bike against the art building.

The security lights flick on. On the wall by the side door that opens onto the courtyard, I hold up my stencils, tape each one in place, spray outlines and repeat the image twice down the wall, taking up the entire side of the building. Outside the front of school, I hear a car come down the drive. The sun's high enough that if anyone were to spot me, they'd have a perfect view. As I stand back and look at the wall, my stomach rolls, part victory – girls will know to stay away from Mr Campbell – part euphoric, hoping Libby will see that I know what's morally right and wrong. And Miss Reed will be interested enough to at least ask questions.

The lights in the teachers' coffee lounge flick on. I push the spray and stencils in my bag, bike through the backfield and along the beach track until school is out of sight. I climb up a sand dune and plop onto the freezing sand, the tide rolling out with each passing wave, while I wait for school to start. The wind numbs my insides. I should be freaking out, sure I'll get snapped, but what can they take away? Nothing. I'd care if I had anything to lose. I've lost everything that meant anything.

A seagull soars over the water and squawks. The scent of salty air circles on the breeze. The coastline and sky are wide open, my chest heavy and constricted. At exactly ten to nine, predictably, the school bell rings. Nausea takes over – everyone will know it's me, they'll gossip and stare. I wouldn't bother going to school if it wasn't for Libby, and the overwhelming urge to apologise to her. A stupid part of me hopes she'll understand why I had to stand her up.

Eight

I wait till the second bell has rung and the corridor is empty before I make my way to art. I peek through the window in the art-room door, my heart wound up; I spot Libby talking to Katie and my stomach rolls. I'm a real spew risk. Out of my bag, I rip a piece of paper from the back page of my art book and write: *Sorry*. I fold the page in half; I contemplate elaborating, but it's pointless, she will never understand why I had to stand her up, that all my hope was tied up in that one shot at SOFA. You'd only understand if you were in my shoes.

I push open the door. The room goes silent and everyone stares, exactly as I predicted. News spreads fast when your artwork is pointed and in-your-face. I walk up to Libby, focus on the ground, heart drumming, and drop the note in front of her. I don't wait for her to say anything. The class is quiet, watching my every move, the silence from Libby deafening.

I take my seat. Through the window I can see Mr Anderson standing next to a policeman who's taking photos. Mr Anderson looks up and directly at me. I divert my focus to my desk. I can still feel people looking at me, and I'm relieved when, from the corner of my eye, I watch Libby walk up to Mr Campbell's radio and switch it on; the school radio station blares. Instead of going back to her seat, she heads towards me, slides a folded note in front of me, and immediately goes back to her seat. I make the mistake of glancing up – I'm being watched, every move I make – and decide to save the note for later.

Katie whispers, "What's that all about?"

Libby takes the seat next to her. "It's nothing."

Miss Reed walks in and stands at the front of the class, a substitute teacher next to her. "Mrs Gibbs will be taking your class for the next wee while."

She scans the room and pauses on me. "Dylan, come with me, please."

I grab my bag, walk down the aisle. As I pass Libby, we make eye contact for a split second and it's like she's about to say something.

Miss Reed is next to me. "Come on." Cold, in a way I've never heard before.

She walks a few steps ahead. She's never purposely ignored me before, but everyone has a breaking point, and I guess this is hers – she'll never have my back again. I swallow hard, fighting to squash the heaviness that wants to fall out. Miss Reed and I will never be the same.

We reach the two seats outside Mr Anderson's office.

"Wait here."

I sit; Miss Reed stands with her back to me. "We've tried calling your dad so he can be in the meeting, but we haven't had a reply." Her voice is clinical, this isn't the Miss Reed I know.

I say nothing; there's no surprise Dad didn't care. I had gotten used to Miss Reed acting in his place.

94

"You do know how serious these allegations are, don't you?" I sense the agitation in her voice. "He was with me that afternoon; I have proof." She shows me the ring on her finger. "Do the right thing and come clean," she says, and she knocks on the door, not waiting for a reply.

I hear talking behind Mr Anderson's door but can't make out what they're saying. Stacked against the wall are a bucket of paint, a drop sheet, blue overalls, and a paintbrush.

Mr Anderson opens the door. "Dylan." He directs me to the seat opposite his desk, next to a police officer who's already sitting. A photo of a shirtless blond man steering a yacht sits on the desk.

The officer stands and holds out his hand; there's an eagle tattoo on his forearm, the wings stretching from his wrist to the inside crease of his elbow.

I shake his hand firmly. "Dylan, sir."

"Constable Mike."

As we take our seats, he pulls a black notebook from the top pocket of his padded vest, which has a sparkly unicorn sticker on the front.

Once the pleasantries are over with, Mr Anderson wastes no time getting to the point. "Two reasons you are here. We'll start with the artwork. The graffiti on the school wall – we have reason to believe it was you? Is it your work?"

My leg jiggles. Silence fills the room. The stares of Mr Anderson and the police officer weigh in on me, suffocating.

"No."

Mr Anderson turns his computer screen around and presses the space bar. "We believe this is you." Sure enough, there I am, spraying the art-room wall. It's blurry, but there's no mistaking the bag on the ground at my feet, the exact same shoes and bag as I'm wearing now.

Mr Anderson goes on and on about needing a support person, and living with the consequences of my actions.

"The exact same artwork is on the front of Mr Campbell's shop," the policeman says. "Is it yours?"

They stare with penetrating eyes, waiting for an answer. I fiddle with the cuff of my school jersey; an excuse to not look at them. It's not like I can deny it.

"Yes," I admit.

The policeman folds his arms. "Was it you who broke into Mr Campbell's shop and stole the spray paint?"

I hesitate. It's not like I can deny that either. "Yes," I say to the ground. If there's a hole to sink into, I need it now.

Mr Anderson goes on about how the shop incident and the school incident are being treated separately. "I'll leave it to the police to follow their process regarding the stolen paint and graffiti on Mr Campbell's shop. But as for your work on the side of the art class, you're fortunate that you will only be suspended. If you'd stolen school property, you would have been expelled."

I clutch the straps of my school bag still on my back, Mr Campbell's stolen graph tab inside, technically school property. If Mr Anderson sees it, he'll assume I stole that, too.

"Suspended."

"Yes. For five days, and you must clean up all the graffiti and apologise to Mr Campbell."

Suspended. That's a relief. I thought for sure I'd be expelled.

The police officer hands me his card. "This is your time and day to meet at the police station. We will go through our process then."

Mike opens the community paper and passes it to Mr Anderson; he looks at the front page, sighs, and shakes his head.

On the front page: Mr Campbell's shop window, my artwork front and centre, and the headline, *Is there something sinister with Mr Campbell's art shop that we ought to know?*

"You're to clean up the graffiti on Mr Campbell's shop – all of it," Mike says.

"Will this give me a criminal record?" I ask the policeman, not sure why that matters anymore either.

"Because you're over eighteen – just – yes."

I look at my leg jiggling. Suspended and a criminal record, there is ZERO chance of SOFA.

Mr Anderson says goodbye to the police officer and sits back in his seat. "Right, the thing we need to discuss."

I look out the window, watch the policeman get in his car.

"About the allegations that Libby has made against Mr Campbell. Were you with Libby at the beach?"

I focus on the police car rolling down the school drive, and ignore Mr Anderson.

"Now is not the time to play games; Libby and Libby's dad have confirmed you were at the beach. We know you were together."

"Okay, I was with Libby."

"Libby is a respected, trusted student, one of our top. Are you aware of the allegations she is making?"

"What allegations?"

Mr Anderson peers at me, his gaze boring into my soul. "Did you see Mr Campbell at the beach with Katie?" His tone is agitated.

"Yes. Well – I think it was him, but I'm not sure; it was hard to see." The walls are caving in.

"Right," Mr Anderson says. He stares at me intently. "I have reason to believe that Mr Campbell was *not* at the beach, that he was elsewhere at the time. He was proposing to Miss Reed. I have photo and video evidence that's captured the exact time and date. It couldn't have been him in the car with Katie." He sighs. "Your actions could have cost him his job, his career, his shop."

Nausea crowds my insides. He wasn't with Katie. So, who *was* Katie with, then?

"We have more investigations to do. In the meantime, you are suspended till Wednesday. I don't want to see you back in my office until then."

Mr Anderson stands and opens the door. He hands me the pail of paint and stacks the overalls, drop sheet, and paintbrush on top. "I'm meeting with Katie next." He closes the door.

I pull Libby's note from my pocket and read the message. *Please don't tell Katie it was me who told Mr Anderson, she'll never speak to me again.*

I stand back and look up at the bombed art-room wall; the word *predator* would be visible from space. Behind me, groups of students eat lunch in the courtyard. I hear their whispers, feel the stares. I slip into the overalls, lay out the drop sheet, open the tin of paint, dip my brush in, and paint a box around the three dinosaurs. I wish my head had been torn off; it would be less embarrassing and a faster way to end all of this.

Behind me, a familiar voice: "Hey."

I turn and see Libby holding a paintbrush; my body tingles with pins and needles.

"Hey."

She rolls up her sleeves and dips her brush in the paint; *Mr Campbell Room 7a* is written on the handle of the brush, which makes me smile. Libby stands next to me and glides the paintbrush down her side of the wall, splitting the box I painted in two, and sets to work her brushstrokes, forming a neat patchwork of grids.

"I guess we were wrong about Mr Campbell. I'm so embarrassed and sorry – you were right," Libby says.

Neither of us looks at the other.

"It's all good." It's really not. But how can I make her feel bad when she thought she was doing the right thing? I should be pissed at her. She's half the reason I'm suspended. But despite all that, I admire the person she is, that she has the guts to apologise, to face me when she knows she made a mistake. This makes it impossible to be angry at her.

I slop my brush onto the wall; paint drips down it in uneven dribbles. As we fill in our sides of the box, we edge closer.

"I'm sorry, too, and thanks for ... you know ... helping." Libby looks at me, her brush pausing mid-stroke.

"Don't mention it." A smile escapes my face. She's here helping me, despite everything that's happened.

Her focus returns to the wall. As she finishes her side with one last stroke, she stands back. "Spot the messy one. You're not a 'colour within the lines' kind of guy, are ya?"

I glance at my messy side. "Really, not."

We stand next to each other again, side by side, her arm dangling beside me, her hand just there. Sun shines on the wall, showing the individual brush strokes, mine messy, in all different directions, the paint uneven; hers tidy in grids with an even distribution of colour.

"I'm sorry ... for standing you up at the meeting with Mr Anderson ..."

Libby's attention diverts to Katie as she storms towards us.

"What the hell kind of rumours have you spread?" she says, stopping in front of Libby. Her face flushes red. "What's up with that shit? You told Mr Anderson all that bullshit?"

Something tells me she's had a meeting with Mr Anderson. The bell blares, and the groups of students head to class, glancing back at us.

I look at Libby. All eyes in the courtyard are on us.

I see the shift in Libby's expression, the moment she realises that if she doesn't say the right thing, her friendship with Katie could be over forever.

Libby fumbles. "Katie, I'm so sorry ... I ... um." Her eyes are wide.

I clear my throat. "It was all me. Libby didn't nark, it was me. I did it ... all me ... I lied so I'd have something against Mr Campbell ... so he'll pass me in art ..." I'm scrambling, but I can see she's buying it. The relief on Libby's face is edging me on.

Katie turns to Libby. "Is it true? You didn't nark?"

Libby nods.

Katie grabs Libby's arm and drags her away towards the field. All I hear is, "I don't get him at all," and, "you're lucky Mum didn't cancel our party plans."

As I pack up the paint stuff, I imagine their party, a room full of stuck-up rich kids drinking liquor stolen from their parents. Luka's arm over Libby's shoulder.

By the time I've picked up everything and returned it to the spare seat by Mr Anderson's office, the halls are silent. I head outside to my bike. Now that I'm forbidden to be at school for five days, I'd do anything to be allowed back, accepted in. So I can see Libby again.

Nine

It's three days into my suspension and the days have dragged. Muffled, unfamiliar drunken voices sing along to some crap '90s remake blaring from the Mitsi. I lie on my cardboard mattress. Dad's made new buddies and they party all day and night. It's eleven a.m. on a Friday, but they're not bothered. Seeing as there are zero houses around, there's no one to make a noise complaint. Police would hit the jackpot if they turned up; they'd find a halo of weed, cars with no number plates, and liquor I know my dad didn't buy.

I'm not sure how much more I can take. My plan was to spend as little time as possible here, only to sleep, which has become impossible as the parties never stop.

I pull my phone from my pocket; nothing from Libby. Bear nudges my bag, which falls over, spilling the graph tab onto the floor.

"I know, girl. I should get drawing." But since SOFA is off the cards, I have zero motivation. Bear buries herself in my bag and pulls out an empty chip packet; she licks what crumbs remain. We're out of food – there's nothing, no human or dog food.

I grab my bike and walk it past the adults.

"Boy, get me some ciggies." Dad turns to his groupies. "Boys, put your order in, and my boy will go get it."

They yell out stuff, clearly none of them having any clue how hard it is to conceal a dozen beers and several casks of wine. They're dreaming.

"Sure, got it," I tell them. I really don't and won't.

I head into town and leave the noise behind. Somehow, I end up at SOFA public gallery. People my age are rushing from one place to another, like they know where they're going. They've got the direction and destination sorted.

I'm not sure why I'm here, torturing myself. The outside of the main gallery is black and painted in epically detailed florals. The artist is mad talented. Inside the basketball-court-sized gallery, split into sections with floor-to-ceiling street art, an artist passes me pushing a trolley jammed with spray – the good kind, the colours a whole rainbow, not hidden in a backpack.

This is the only place where street art is valued. Hell, it's embedded in its culture; it makes up its soul. Without street art, there would be no SOFA; it's immortalised on every wall. For a conservative city with a zero-tolerance policy on street art outside of these doors, SOFA is hitting back hard; the community here backs their artists and art hardcore. I take in the place – this is what it feels like to be home.

I stop at the lady behind the desk. "How much to get in?"

She lifts her thick-rimmed glasses. "Honey, are you with the school group at eleven thirty?"

I am if it means I don't have to pay to get in. "Yes, I am."

"Oh, sweetheart, you wait over there, and your class will start soon."

A stream of people flows in. I sit in the couched area opposite a two-storey wall hung with portraits painted in popping candy colours that match their happy faces.

As the spot where I'm sitting fills with students – by the number of people wearing SOFA hoodies, this is the first-year class – the lecturer comes in.

"You must be new," she says, and she hands me, along with everyone else, a thick pad of white cartridge paper, a metal tin of watercolour pencils, and markers – the expensive ones where the colours pop off the page. The type Mum would drool over in the art shop but could never afford to buy herself.

"Follow me," the lecturer says.

We follow the small, blonde lady with the pixie haircut to a studio, where easels are placed in an oval around a bunch of random objects: a large vase of flowers, a car engine, and a mannequin.

I copy the other students and take my place in front of one of the easels.

"Hey, man, over here." A dude I've never met hands me a stool and sits at the easel next to me.

"Thanks, thanks heaps." I feel like my kind is welcome here – I feel like I'm where I'm meant to be.

The lecturer turns on some music, and I watch everybody open their art folders and pull out half-finished drawings, presumably from a previous class. I sketch a portrait of Libby, set in a background of technicolour flowers. I block in colour.

The guy next door leans over. "Nice skills, love the street-art vibe."

I don't know what to say; I have no words. I look at his work, a completely different vibe, an intricate, black, lifelike flower. "Amazing, the detail."

The lecturer stands behind me, and my heart picks up its beat.

"Street-art style – love it. We need one in our group. Keep it up."

I could be in a dream.

A few hours later, the lecturer announces, "Until next time."

I pack up and hand her the watercolour pencils and card.

"They come out of your fees," she says. "You keep all materials in this class."

The guy from before walks out with me. "What class you got next?"

"Er, the exhibition."

"It's cool that you get real practice making and hanging frames, aye." And he hurries off with the others, most in different directions, I assume to get to their next class.

I have no idea what he's talking about, what class I described, but I want in.

I walk around the other galleries, which exhibit every art style you can imagine, from teeny watercolours to giant murals. I look up at the mural taking up the entire back wall of the last gallery: a forest, in intricate detail. The artist blurb reads, *Dan Miles. A muralist, street artist, illustrator.* Here you can be any kind of artist you want, but most of all, you can be who you *really* are.

I head out of the gallery, and I'm unlocking my bike when my phone beeps. Libby's name on my screen. My insides glow. There's no actual message, but a picture of Libby and Katie as little girls, Libby dressed up as a policewoman and Katie as an artist. *Come celebrate Libby and Katie's eighteenth birthday party,* followed by an address and time and *BYO.*

It's tomorrow night. The fact she picked my name from her contact list as someone she wants to spend time with, I'm luminous. But only for a nanosecond. She's got a boyfriend, and I'm sure he'll be there. And even while I think it's not a good idea to go, I'm replying: *Cool, see you then.*

She replies with one smiley rosy-cheek emoji.

I'm feeling that emoji hard. I bike towards the supermarket. I'm not a fan of BYO of any sort, but I want to blend in. Plus, we need some essentials.

I lock my bike outside the supermarket where the rich people shop; where the staff don't watch closely, like there's an expectation you've got lots of cash. I pass through the doors and pick up a basket. The thing about lifting stuff – you've gotta fake it, pretend you have a stack of cash, then you'll blend in. The trick is confidence.

I walk down the pet food section. A jumbled list forms in my mind of what I need for the party. Deodorant, soap, booze. Do I need to bring a present? I have nothing she'd want and no money. As I stack five small dog food tins in the basket, I slip two up the sleeve of my jacket, balanced in the palm of my hand and hidden from view, then drop them in my jacket pocket. I use the same technique at the mini salami and pita bread section until my pockets can't take anymore without being noticeably stuffed. You can't be greedy; it's a sure way to get caught by the supermarket staff, then questioned by the police in front of everyone. I can't take that again. And just to top things off, they stick your photo on the shop doors; it's a new thing.

I wander the deodorant and body wash section. Even the aisle smells clean – cleaner than me. All the bottles are neatly lined up; they remind me of Libby and how great she was with Jack. I focus on the smallest bottles I can find, which come as a travel pack of mini things: deodorant, soap, comb, toothpaste, body wash – no hair gel, but otherwise, it's perfect. If I'd taken the bag of stuff Libby offered me at the library, I wouldn't be here right now.

I drop the packet of travel minis in my basket and look around, which is a rookie mistake. I try the stick-them-up-my-sleeve thing, but the packet is too big, too obvious. I watch the passers-by while I wait for another chance. I try again, checking both ends of the aisle, a supermarket worker now at one end. A lady wheels up a trolley of stock and slices the box with a craft knife. Before she lifts the handful of shampoo bottles onto the shelf, she looks over at me. The rectangular packet is now half wedged up my sleeve, stuck, half in, half out. I turn in a way that hopefully hides my hand. The lady holds her focus a little longer than is polite.

I pretend to look intently for something on the shelf when I hear, "It's newspaper curtains boy." Luka and an older-looking twin appear next to me. My gut sinks.

His brother looks confused. "What?"

Luka explains in detail about me nearly backing over him and the significance of the newspaper.

They laugh hysterically. I edge away, and my only option is to move towards the supermarket lady. Passing Luka and his brother means navigating past an elderly lady, but her trolley is stuck in the middle of the aisle and I need a clean run. That or I'll drop what's in my hand.

All I can do is ignore them so as not to attract more attention. Turns out being seen is overrated.

"What's that in your pocket – newspaper curtains?" Luka yells, purposely looking at the supermarket lady. "Looks dodgy to me."

I edge between Luka and the old lady and walk down the aisle towards the checkout. I drop the basket, still balancing the travel bag in my sleeve, secured only by the palm of my hand.

They follow behind. "In a hurry? What's in your pocket?" he repeats down the aisle.

Two ladies at the customer service look at me, then behind. One holds a walkie-talkie to her mouth. At this point I can drop what I've got and run, or just run. It's lunchtime and the aisles are now filled with uniforms, so I go with a third option, playing it cool by the checkout and pretending to ponder the newspaper. I recognise Mr Campbell's shop window on the cover, a dinosaur tearing Katie's head off.

The supermarket lady edges between me and the newspaper. "Can I help you?"

They know you don't need help; they're trying to stall so they can get their reinforcements ready, aka the local policeman.

"I'm good, thanks, just reading." Trying to act casual.

Entering the checkout with his brother, Luka stacks a dozen beers on the conveyor belt. He's behind the lady, making faces. He holds up a can of deodorant. "This one's good, I hear."

"Sir." The shop lady sounds impatient. "Come this way, please. We would like to have a little chat."

The dude with *Manager* on his name tag puts one hand on my shoulder and escorts me to a chair at the front of the shop. I take a seat while he stands in front of me.

Shoppers watch, like I'm a spectacle, a sideshow for their cheap entertainment.

There's no point in denial – it only extends the time they interrogate you.

"What's in your pockets, bud?"

I say nothing and empty the stuff from my sleeve and front hoody pocket into the basket.

"Anything else?"

Luka and his brother move out of the checkout, and Luka holds up his phone as the policeman from school appears next to me. Luka snaps a few pictures or video, which I'm sure he'll gladly share with Libby and the rest of the world.

"Dylan, we meet again. You'll need to come with me to the station."

I follow him out of the supermarket, past the photos of the other criminals stuck on the shop's front window. My picture will be there by day end for all to see. I'm sure Luka will post that, too.

The police officer starts the engine, and we drive through the car park, passing Luka, his brother, and Katie, who's slipping into a white station wagon. I duck down from view.

We pull up at the police station. The officer takes me to a room. The last time I was here I was under eighteen, and they made me wait for a parent to arrive, which didn't happen, and they eventually sent me home with a note on my record that child services would pay a visit.

The policeman sits at the table opposite me.

"Who can I call, mate? Your caregiver?" And then he does something no other policeman has done before. Out of a cupboard in this dingy office, he brings out a box labelled *Homeless essentials* and rests it on the table. "Help yourself to a few things." He hands me a bag.

The box contains an eclectic mix of tinned food, toothbrushes, and hair ties. I pick out two tins of dog food and place them in the bag. "Thank you."

"Here – this and this," he says as he loads the bag till it's bursting.

"Thanks."

I'm not sure what to make of this.

"I know you boys do it rough – your pets, too."

Is it that obvious?

He sits back at the table and asks me a bunch of questions, then gives me a lecture on how my future is dependent upon not adding any more to my permanent record.

"Unfortunately, you're eighteen and an adult under the law, so this will go on your permanent record."

A lady pops into the office. "No answer, I'll keep trying."

"I've tried calling your dad, but so far there's no pickup."

"He's at work," I lie.

"And where's that?" He has his tablet, and I can see he's waiting for me to tell him so he can update the data. The problem is, I can't remember what lie I told them last time.

"The pulp and paper mill."

"Oh, right – so same place."

"Yes."

Basically, there's nothing he can do. I sit there for three hours until he abandons hope that Dad will turn up and dishes out another warning.

"Look, I know you're doing it rough. There are services that can help with the essentials." He passes me a list of websites, the Red Gallery Café included.

I know most of these services – most people living rough do. In stealing food, I at least feel like I'm doing something to help myself, rather than relying on the pity of others. But sometimes there's little choice.

The police officer has been nice, a refreshing surprise. "Thanks."

And like that, he lets me go, even helps pull my bike out of his boot.

"You got talent, kid. Direct it somewhere positive."

I'm so taken aback at his use of the word "talent" that I'm slow to connect the dots. Now that he knows my work, he'll recognise it all around town.

When I get back to the tent, the music has stopped, and bottles and rubbish are scattered everywhere. All the people have gone, including Dad and the Mitsi. I check on Bear in the tent. As soon as she sees me, she races to her bowl outside the bathroom wall and nudges it with her nose. Out of my bag, I grab one of the tins the policeman gave me and drop food into her bowl, then refill her water dish.

My bomb stares back, the home-with-the-tent scene. I walk around to other side of the bathroom, which is unpainted, drop my bag in front of the wall and bomb the wall in black. While I wait for the paint to dry, I pick up all the bottles and rubbish, filling the public rubbish bin and repacking the empties into the beer-bottle boxes.

Back at the wall, I spray a portrait of a guy with rat features, but not in the ugly way most associate with rats. Knowing eyes, tidy fur, glasses, rounded ears, and a mischievous smile.

And I spray the definition of vermin: *Perceived as despicable and as causing problems for the rest of society.* I put an X through the sentence and spray *misunderstood* in black. I pull out the graph tab to take a picture ... battery dead.

Back in the tent, I text Marv. *Keen?* I attach the picture of Libby and Katie's birthday party invite.

I get an immediate reply. *Always, bro. Come by work at 9.*

Ten

Dad didn't text to say he wasn't coming home last night. I heard him and his buddies take off somewhere, but he didn't mention where he was going or when he'd be back; he never does.

Bear crawls up from inside my sleeping bag and licks my cheek. Last night was polar, the coldest night in the tent so far. Even wearing every item of clothing I own and triple socks, the freeze takes over my core and won't leave.

I pop my head out of the tent. Frost covers the sports ground, glistening white. It won't be long till the first snow arrives.

A car parks out front, and the dodgy Santa-looking dude helps Dad out of the car, flopping him over his shoulder.

I give a parental eye roll. "What's he done now?"

"He mixed up too many things." Even dodgy Santa dude rolls his eyes. "Name's Ginge. Where you want him?"

I lead the way to the tent, open the zip and hold back the door flap; he ducks in and lays Dad on my mattress.

Bear scrambles out of my sleeping bag and curls up next to Dad's grey face with its sunken cheeks. I watch Dad's chest rise and fall; he's alive, he only looks dead. At least someone else was doing the rescuing for a change.

Ginge's head skims the tent roof. "Your dad was tryna convince a guy to let him live rent-free in his house, in a room barely big enough for a single mattress – he was tryin' it on with offers of free weed and booze. Didn't work, though."

It takes a moment for the words to sink in. He's gonna ditch me for his own place. I shiver; he didn't even give me a heads up. My body tenses, ready to burst through too-tight skin. Unable to hold the pressure inside, I stomp out of the tent to the bathroom block as the lump in my throat threatens to cut my air supply. I pull my hand back and slam it into the bathroom wall. Hot searing pain radiates through my fingers into my fist and up my arm; the sense of release is electric, the red frustration dripping away, and I fall to the ground, alone in the dark.

Ginge appears and pats my back. "He'll be right, just needs to sleep."

He's missed the point. Dad was going to ditch me. I flashback to Mum in the hospital, a day before her eyes closed forever, the stupid promise I made her.

Ginge helps me back to the tent; Dad's asleep. I fight the urge to shove him – he wouldn't care, and the inferno in my chest dies. There's only so much energy you can give toxic people before you stop talking, before you give up and go numb.

I swallow hard. "Thanks," I say, my voice cracking. And Ginge leaves me with Dad.

I shake Dad's shoulders violently. "You're going to ditch me, you piece of crap?" He's out cold. I could leave him alone – has he thought of that? I wouldn't, because he's family, and if arse-kicking could happen from heaven, Mum would be on to it.

For the rest of the day, Dad sleeps. I distract myself with a sketchbook and making a birthday card for Libby, which feels lame, but without any money and her party in three hours, it's my only option. I picture her unwrapping a present from Luka, some blingy, expensive piece of jewellery. I *could* get her something better, but it would mean stealing, and it wouldn't feel right. Nothing I draw is good; I rip out the page of flowers I've drawn, scrunch the page in a ball, and basketball-throw it into the bin.

It's eight thirty when Dad comes outside. "Got any food?"

"Get your own. I hear you're looking for a place of your own."

I hate how my throat catches and the words quiver, sounding less pissed than I wanted and more on the verge of crying. I swallow hard and manage to redirect the mounting frustration, desperate for Dad to say something – anything – hoping it was all a misunderstanding. But I know it's not.

"Don't be like that, boy. Where'd Ginge go?" He walks off towards the Mitsi, ignoring my question. Avoiding all emotional confrontation is his thing.

I follow behind him. "Are you gonna even answer me?"

He doesn't turn back, doesn't look at me, doesn't acknowledge my existence. Even as he backs the car, there's not one look or one word. It's what he does when people are angry at him; he runs away, a coward afraid of facing the facts – Mum dying was his fault.

I watch the Misti leave; I feel like a shaken Coke bottle, desperate to release pressure. I swing my good hand back and slam it into the bathroom wall again. The pain takes my breath away. "Fuck it!" I yell, and once the sound stops echoing through the stadium, it's deadly silent, and I know I'm on my own.

I ride through Central Garden Square on my way to pick up Marv. Food trucks line the edges of the square; the trees are lit with fairy lights. People chill out on the clock tower steps, stuffing fat souvlakis into their mouths, wiping rust-red sauce away from their cheeks.

I sit on the bench seat opposite the souvlaki hut. A line forms from the clock tower down to Marv, who's filling flatbreads. Behind Marv, Mr Antoni puts a handful of meat onto a hot skillet. The oil sizzles and crackles, and a cloud of smoke billows from the cart. The aroma of barbequed lamb fills the air. My stomach groans, but I'm in no mood to eat.

Next to the souvlaki truck is a coffee cart filled with small bunches of brightly coloured flowers for sale; they remind me of Libby.

Marv holds up one hand and mouths, *Five mins.* A souped-up metallic car passes, releasing its blow-off valve. It drives down the street and past the Red Gallery Café. Libby will be at the party by now.

A sparrow jumps around at people's feet, pecking at dropped burrito and souvlaki crumbs. The bird takes to the sky, its wings outstretched, and hovers over people eating. Occasionally it flies in for the bite, but bails as soon as someone makes a sudden move. It's beautiful and brave.

I pull out a page from my sketchpad and fold it into birthday-card size. On the front, I sketch the sparrow mid-flight, wings outstretched, wide eyes, round face. I shade in the footpath behind and write in tidy letters, *You're beautiful.* For a nanosecond, I think about leaving them there.

I shade over the letters, blend them into the footpath. Inside the card, I write:

Libby
Happy Birthday.
Dylan.

Marv hangs his head over my shoulder, balancing on his bike.

"Deep, bro."

"Ready?" I slide the card into my bag. I'm not sure if I'm lame enough to give it to her.

We bike through town and wind up at Ocean View Road. The houses get less ghetto and more flash the higher we ride. With each pull on the handlebars, the cuts on my swollen hands send sparks of pain through my fingers. My lungs gasp for air. I pull over at the top and catch my breath, the city below a kaleidoscope of lights. In the distance I spot where the main road follows the sea, the dark, tree-laden gap where Dad should be.

We bike along the ridge of the hilltop. Music booms louder as we grind our way up the hill. I stop outside a black fence. "This"– I suck in a breath – "is it."

The fence is thick with jasmine, the gaps too small to see through. The bass of a SIX60 song bounces off the hills.

Marv presses the button by a speaker next to a sign that reads *Sustain Architects Ltd* in green block letters.

"Hello."

No one replies. The black metal gate in the fence swings open. At the top of the drive, two flat-roofed rectangular blocks sit side by side, connected by a glass-walled corridor. Solar panels cover the roof, and lush green plants blend the house into the bush surroundings. A garage, bigger than most houses I've been in, booms with music and overflows with people.

Too many people.

We lock our bikes to the front gate and make our way up the steep drive. My stomach twists, and I'm very aware we're being watched; we're outcasts invading new territory.

The crowd outside the garage is all girls with wide-rimmed glasses, dudes with man buns, and guys wearing hoodies with *Beachlands High Football Club* printed on the back. I search through them for Libby.

We walk through the crowd and into the garage, and the bass vibrates through my body. I scan the room; people dance in waves to the music.

I spot Katie in the corner. She lowers her eyes, whispers to the girl next to her. I know when I'm not welcome.

Katie disappears into the crowd, then appears in front of me. "Why are you here?"

"Libby sent me an invite." I pull out my phone and show her the message.

"Fine." She storms off. Maybe I should have started with "Happy birthday."

Marv shrugs his shoulders. "Know when I'm not welcome." He turns to leave.

And then I see her on the front steps, leaning at an odd angle, a wineglass in her hand. As I walk towards her, Luka tops up her glass and pushes it up to her mouth. Libby giggles; wine sloshes over her jeans and the arm of her black leather jacket. Luka tries again.

I place my hand over the glass. "She's had enough."

"Dylan," Libby slurs, her eyes half-open – the same way Dad gets when he's nailed. It's unattractive, but the electricity is raging.

Luka pushes me away. "Loser! Get lost. You don't belong here." He faces Libby. "Caught this idiot stealing. Got a video of him being taken away in a police car." He roars with belly laughter. "And get a load of this photo. What have we here? Is this your artwork?"

The back of my neck tenses.

He pulls out his phone. "Share, to all." He taps his phone.

He laughs so hard he can barely finish the sentence.

That familiar lump builds in my throat, and my cheeks heat up. If this guy doesn't shut it, he's gonna get it.

"How do you like this?" Luka pulls Libby's face towards his and tries to kiss her; her face flops side to side and she swats him away, which breaks her balance, and she slides to one side. I catch her before she falls off the steps. All her weight falls into me.

"Get me out of here." Her face is pressed into my chest, extinguishing my rage. He's lucky – the mood I'm in, I wouldn't have held back.

And that's when Katie fires me a look, a thanks. She's hard to read.

"I'm sorry, Katie, for causing trouble," I say. Libby tries to stand and falls onto me.

Marv grabs Libby's arm and helps me steady her. "Let's get outta here, man. Ain't our scene."

Libby's head flops onto my shoulder. "I want to go home."

I pick Libby up and haul her over my shoulder. I know I'm an idiot; this is not the smartest move. Luka is not a stable person, or trustworthy.

"I'll take her home," I call to Katie, who's mid–intense conversation with Luka. She looks over, teary, but mouths, *Thank you.*

"I'll call a taxi and get her bag," she says.

Luka catches up to me. "Put her down, or else."

"Settle, dude. I'm not stealing your girlfriend. You heard her. She asked *me* to take her home, where she'll be safe."

I speed up. Flopped over my shoulder, Libby bounces as I walk down the drive.

I'm not sure why Luka doesn't follow, but suspect Katie has something to do with it.

Marv matches my pace. Libby's arms around my shoulders are creating a warm imprint. She fits perfectly to the shape of my back. At the bottom of the drive, I lean her against a tree and rest one hand on her shoulder to stop her from sliding down the trunk.

Marv laughs. He joins his hands together to form a heart shape. "Bro, ya'll got the sweeties for her." He lights a ciggie and takes a drag, blows a puff of smoke into the night sky.

Libby picks up a handful of sycamore seeds and laughs as they helicopter to the ground.

At the top of the drive, Luka watches us as he gathers his entourage.

Katie walks down the drive with Libby's bag, cell phone to her ear.

I take the bag and grab a packet of tissues from inside. Libby crawls away from her vomit pile and sits against the other side of the sycamore tree. The smell reminds me of Dad – not attractive, but that's the booze talking. I kneel in front of Libby and wipe her mouth with the tissues. She looks at me, eyes half-shut, glassy and green. I'd never have picked her for a big drinker. She's always seemed cautious, almost like she'd be morally against it. But that's the thing about booze – it sucks the real life out of people and spits out an annoying version.

Libby rests her hand on my knee. "You're a sweetheart." Her body slumps as I remove my hand. Booze makes people talk either complete bullshit, or brutal honest truths they'd never have the guts to say sober. "I don't usually drink," she says, and swings her arms around my neck. "Huuugs."

I wrap my arms around her and hug her back, and we're perfectly connected, like Lego.

I throw Katie the spare top from my bag. "You change her."

Katie doesn't argue.

Marv lights another ciggie as we turn our backs.

Libby giggles, copying Katie when she says, "Hands up." Then she says, in a shouted whisper, "Shhhh – it was me who told Mr Anderson about Mr Campbell."

"What the hell?" Katie snaps back.

Libby's timing is poor, another downside of booze. She attempts to stand, using me to pull herself up.

"She was trying to look out for you," I say.

"I'm done," Katie says as the taxi van pulls into the driveway and beeps.

Libby pulls my t-shirt away from her stomach, unaware Katie has stormed off and is already at the top of the hill with Luka's arm draped over her shoulder. "We be friends, aye, Katiekins?" she says as she checks out the picture of Frida Kahlo on my t-shirt. I love that something of mine is wrapped around her body.

The cab beeps again, outside the gate.

Marv and me link our arms around Libby's waist and walk her to the cab.

"If she's sick, you pay to have it cleaned," the taxi driver says.

Marv slides the van door open. I help Libby into her window seat and sit next to her. Marv rides shotgun. Libby slumps onto my shoulder; her perfume peeks through the reek of booze. I stick my bag next to me, open and ready if she needs to spew again, and grab the card I made, slipping it into her bag.

As we wind our way towards town, I text Marv: *Got any cash 2 pay 4 the taxi?*

He replies: *Nope.*

The taxi misses the shortcut to the city. I'm stoked Marv doesn't say anything. Libby sleeps on my shoulder, one hand on my knee. It feels so right, connected, but so wrong because she's got a boyfriend. We're fundamentally different. She's somebody going places, gonna achieve big and beautiful things. I'm going nowhere, fast.

The van turns the last of the hairpin corners.

We come to a stop outside the souvlaki hut. Neither of us has any money.

"That's us, then. It's all been taken care of," the taxi driver says as Marv helps me steady Libby out of the van and onto the pavement.

"Think your uncle will let me IOU a souvlaki?"

"Yeah, man." Marv pulls the bikes out of the taxi and lays them on the ground. He disappears through the side door of the souvlaki truck. I set Libby on the bench seat, and she rests her head to my shoulder again. Mr Antoni squirts sauce over a flatbread and wraps it in tinfoil.

Libby shivers. I swing my arm around her shoulders. The stars are out in force, illuminating the deep indigo sky. Libby relaxes into me as Mr Antoni brings over a blanket and drapes it over us, and I feel it's me powering the night sky.

I remind myself it's easy to get the wrong impression from drunk people. But I'm happy to enjoy the lie right now.

Marv steps out of the truck and hands me a coffee in a polystyrene cup. Steam rises against the frozen air.

"I'm outta here." Marv pumps my hand. "Laters, bro." He bikes off up Main Street.

I hold the souvlaki to Libby's mouth. She takes a bite, chews with her eyes closed, not moving her head from my shoulder.

Libby falls asleep between bites. It takes two hours to get souvlaki and coffee into her. I can't remember the last time anything felt this good, warm and cosy. I watch the food trucks feed the drunk and disorderly, before packing down their workstations and locking up for the night. I'm not about to disturb Libby.

Libby wakes, lifts her head and glances around, peers down at my t-shirt.

"Thanks for looking after me ... and for the clothes," she says in a husky voice. This time her eyes focus on mine. Her mascara smudge makes the green of her eyes pop.

"Want some?" She lifts the takeaway tray, with the soggy end of souvlaki, towards me. And beams a smile – dimples pop, one in each cheek. And there it is. Electricity fires through me, illuminating every cell in my body.

"I'm good." I laugh with her.

Libby checks her phone. "Oh shit, the time." Her smile turns to panic as she grabs her bag and stands. "I've got a million missed calls from Mum." Libby wobbles as she stands, as she texts.

I catch her as she falls. "I'll walk you home."

"Okay." She loops her arm around my waist, steadying herself. My insides glow, luminous. We edge closer to the Red Gallery Café.

"I love your work around town; so does my mum." She stops along the street, points to a faded heart bombed on the concrete wall that separates two shops. "It's yours, right? That's the gold you always use to edge stuff."

"Yep. Mine, from when I started out." Right after Mum died, but I don't mention that.

We cross the road, and when we reach the red door of her apartment, Libby unhooks her arm from my waist. "Well, this is me." She looks at me. Our gaze, our smiles, it's like they're connected.

A woman's voice comes from behind the door; the café next door is shut up, black. "That you, Libs?"

The lock releases and the door swings open. A woman with short, frizzy, orange curls steps out. Same eyes as Libby. "You smell like a brewery." She looks Libby up and down, stops at her t-shirt.

"This is Dylan. He rescued me, fed me souvlaki and coffee."

"Hi, Libby's mum," I say brightly, and extend my hand.

"Thank you for looking after Libby," she says, ushering Libby through the door.

"No worries." My eyes fix on Libby, and she grins.

Libby waves as her mum closes the door. I stare at the door like an idiot, listen as they climb the steps into their apartment, and wish I could do the night all over again.

I float back to my bike in Central Garden Square, ride down Main Street and take the underpass down into the train station. The screech of my brakes echoes through the tunnel as yellow dome lights flick on. A couple are asleep, leaning against the wall, next to them a pram with bags draped off both handles, the baby just visible under a mountain of blankets.

I stop next to a sign that says *No sleeping, camping, or loitering* and lean my bike against the white concrete wall.

I spray the outline of Libby's face, mad big hair piled into a messy bun, a red pencil, *Artistry* etched into the non-pointed end. I spray her eyes green, and her hair streaked with bronze and gold, lips watermelon pink, with a sea of hearts that float out her mouth and down the side of the wall.

My phone beeps and my stomach drops when I see Libby's name: *Thanks for walking me home and for the card.* And a picture of it pinned to her noticeboard surrounded by hand-drawn anatomy parts.

Glad U like it. Happy Birthday! PS epic anatomy drawings.

I wait for a reply, staring at my phone like an idiot. It beeps, and my heart repeats.

No words but an excessive number of smiley-face emojis. I know I'm smiling like an idiot.

On the wall, I spray two portraits, both exactly the same. Above one, I spray *homeless*, and above the other, *not homeless*. And inside both, in the exact same way, I fill in their anatomy, inspired by Libby – the arteries, veins and muscles in popping rainbow colours. Both with the biggest fattest pink heart. At the top, I write *SAME SAME*.

In reality, the heart of the homeless person is exploding.

I glide home, every cell in my body fired up with electricity. I could light up the city. Strike that – the universe.

Eleven

It's my first day back at school after being suspended. The high of walking Libby home after the party rages; we've texted nonstop. I sent her pics of my visit to SOFA and she loved them so much, she and her mum visited the gallery. Shamefully, I've become glued to my phone for FOMO – a fear of missing out on a text from her. Each one is a warm surprise, like I see life through a new filter that masks the fact that me and Bear are two tiny, lonely specs at the end of a deserted road that leads nowhere.

I ride towards school past the beach; black clouds, choppy waves, a freeze in the wind that numbs my fingers. At the lights, my phone beeps and, like every time Libby's name appears, my body tingles, excited.

I open the picture she's sent, of a detailed watercolour pencil drawing of a heart, each anatomical part layered in popping colours. She's got mad talent.

Work number six for my portfolio. What number are you at?

Since I avoided her question about my portfolio and where I'm at with it, she's been harassing me to not give up applying to SOFA. Like a cheerleader, she sends me GIFs of dancers holding pom-poms with captions that say, *don't give up*, or *you got this*, or *you can do it*. She's convinced SOFA wouldn't turn down the right artist. I want to get swept up in her enthusiasm. I'll admit it's rubbed off a little; combined with my new filter set on optimistically enthusiastic, I *want* to believe her. What she doesn't know is the extent of my criminal convictions. On the SOFA application form, I'd have to tick the box admitting I have a criminal conviction, and that would be the end of it.

I turn off into town, passing a neon orange crash sign, a colour I can't use anymore. Emergency vehicles block the street, and two paramedics rush around a body too *still* beside a beat-up car. My body shivers and a familiar sting hits the back of my eyes. I'm hammered by memories of Mum, and I'm reminded she didn't get to live out her dream to finish art school or see me live out mine. Like she's here cheering me on, the crash is a reminder that life is unpredictable, and there are no guarantees – that I shouldn't give up on SOFA, not at least until I can say I've fought hard.

I text Libby, surprised by how amped I feel. *SOFA comp is on. We back, baby!*

Her reply: *YAYYYY!!!!!* And of course, a GIF, more pom-pom cheer-leading; the girl is obsessed, I'm loving her vibe.

At school, Mr Campbell's white station wagon is parked in the lot. I push my bike into the bike rack. People watch and whisper.

Pinned to the side of the administration block is a banner: *Join the Ball Committee*. Katie stands behind the desk, talking to a senior. "We need all the help we can get." Her voice is upbeat.

I stare at the ground, quicken my pace as I pass in the hope I'll go unnoticed. I'm already inside when I hear, "We could use your help with the artwork. You are, after all, experienced." Her tone is no longer upbeat, and has a pointed edge to it. And she's right next to me, taking two steps to my one.

124

"I'll do the ball art." I don't look at her, keeping my focus on the art-room door at the end of the hall.

"Perfect. It's a deal, then."

I look at her intently and say, "If you don't tell anyone about my art or anything about me."

"Sure."

Before I can read her expression, she turns and slips back to where she came from, but it was worth a shot.

From behind, I hear Luka's and Libby's voices. "So, the band is booked for the ball, thanks to your dad agreeing to pay for it." I slow my pace. I'm desperate to turn, to see her face, my body in a battle with my mind. Until I hear Luka's voice as they argue over songs that should be played. She'll go to the ball and dance with him. They are together; he's her boyfriend – a very, very irritating fact.

I'm relieved art class is empty and take my seat on the back bench by the window. My leg jiggles, my eyes are on the art-room door. Usually, under these circumstances, I'd sketch out a bomb, art the nervousness away, but my mind is too hyper to concentrate. I haven't seen Libby since the walk home.

The door pushes open and she walks in, followed by Luka. I look outside at trees flustered by the wind and the rain lashing the concrete at sideways angles.

When I finally look to the front of class again, they're sitting upfront in their usual spot. Libby cranes her head back and glances at me with a slight smile, and it's as if a floodgate opens. My body has zero control and I grin back – don't even try to fight it.

Mr Campbell barges into class. Everybody looks at him and then at me, like a game of awkward tennis. He turns to the whiteboard and writes:

1 SOFA class trip and compulsory assignment

2 Emerging Artist Exhibition at the Red Gallery and Café.

"About the class trip tomorrow," he says. "We'll visit several locations, starting with SOFA, continuing with the topic of art in our community. The assignment that goes with the trip is due Monday, nine a.m., no exceptions. It's compulsory."

Half the class groan. I don't know what they're worried about – it's easy grades.

My eyes end up back on Libby; it's the hardest thing to not look.

"Moving on to number two," Mr Campbell booms. "Our class has been given free entry to Francesca Green's exhibition at the Red Gallery Café for this Saturday at six. I've given Francesca a list of names; so, to get in, you need to say you're from this class."

Does that include everyone in the class? Is my name on the list, or is it only the students he's selected, those deemed worthy?

Libby turns to the class. "If some of you don't mind coming a bit early and helping to set up chairs, hand out food, that kind of thing, that would be awesome."

Luka pipes up. "Dig deep, people; we are a team. Let's pitch in and help out." It's as if he's motivating his team of footballers. From the stare he fires at me, I assess that invitation excludes me.

Mr Campbell instructs the class to pull out their laptops and open to a page. "Dylan, you can use the computer in the resource room." His tone is friendly – and loud, so that everyone understands I'm too poor for my own technology.

I walk down the aisle, past Katie on her mint graphics tab. She doesn't look up. I get it. For a split second, when I pass Libby, we're centimetres apart; she looks up and my insides drum. She whispers, "Hi."

I grin back and say, "Hey," egged on by Luka's grimace that Libby has acknowledged my existence.

I start up the computer in the resource room and access my school page. I stare at the blank Word document, distracted by the hum of the class gossiping, not working. For the rest of the time, I try to focus on the assignment and retype the same sentence a billion times. When the bell rings, I wait until the class is silent and I hear Mr Campbell leave out the side door.

At lunch, I walk to the beach the long way, to avoid the backfield packed with staring faces and to minimise the chance I'll bump into Mr Campbell or Luka with his arm over Libby's shoulders.

My phone beeps. Libby's name pops up in my inbox. I legit am a smile-face emoji.

Where are you?

I take a picture of the black brick building we sat against, with the beach in the background, and hit *Send*.

I wait for a reply, but after half an hour give up and skim pebbles into a puddle. I lean back against the black wall; in the distance, the school bell rings. As I stand to leave, Libby appears, and I kid you not, at that moment the sun bursts through black boulder clouds and my nerves tingle.

"Hey," she says in front of me. When she was drunk, it was easy to talk to her, to make eye contact.

"Hey." It stumbles out.

There's an awkward silence, me beaming like a fluorescent idiot. I'm not sure what comes over me. I sit down and pat the ground next to me. "Want to sit?" I'm unsure where the courage comes from.

Her smile fades, and she looks behind her at Luka walking towards us.

The neon colour dies and I'm embarrassed I got it wrong, stupidly thinking she wanted to hang out.

In a flurry of words she says, "I'm wondering if you'll help with the art-work for the school ball – the banner? A photo booth? I wanted to ask you in person. Katie said you agreed to, but I wanted to know if –"

The words speed out, flustered, no gaps in between. She stops mid-sentence when Luka stands next to her.

He doesn't acknowledge my existence as he turns to Libby. "I told you Dad said he'd pay for an artist."

Libby rolls her eyes and snaps, "And I said why pay all that money when we know an artist." Is she referring to me? I'll take it. "He's got experience painting large works in the style that matches our theme."

"He does not, and Dad could find someone better."

She sounds agitated; they both do.

They're face-to-face arguing. "It's the Gatsby theme, Luka, not rich artists who paint weird stuff. I live with someone who does that."

Luka glares at me. "He's a vandal. Think about it – it doesn't look good."

And that's when I've had it with Luka. I stand up; the action breaks their steamed conversation.

I turn to Libby. "Happy to help. I'll draw up some sketches. You can take them or leave them."

"He can't do Gatsby. Look at him. I doubt he even knows what that is." He laughs.

My throat begins to tighten, my warning that if I let him get to me, I'll punch him to the ground. "You've made a lot of assumptions there," I snap.

He assumes I'm stupid. I grip the straps of my backpack because if I don't, my fists will do things they'll regret.

I walk towards school, listening carefully to their conversation behind me.

"See, he's happy to, problem solved." Libby shouts, "Thanks, Dylan. I'll text you about the next ball meeting."

And I could fist-pump the air. I can set aside that I'm morally opposed to balls on account of them being lame, but it's a legitimate excuse to hang with Libby, and that aside, she asked for my help. Not gonna lie, it feels good that she wants and needs it.

I have graphics and study period in the library, and I manage to stay undercover and out of sight for the rest of the day. I get some dope concepts sketched up for the ball in the back of my graphics workbook, while half-distracted checking my phone for new messages.

When I get home, Dad and Bear are still gone, and there are empty booze bottles everywhere.

Twelve

I work on the ball art until stupid o'clock. I should be focused on assignments. Thanks to the sweet graphics program on the graph tab, I'm stoked with the dope banner options I've come up with. They'll look mint on the back wall of the hall. I design moustache and crown cut-outs for the photo booth, the kind that you attach to sticks and hold up to your face. I'll be gutted if Libby doesn't like them.

As I flick through the pages of designs, a worry creeps in. What if she *doesn't* like my stuff, and regrets asking me?

Before the graph tab runs out of power, three percent left, I open my messages, tap in her email address and attach the files.

Hi Libby,

Here are the designs for the ball. Totally cool if you don't want to use them. Let me know what you think.

Why are you with Luka? He's a dick.

I delete the last line.

Dylan

and hit *Send.*

Outside I hear the chug of the Mitsi. It screeches to a stop, the door opens, then closes and the engine revs as it drives off. I walk the frost-covered path to the carpark where I'm met by Bear and watch the Mitsi drive away until the glow from the headlights disappears. Not one word. Guess he's got better things to do. I breathe into my hands and jam them in my pockets.

Back in the tent, Bear sits up next to me, one ear pointed up, the other flopped down as she tilts her head to the side. I reckon Libby would think she's cute. I refresh my emails. It's three a.m.; she'll be asleep. I push the graph tab into my bag.

I pat Bear. "I'm not myself, girl."

In the centre of Garden Square, I lock my bike to a tree. I'm the first to arrive for the SOFA class trip, and I walk the concrete steps to the statue of a dude with a leaf covering his privates. If I was that ripped, why not? I sit on the steps to wait, and glance down the path leading through the square to Libby's apartment.

The rest of the class starts to arrive. Libby and Luka appear, holding hands. I force my attention to my phone and mindlessly scroll through my Instagram feed, which I've paid no attention to for a year.

Libby comes over, hair out, no pencil today. She beams. "I *love* your designs – they're perfect! Thanks so much; I'm super excited. The hall is going to look *so* beautiful thanks to you." The excitement bubbles out of her; it's contagious. Her happiness makes me comfortable.

"I'm stoked," I say, but it's more that I'm epically relieved – not that I'll tell her that.

"Mum's set aside a bunch of paint for us."

I could get used to that.

Then her mood switches to panic as she lists off all the stuff left to organise. "Ahhh, there's so much to paint, to create."

"Give me everything that needs painting, and I'll do it."

She sits down next to me. "Are you sure?" She opens out a list on her phone labelled *Stuff to paint*.

I scroll the list. "Easy."

She breathes a sigh of relief.

"You're a lifesaver, thanks so much." She lets out an excited squeal. Her enthusiasm is cute. Maybe balls aren't lame after all.

I watch Luka's eye roll, and as Libby stands, he swings his arm around her shoulder. I dip my focus to the ground. It's not that I forget he's her boyfriend, it's just that when we're together, the world fades in the background, everything and everyone forgotten, only her and me in focus. And Luka is killing my buzz.

She faces Luka. "Oh my god, you've got to check these out. They're adorable." She opens her bag, pulls out the moustache and crown already attached to sticks, holds the oversized black sparkly moustache above her lip. She's adorable. I laugh; she's too funny, and I can't contain it.

Luka groans. "They're lame," he snaps, and storms off, possibly to have a cry.

I'm having the best time.

Libby passes me the oversized dusky-pink glittery crown. I hold it above my head and she giggles. "You look beautiful," she says, and a grin sweeps across her dimpled cheeks.

"I really do." And we're both in fits of laughter.

I can't remember the last time something was this funny.

"You know you're officially part of the ball committee?"

"Sure." I'm gutted when we see Mr Campbell arriving, snapping us back to reality.

"I'll text you about the next ball meeting. Any days or times work best for you?"

"Anytime."

"Cool." She opens her bag, drops the crown and moustache in and goes back to standing next to Luka.

Mr Campbell, ready to start the class trip, hands out a map, worksheet, and assignment questions. "Find all the public art and answer the questions."

My phone rings. Mr Campbell stops talking and throws me a death stare. I grab my phone from my pocket, fumbling to silence the unknown number. I stick my phone back in my pocket and Mr Campbell resumes his conversation.

"Write the essay and hand in –"

My phone rings again. Mr Campbell's hands fly to his hips; his eyes bore into me. "Mr Marshall, silence your phone or hand it over."

I glance at the screen, at the same unknown number. Pushy, much? I look around; everyone's eyes are on me, including Libby's.

Luka groans. "Turn it off."

I hang up the call. No one ever wants to get hold of me enough to ring twice. My worry turns to Dad.

"Finally," Mr Campbell says, and resumes speaking. "All of this is due Monday, nine a.m., no exceptions. You can stay in groups or go solo; it's up to you."

My phone rings again, and agitated sighs erupt from a few still waiting for Mr Campbell to tell them they can leave. Worry gets the better of me. Who calls three times?

I walk away from the group. Mr Campbell raises his voice. "Late assignments or an inability to meet the rules will result in a fail. It's that simple."

I pace the sidewalk and answer the call. "Hello?"

Libby and Luka walk off; Libby glances back as someone says, "Is this Dylan?"

"Yes."

"This is Ginge, your dad's friend. You need to come to the hospital. It's your dad."

I don't wait for him to fill me in with details. He doesn't need to. I drop my phone in my bag, letting go of the assignment sheets in my hand, which float across the ground.

It's as if the world hits *Fast Forward* with no way to hit *Pause*. What if I get there and it's too late? All I can process is getting to the hospital. You never get used to the adrenaline; it's the same every time.

I don't care that the class is staring or that Mr Campbell is talking to me. I can't process his words, my hands shaking as I unlock my bike, the shivers setting in as I speed down the path, past Libby and Luka. I pound it towards the hospital as fast as I can.

As the hospital comes into view, sirens scream past. As hard as I pedal, it never feels fast enough.

I make it to the emergency department, a stitch in my side, drop my bike, heave air and run through the double doors. I stand in line to talk to the administration person. An elderly lady takes a lifetime to describe the exact location of her headache symptoms. I lean side to side to see past her, like I'm in another dimension.

To the left of the administration desk, the door swings open as a doctor enters. I burst past on autopilot. Someone yells, "Stop!" I don't care.

I reach the ICU receptionist. "Gary Marshall," I puff.

"Room five. But you can't –"

I speed down the hall, scan the numbers on the doors. I find his room and stand outside, frozen. The last time I walked into a room in this ward, Mum lay dead. I can't do that twice.

A nurse taps my shoulder. "Would you like me to go in first?"

"Is he alive?" I fight tears, not sure how long I can hold them back, like I'm trying to hold up the universe with one finger. It's only a matter of time before it falls and breaks.

The nurse nods and says, "Yes," as she opens the door.

A respirator puffs. Tubes run into Dad's nose, his chest rises and falls, and relief washes over me. Beyond my control, the floodgate opens. I bat away a few tears, swallow the rest.

Dad's skinny frame sinks into the mattress; his collarbones and cheekbones jut out, his skin has a grey, yellow tinge. I know he's seriously unwell. The adrenaline that got me here vanishes. It's like my insides have been emptied, the electricity cut, and what remains is devoid of life, black and empty, nothing inside left to give.

I sit on the seat next to Dad. "He's alive," I huff out.

The nurse pats me on the back and rests two trays of food on the side table. "He's going to be okay. Lunch if you want it."

It's kind of her, but I'm in no mood to eat.

I jolt awake, unaware I had fallen asleep. A doctor comes in and states the obvious – if Dad doesn't stop drinking, and whatever else he's on, his heart will give out. I listen, nod in all the right places, the gravity of the words too deep and painful to fully comprehend.

The doctor leaves. I force my focus on the class trip I missed today and the compulsory assignment I still have to get in.

I pull out my phone to text Libby, and there's already a message from her: *You okay?*

I ignore her question and text back: *Do you mind sending me a picture of the assignment?*

Libby replies with three images: the assessment sheet, map, and a photo of Libby outside the school van, SOFA behind her. Along the wall next to the van, a bomb I did ages ago, a line of hearts, one with a sad face, one happy, another angry, the last empty. The caption: *The Street Has Feelings*. *Xavier* in the corner. I expand the photo. Someone has coloured in the empty heart with intricate details of a healthy-looking heart, lifelike with chambers and valves.

Thanks! I wait for a reply, dying to know if it was her who coloured in my heart. Too impatient, I send another text: *I like what ya did with the heart* with an eye-wink-smiley emoji.

I've made an enormous assumption it was her, but as I zoom in, the style is definitely hers.

Haha! Hope ya don't mind, couldn't handle the heart feeling empty when there's so much love around!

It's like we're dancing to the same heartbeat, like a perfect symphony. She gets me.

Not at all, it's perfect! And I'm tempted to send a perfect line of hearts, one in each colour, but I delete them and choose a plain smiley-face emoji instead. I can't let myself get carried away. Something tugs at my insides, warning me to pull back, not go in too deep.

The mornings become a routine. I block the door of Dad's room, as he makes it half out of bed.

Dad yells, "You can't stop me."

"You're not leaving. You have to stay to get better."

And he launches for the door like I'm not there.

"You won't control me. The last time I looked, this was a free country, and this isn't no prison."

He rips the IV line from his hand; blood pools. The tantrums are normal, expected; it's part of the withdrawal process. I've seen Dad in two modes: drunk or in withdrawal. To get into the rehab programme, he has to go two weeks sober. He's never made it more than a few days, and after the free food and warmth, he gets strong enough to fight back and eventually escapes.

"Don't you want to get better?"

He doesn't listen; he never does. He rams into me and before I can regain my balance, escapes past me and runs down the corridor. But he's easy to catch. I push him back to his bed as he nuts off at me, and drop him on it. I hold him down with a firm grip and all my weight leaning into him; he flails his arms, bats at me, which sets him on a full-on meltdown.

"Get the fuck out of my way before I hurt you," he screams.

I strengthen my grip. "No."

Dad fights back, but I know he can't move. The power feels better than it should. I'm not proud; I can see my weight and grip hurt him, but I can't stop myself.

A nurse rushes towards me. I release him, immediately filled will guilt.

"I don't need you," he snaps. "I'm getting out of here! You can't make me stay."

My neck stiffens, teeth grit, and I know I'm at a point of no return, all control lost, no longer able to contain all I've kept buried. I know I shouldn't say what I'm about to say, but the words shoot out: "You killed Mum; it was your fault."

Years of wanting to say those lines.

I watch his face drop. I know I've hurt him. But I can't stop myself digging it in further, the years of pent-up rage I can no longer bury.

"Mum would still be here if you hadn't been off your face drunk and slammed the car into a power pole."

I storm out, too red hot, not proud of how it felt good to let it out, to be heard.

I ride back to the tent and feed Bear, replaying the conversation over and over, yet numb to what I said. I try to sleep and lie awake for hours before guilt consumes me and I ride back to the hospital to say sorry.

I sulk back to Dad's room. And when I open the door, the room is empty. I check the drawers, but Dad's stuff is gone.

The nurse making the bed says, "Sorry, he checked himself out."

For the next week, Dad doesn't show at the tent or answer any of my messages. And I know I was wrong – I shouldn't have said those things. I'd do anything to say sorry, to make things okay so he'll come back to the tent.

Thirteen

Each day I search in Dad's usual spots, desperate to find him and apologise, even if it's not all my fault; to release the guilt that's consumed my thoughts, that's gripped every corner of my body so heavy it's hard to think of anything else, or sleep or eat.

I call Dad's phone and leave my sixth message: *"I'm sorry, I shouldn't have said those things. It was an accident. I know you miss her too. Please come back."*

As I hang up, there's that familiar lump in the back of my throat, more mountainous than ever before. I swallow my lies; technically it was an accident, but the fact is Mum would still be alive if he hadn't been drunk. I thought it would be easier without him. But now he's gone, I can't be homeless and alone.

I lie in the tent, curled in a ball, my sleeping bag over my head, huddled into Bear. Nothing matters – not the freezing cold that never leaves, or my stomach that constantly rumbles; not Libby or SOFA, or that we are homeless. None of it matters if I can't make things right with Dad. I lie there till the sun rises, hoping that going to Libby's mum's gallery event will be a distraction.

I ride to the Red Gallery Café. Libby is kneeling down writing on a blackboard: *Emerging artists exhibition: on now.* One of her artworks hangs in the window.

I lock my bike against the streetlamp. Libby hasn't seen me yet.

Act normal, keep it together.

I'm right behind her. "Heya."

Since when did I say "heya"?

I tilt my head at her drawing. I can't make out if it's a mouth or a cup with foam gone wild.

She looks up at me and smiles. "Hey, is it bad?" And she grins at me cheekily, which immediately brightens my insides.

"If you're going for a dog's mouth leaking masses of foam, then you're onto something." I can tell by her smirk she knows it's terrible.

Libby laughs. "It's better than I thought, then."

I return the cheeky grin; she pulls a cloth from the pocket in her apron and wipes the board clean.

"You try." And she hands me the chalk.

I redraw the coffee cup in the style of a keep cup: glass canister in white, sky-blue rubber grip around the middle, and the same blue for the lid. I form the steam from the cup into words that say *Keep Cups Inside.*

Libby contemplates my work. "Way better, thank you. You are a maestro of your craft, my friend."

And there it is, the warmth spreading through me. I relax my shoulders, relieved the distraction is working.

Libby's mum – Francesca – pops her head out the door. "Awesome cup." She scans up and down the street. "No one's here to help yet?" A frown stamps her forehead. She looks stressed, a woman on a mission with shit to get done.

"Sorry, Mum," Libby says, deflated. "Dylan's here to help." Excitement rings in her voice.

"Happy to help," I say, facing Francesca.

"Really appreciate your time, thank you." She emphasises the *thank you*.

I'm pretty sure my cheeks have gone red, an annoying trait when I'm embarrassed – well, in this case, stoked – that my offer of help is needed. Tragic as it may be, it's nice to feel needed, and for something positive.

"Can you start now? Not much time left." Francesca's tone is fast and snappy.

Libby looks at her phone. "We'll start on those chairs." Her phone beeps, and her face drops as she reads the message. "Luka will try and make it." That brightness fades from her face.

Francesca waves us through the café door. "One is better than none. Let's get going."

We follow Francesca inside. Sun streams through the café windows. The roar of the coffee machine grinding beans does nothing to drown the buzz of people talking. On the back wall, a life-sized painting of Francesca, red frizzy hair, drinking a cup of coffee, *The Red Gallery Café* written in looping clean-cut vinyl.

We turn down a corridor to the back of the café and into a large gallery with white walls, wooden floors, *Emerging Artists Exhibition* in cut vinyl letters. A crazy variety of art fills the walls, from teeny delicate water colour abstracts to floor-to-ceiling murals. One, a detailed anatomy of a heart, I recognise immediately as Libby's pencil work. It's more than beautiful; she's incredibly talented. I lean in and spy the overlapping layers in the muscles, the tag on the corner – *Title*: Art Comes from Within; *Artist: Libby Green*. I imagine my work in a real gallery. It would be living the dream; being here surrounded by artists and art, it feels like how home should, welcoming, and like I belong.

I glance over at Libby talking to her mum. I take a picture of Libby's heart and send it to her with the words: *impressive, you have mad talent.* She glances at her phone briefly, still talking to her mum, and beams a smile. And for a second, she looks back at me, like we're connected.

She texts back: *I dabble* and *thank you* with smile emojis with heart eyes. Out from the wall, a trestle table sits loaded with café food waiting to be unpacked. Libby helps two of the café staff load stuff from trays onto a table.

"Start with the chairs," Francesca says; she draws where with her arms, the semi-circle taking the best view of the podium set up with a microphone.

I pull out a stack of chairs from against the wall. In front of me is a black-and-white photograph of a naked woman sitting in a Perspex box. Her head hangs down, hair falling over her face and touching her arms, which are wrapped around her knees. The only colour is a massive diamond-and-ruby ring on her wedding finger; the tag under the photo says LADY IN CAPTIVITY, *artist: Francesca Green, price tag: PRICELESS.* It's brutal honesty. I like it.

I unstack a chair and start building a row where Francesca indicated.

Me and Libby get into a goofy rhythm, me forming one side of the row, her the other, until we meet in the middle. I have to force myself to stop glancing over at her.

An hour later, the chairs are set up. Libby sits in the back row, head hung, furiously texting.

I sit next to her and take in the gallery. It's an impressive space.

"Thanks for helping," Libby says, her focus still on her phone.

"No worries." Where *is* Luka – and Katie, or anyone for that matter? I don't say anything, but I can tell what she's thinking by the broken expression on her face.

Francesca comes back into the gallery with a fresh batch of food to be loaded on the table. I get to work, setting up stacks of plates and cups and arranging the platters.

Francesca breathes out a sigh of relief. "Great, thank you. It's nearly go time." Her voice is quick, flustered, as she shuffles through cue cards for her speech.

"You'll be awesome," I say.

She pauses. "What if no one comes? Don't answer that. Thank you, Dylan. Public speaking is not my forte." And she hustles off to check the microphone on the stage is working. She blows into it; no sound comes out.

I grab my phone, write on the class Facebook page *Gallery Talk by Francesca Green*, link the location, and share it with the class and all my contacts.

I walk over to the sound system. Francesca pushes at random buttons.

"Err, not that one," I say.

She stands back as I reinsert the cords in their correct sockets. "Try now."

The microphone squeals, and Francesca's voice – "testing, testing, thank you, Dylan" – booms through the gallery.

I sit back down next to Libby. "They'll come."

She nods. "Yeah, I guess." Her tone is downcast. "Thanks for helping Mum. You're sweet, you know."

I shift on my seat, racking my brain to think of the right thing to say, ignoring her statement that right now makes my nerves fizz. "I'd love to see more of your drawings."

She giggles. "You've seen my work."

I smirk. "Oh, right, the foaming dog mouth. Surely it's on the wall here somewhere?" I crane my neck in exaggeration, looking around the gallery. "It'll go for millions."

Libby laughs. I did that; a happy hum radiates through my body.

Her attention diverts to Katie, who's walking in. She glances at Libby, and as if she hasn't seen her, begins to stroll around the gallery checking out the art.

Libby walks over to her. "Hey." Upbeat, as if nothing has happened.

"Hey." Katie's voice is flat, almost uninterested.

Luka struts into the room. Flustered. "So hey, we're here." He backtracks. "I mean, *I'm* here."

Libby, not listening, swings her arms around his shoulders. And I'm not gonna lie, it sucks to be me right now. I can't watch; I sit back at my seat, curious as to why Katie has stormed off.

Francesca sits next to me, wearing flashier clothes than before, plus lipstick and dangly, feather-shaped earrings. "Libby has told me about your work. I've seen it, actually."

I glance at my feet. "Oh – sorry about the work on the back wall of your shop." I'm embarrassed; she's looking intently at me. "I can clean it off. I'm sorry, won't happen again."

"No, leave it, I like it. You're a talented artist." Her reply floors me.

Francesca places a hand on my shoulder. "It looks better than what was there before."

She scurries off to talk to a group of formally dressed, serious-looking people entering the gallery.

In shock, I replay the conversation, questioning if I heard what I think I heard. I wish I'd said thank you. She has no idea how much it means to hear such a compliment from her, a real-life working artist I respect, who the art community respects.

Around the gallery, artists' work is on display for all to see, their hearts and souls cut open on the walls. And it hits me hard how right it feels to be here, amongst art, and the art community; how much I need art to fill my life, that I can't live any other way. Becoming an artist, it's not what I want to be. It's who I am.

Katie and Luka take their seats a few rows in front of me, whispering. It sounds like a tense conversation, and by the number of times they look back, they don't want me to hear.

The near-full gallery hushes as the lights dim. Francesca takes the stage; Libby wraps her in a hug, walks down the middle of the gallery between the two blocks of seats. She glances at me for the briefest of moments before her attention diverts to Luka, and she squeezes down the row of seats and sits next to him. My heart deflates.

Francesca begins her speech, introduces her work, herself, and thanks everybody for their help. "This is one of many exhibitions. The gallery's sole purpose is to represent emerging artists in our community."

Libby turns and smiles playfully. I grin.

The exhibition preview ends, and I survey all the work, visit each piece. No matter how much I try to not look at Libby, my gaze ends up in her direction. As she hurries Luka to each piece, her excitement bursts in her explanations and he couldn't look more uninterested; I count six times he checks his phone.

"When can we go?" he says in a monotone. "Let's go upstairs to your apartment."

Libby's face drops, deflated.

Katie stands next to me as Libby and Luka leave. "Where are those two going?"

I'm shocked she's speaking to me, her focus on Libby and Luka as they disappear out of the gallery.

"I'm not sure – to Libby's apartment, I guess." I hate that I'm jealous.

"I'm getting outta here." She stomps out of the gallery. I follow her through the café.

"Why are you following me, weirdo?" As we exit the main doors, the outside chill stings my face. The first of the winter snow dusts the road.

Katie crosses into Central Garden Square. It's pitch black; the place is legit freaky at night. She shouldn't be alone. I unlock my bike and follow her.

"You shouldn't be alone at night, especially in here. I'll walk you wherever you're going."

She slows her pace. "Fine ..." and a few seconds later, "thank you." Her tone sounds meek, broken. She slips her fur-trimmed hood over her head. I wish I could do the same; my thin school jacket is doing nothing.

We walk to Katie's home in silence. I get quiet is what's needed sometimes, and don't bother her with mindless chitchat or push her to tell me what's up. I don't know her well enough to ask. At her gate, she grabs a key and slips it into the lock. "Thank you, and sorry for calling you a weirdo. You're not." Then, in a brighter tone, "Wait here." And she runs up her drive and into the garage, returning moments later with a puffer jacket. "Keep it, it's freezing. My dad won't mind."

"Thank you, appreciate it." I really do. And as I sling my arms inside and do up the zip, I watch as she shuts the gate.

I pull the hood over, it's supremely warm, and I feel my body relax into it. I'm relieved that tonight's sleep in the tent won't be so polar.

I'm not sure why Katie was upset. She could have hailed a taxi. And then I remember – maybe she didn't have the money, maybe she needed the walk to sort her head. I get it.

Because I'm a sucker for punishment, I bike back to Garden Square. I peek through the trees at Libby's apartment. The light is on upstairs. Has Luka gone?

I walk up the steps to the concrete statue. On the wall next to it I spray a thick black outline of a heart-shaped balloon, deflated, and I leave it empty.

146

At the bottom of the steps, I spray a section of the concrete to appear as if it's peeling off, revealing the homeless faces hidden underground. I add a bubble and write: *Empathy: always empathy.* I spray *Xavier* and save the photos, emailing them to myself.

I finally make it home, disappointed Dad isn't there.

I curl up in my sleeping bag, Bear at my feet. The roof of the tent is stooping from the weight of the snow. It's dead quiet; there's no one but me for kilometres. The solitude is deafening, being here alone, not knowing where Dad is.

My phone beeps. Libby's name: *Thanks for today. Mum really appreciated your help; she's left a food voucher for you at the café desk. FREE FOOD!!!!!! Are you free Wednesday after school to meet at the gallery to start the banner?*

I re-read the text a million times. What's up with the free-food voucher, and FREE FOOD in capitals with six exclamation marks? They're legit yelling at me, a reminder that I'm homeless and can't afford food, like I'm some charity case.

I reply: *Wednesday works for me.* And I attach a GIF of a kid stuffing his face with cake. I wait for a reply until I give up; she's probably loved up somewhere with Luka.

Fourteen

Sunday, I spend the afternoon in the public library working on my assignment, which is due tomorrow. I spent the morning biking around to all the locations of public art and answering the questions on the assignment sheet, and I've just got the essay to do.

I scan the line of library art books, searching for the number that matches the ones on my list. Seeing as it's Sunday and the school library doesn't open at weekends, half the art class is here, but no Libby. I glance down the aisle of desks and take the last empty space. My phone beeps, and it's as if she knew I was thinking about her. My insides tingle.

You working on your assignment? What's with those obscure references? Trust Mr Campbell to make it hard, and a line of crying emojis.

I reply: *Just started; they're impossibly obscure,* and I add the frazzled emoji.

The art books I need are out, but I find a few that I can use to make a start, and I begin to draft my essay.

Libby: *Took me an hour just to find that last ref online*, and a GIF of SpongeBob SquarePants' brain exploding. *Just a final read through, and I'm done* and a GIF of an orang-utan doing a happy dance, which is hilarious.

I know I'm losing precious assignment writing time; I have under two hours to get those references.

I read through what I've written; the words glide past, their meaning lost, my focus gone.

Once I push Libby out of my mind, it doesn't take long to write the first draft. It's all there. All I need is the one obscure required reference.

I re-check the book stack to see if anyone has returned the book I need. At the library computer, I find the ecopy of the book, but you need money and a library card number, which requires a permanent address. I don't have either.

My last resort is to look around the library for someone using the book, and beg. I find Katie on her graph tab with the book I need.

"Hey, mind if I borrow that after you?"

She looks up, eyes back to her graph tab; she's mid-essay too. "Luka's after me, then it's yours. I'm slammed." She looks desperate and whisper-shouts, "Why'd Mr Campbell have to use hard-to-get, obscure references?"

It was clever, like a treasure hunt; to get one reference, you had to read the previous. A clever, pain-in-the-arse plan that forces us to read all the articles.

"Yeah, sucks." I need that book.

In a sarcastic tone, which I think is Katie's attempt to sound like Mr Campbell, "A fail if it's late and no re-sits."

I notice the empty desk next to her and recognise Luka's bag open on the seat. "Yep, sucks. Luka isn't here. I only need a few minutes, max."

Katie ignores my request as Luka appears behind me.

He places his hands on Katie's shoulders. "Finished?"

"No, share the page with me." And she pushes him away. "Dylan has the book after you."

He looks me up and down and smirks. "Well, I need it so ..." He glances at the library clock. "Not a lot of time left; I'll need half an hour." Very convenient that the library shuts in exactly that amount of time.

He returns his focus to sharing the page with Katie.

I breathe in and try to relax my shoulders. "All I need is two minutes." It comes out more direct than I intended. And the more he pretends I don't exist, the more I want to grab the back of his top and push his face into the desk. I need that reference to pass art. My SOFA plan depends on it. "I'll come back in five."

He ignores me; I know he's heard.

My phone beeps; Libby's sent a GIF of Frida Kahlo moving her eyebrows in a Mexican wave, and a smirk wipes my face ... if Luka only knew. I reply with a Minion wearing a G-string, strutting, and we go back and forth for five minutes sending hilarious GIFs.

After twenty minutes, Luka closes the book, and Katie's laughing at Luka's tragic attempt at impersonating Mr Campbell.

"Looks like you're finished." I reach for the book.

Katie, still laughing, says, "Yeah, it's yours."

Luka snatches the book and shoves it in his bag, closing the zip. "Nope, I still need it."

Katie says, her tone staunch, "Come on, you're finished. Give it to him."

"Na, I need to change a few things." He glances at the library clock – five minutes till the library is due to close. "I'll be done in five."

I pick up his bag; my arms tense as he grabs the book back. I heave air, and it takes all my energy to not push my free fist into his smug face. "Give it," I say with gritted teeth, and he laughs.

My jaw clenches as the librarian rushes over. "You boys, split up or get out."

I push down the rage, swallow hard and walk away. Lucky she came, otherwise I'd have pushed him to the ground. I've been evicted from this library more times than I can remember, and I can't risk any attention. As I reach the exit, the library's closing message blares over the speaker.

I text Libby: *Do you have a copy of that obscure book we need for the assignment?*

I bike to the café at the petrol station, take a bench seat and plug my phone and graph tab into the power sockets – free power and Wi-Fi till they kick me out. I search the net for a pirated copy of that book; no luck. To get it you need a credit card.

Libby replies: *No book, but login here, it will get you what you need.* She attaches a link to an art journal subscription with her email address and password.

Thank U!!!!! I add a GIF of a cute dog smiling with *thank you, thank you, thank you.* I add one emoji that sends hearts floating up the screen, fully got the feels for that, but I delete it before I hit *Send.*

Libby replies: *All good* with a GIF of a Yoda saying *welcome, you are.*

Once I'm on the website, it's easy to access the reference. Just in case I'm asked to leave the café, I take screenshots of all the pages and passwords, and I'm about to insert the references within my essay when, as I predicted, the petrol café lady appears next to me.

"Are you going to make a purchase?"

"No, sorry."

I don't hang around for the lecture on using their power. I unplug my phone and graph tab and dump everything in my bag. I just need to swing by free Wi-Fi somewhere in the morning and email it to Mr Campbell before school.

The back wall of the petrol station is in full view of the expressway that heads out of town. I'm not sure why there's perfect lighting, but it looks like an opportunity to me. The assignment was community art, after all. It's rush hour, and cars zoom past on the freeway. I push an abandoned rusted ladder up to the wall. Taking up the entire back wall, I outline two people sitting back-to-back; one sits in a home, the other is homeless on the street. I add heart-shaped text bubbles above their heads, a question mark in hers, a heart in mine. At the top, I spray *LOVE IS LOVE.*

I spray *Xavier* in gold in the corner, take a picture with the graph tab, and add it to the file labelled *SOFA PORTFOLIO.*

My phone beeps, a message from Dad. I nearly drop my phone. I call him immediately, but he doesn't pick up.

You comin hom tonighkljt

The spelling tells me he's already bombed.

U okay? I'm coming home now, don't go anywhere.

Dad: *Justs nerd uoy to cime hime.*

I can't bike fast enough to tell him I'm sorry, to make things right.

Back at the tent, I lean my bike against the toilet block. Parked up next to the Mitsi is a technicolour Datsun, a shit-ton of spray wasted in an attempt to hide the rusted dents. The Datsun door creaks open. Ginge steps out in black jeans and a leather jacket.

"Gary here? He owes me," he says in a smoke-a-pack-a-day voice.

Is this why Dad wanted me here? Is he hiding somewhere?

"Not here, sorry. Want me to pass on a message?"

I avoid looking at the tent.

"He owes me a package or my money." Irritation edges his voice.

Yep, I was right. A deal has gone down, and Dad wants my help. I've bailed his arse out of too many sticky situations, and this feels too familiar.

"I'll tell him when I see him."

"I see." He strides to his car and opens the door. "I'll come back later to get what I need." And he gets back in his car. The engine roars, splutters, and stalls.

He gets out and kicks the car tyre. "Piece of shit."

I jump behind the vehicle, ready to do anything to get this guy gone. "I'll push."

I ready my hands below the back window; on the back seat are a box of beer and library books, the one on top an introduction to graphic design.

"Go," he yells.

I turn my legs over as fast as I can, and push. The car pulls away and takes off down the road.

I dart to the tent. Dad's passed out in my sleeping bag. There's the stench of hard alcohol. He'll never change. But he's safe, and here. I tap his shoulders, which does nothing to wake him. The relief is so great, even though he's asleep and off his face.

"I'm so sorry, Dad. I love ya, man. I shouldn't have said those things at the hospital." And I leave him to sleep.

I lie next to him and re-check that my bag has everything I need to get my assignment sorted for tomorrow: graph tab, alarm set, charger, and push my bag against the tent wall. I lay a towel over the ground and steal Bear's blanket. She slips underneath and curls into my chest. For the first time since I last saw Dad, I fall asleep easily.

Fifteen

When I wake, Dad isn't here. I peek out of the tent and the Mitsi is gone
again. At the hospital, I pushed him too far, said too much, and now he
can't face me. I'm a constant reminder of Mum and what he did. What if he
doesn't come back?

I search for my graph tab; it's not on top of my bag next to my phone
where I left it last night. Panic sets in; I tip the tent upside down, pull my
sleeping bag inside out, forcing Bear to reluctantly move from her warm
spot. I have to find it to get my assignment in. I re-check again, and again ...
my graph tab is gone. Deep down I know Dad has taken it. I search through
everything again. I need to find it to prove myself wrong – that Dad wouldn't
do something so stupid.

It's gone. And I know Dad has taken it. I can't believe I was feeling bad,
that I was actually missing him. All the worry about what I said, about him
not coming back, vanishes, and I'm split in two. Rage overtakes one side,
sadness the other, that he would do this. But I have zero time to fume or

smack walls, and I force the pressure down, cap it; it's building below, about to boom. When it'll take over and consume me – explode – I don't know. It's 8.10, and my assignment is due by nine. I've got to get gone.

It's hard to ride when you're mad as hell. Dad set me up. He asked me to come home last night so he could steal the graph tab. My chest tightens, pushing out what little respect I had for him. What remains has always been there, but it's only now I see it clearly and can admit what I've always known – that he doesn't give a crap about me. And for the first time I want to give up on him, and admit part of me hates him.

I race down the school drive and park my bike outside the library.

I plug my cell phone in at the computer station – 8.58 – and wait for my phone to do its start-up thing.

In the far corner, Katie and Libby flick through old fashion magazines. I don't have time to be distracted. The fact that they are together and seem happy is good; I'm glad for Libby that they've worked things out.

Libby giggles. "Oh my, this one." She holds up the magazine with the picture of an old-fashioned ball dress. "Do you think Luka would like it?"

Katie seems less enthusiastic. "I suppose."

I log on to the computer, find my emails and open the essay I emailed to myself last night.

Libby says, "I just love it. I can't wait for the ball; Luka's got a limo."

Gutted.

I force my focus on the assignment; I don't have time to read it over or to obsess over Libby and how much she's in love with Luka. I find the photo I took of the references and add the citation into the body of text and on the reference page. As I attach the file to an email to Mr Campbell and hit *Send* – the time 9.04 – I'm legit worried he'll be pedantic over four minutes; it would be his style. I overhear Luka's voice and sneak out of the library unseen.

I ditch graphics, walk across the backfield towards the beach, and sit against the toilet block. Without the graph tab and with no paper left in my art book, I can't draw.

Winter sunshine soaks my face. A shitty white station wagon parks up, and I'm struck with déjà vu from when Libby and I thought we saw Katie and Mr Campbell. It's the same car. I lean back, hidden by the toilet block, and peek around the corner. Through the back window I spot Luka and Katie.

My stomach rolls as he plants a kiss on her – not in a friend way, in a way-more-than-that kinda situation.

What the actual hell?

My mind's a mess, imagining the moment Libby finds out, how her face will drop, how I'll spot the second her heart falls apart. I should be fired up, want to smash Luka's face and shout at Katie; but I know what it's like to think someone loves you deep, and how it carves out your soul when you find out they don't, till all you're left with is empty nothingness. Libby will be broken.

I snap a picture of their conjoined heads playing tonsil hockey, then sit back against the wall, unable to process what I've seen. I take another look just to make sure I'm not seeing things. And it's the same. I have to tell Libby.

My phone beeps, and if this moment could get any weirder, Libby's name appears.

You still free to help with the ball banner on weds after school? Meet at the gallery?

I type in a reply and attach the picture, and sit there for ages staring at the screen without sending. I delete the image, and decide that kind of news shouldn't be dropped in a text. It's better if I'm there when I tell her.

Sure, see you later. And I add a cute GIF with a cat jumping away from a cucumber, because I know it will make her happy.

What if she doesn't believe me? It's not like I've got the best track record to go by, and they're gonna deny it; it's Luka, after all.

I wait for the traitors to leave as black snow clouds set in and the bitter wind stings my face. I check the weather forecast – and colossal snow is forecast for tonight. Before the snow sets in, the tent needs reinforcing. It won't stand up to a huge fall. It would bury me and Bear alive.

I'm happy to ditch class to avoid seeing Libby, Luka and Katie, so I go back to the tent. I search the forest for long solid branches, prop up the tent's middle, and reinforce the side poles by adding more sticks and hammering them further into the ground. The tent material is thin and old and no longer waterproof, and after a while, I realise it's not the structure that I need to worry about; it's that the canvas will tear under a heavy fall.

By the time I finish, the sun is nearly down and snow has started to fall. My phone rings. I immediately think it's Dad, but Libby's name pops up.

"Hello."

"Hey, Dylan, it's Libby." Her voice is warm but has a quick, worried tone about it. "I'm delivering food to the library, and I've come across Jack. He's pretty upset about something, but I can't quite get what about. Are you around? He said only you can make it better."

"Of course, I'm on my way."

"Great, thanks, see you soon."

I ride the track towards the library, distracted by thoughts of what Jack could be upset about and nervous about seeing Libby.

I ride through the library car park dusted in snow, and immediately see the free-food van. Libby sits next to Jack, the appropriate distance away from him. He hates to be touched.

My eyes immediately meet Libby's.

"Thanks for coming."

A gush of wanting to hug her overcomes me, and what I've discovered wants to explode out in a burst of uncoordinated worried words.

I lean my bike up against the library entrance; Jack follows, his arms wrapped around his chest, concealing something.

Libby lifts a stack of empty trays into the back of the van. "He won't show me what it is." She's working solo tonight.

He rocks back and forward; I point to the seat, and we sit next to each other.

"Whatever it is, bud, it's gonna be okay."

He groans, rocks. "You'll be mad, mad, mad, Dylan." He tightens his grip around whatever it is he's hidden under his jacket.

"Na, I promise Dylan won't be mad." I say it in third person; it calms him when he's stressed, like it takes the focus off what or who he's worried about.

"Want to show Libby first?"

He nods repetitively. And out of a box wrapped in happy birthday paper, he shows Libby my graph tab. And now it makes sense. I see the likeness – Dad's dodgy friend Ginge. Same eyes, same hair.

I gaze at Libby. She looks confused. I'm not about to explain Jack has my already stolen graph tab as a birthday present.

The urge to snatch it from Jack and check all the work for my portfolio hasn't been wiped is epic. That will freak him out; there's a way, and it's gotta be on his terms.

Jack opens the folder labelled *SOFA PORTFOLIO* and flicks through the images, confused. "Why, Dylan? Why?"

I'm not about to explain to him either that his dad stole his birthday present and in doing so unnecessarily upset him, or why I'm so relieved no folders have been wiped.

Libby has finished packing up the van and closes the back door. I frantically try to think of something that will make her stay longer, but I know she'll have other places to visit. Now's not the best time to tell her about Katie and Luka.

"Dylan, your hand – it's bleeding."

I look down at the specks of blood that have smeared on the graph-tab screen, which turns out to be the best thing to distract Jack, who's squeamish. He thrusts the graph tab at me as he gets up and stands by the front doors of the library.

Libby jumps back into the van.

I can hear Jack moaning.

"I'm fine, buddy."

Jack repeats, "Dylan needs a plaster, plaster, plaster."

Libby reappears and sits next to me, opening a first aid box.

"Pass me your hand." It's a graze from cutting sticks.

She's all smiles – we both are – and our eyes do that weird Lego connected thing. And I'm so distracted that she's sitting so close, her leg almost touching mine.

I hold out my hand; she peels the back off a plaster and sticks it on my hand, then repeats, covering three scrapes.

"Done." She beams at me, and I want to beam back, but I can't; it's like I'm pre-empting the sadness I know is coming her way when she finds out about Luka and Katie.

I take my hand away. "Thanks so much."

"I'd better get going; need a lift home?"

"Nah, I'm good. I'll hang out with Jack, make sure he's okay." I look back, but he's gone. I'm guilty I've used him as an excuse, but there's no way she's seeing my home.

Libby jumps in the driver seat. "Think he walked back to the men's night shelter; he hates blood."

"He really does."

"Sure you'll be okay?"

"Yeah, I got some stuff to do," I lie.

"Thanks again."

I can't think of anything else to say to extend the conversation naturally without sounding weird.

"See you at school – oh, and on Wednesday," she says.

"Definitely." I wave as she drives off, racked with guilt that I could have told her but didn't. I should tell her about Luka and Katie. But awkward emo situations have never been my thing. Like my mind can't string words together in case I say the wrong thing.

I settle on Wednesday; I'll tell her then, maybe.

Sixteen

Snow falls all Tuesday and I'm gutted school is closed for the day. Me and Bear are living in an actual freaking freezer. It's impossible to sleep, even with every item of clothing wrapped around us inside the sleeping bag, with the top pulled tight over our heads, leaving a gap just big enough for air. The cold grips my core and I'm unable to feel my fingers, toes and nose.

Wednesday morning I refresh the school webpage, relieved to see, in red: "Snow update: school is open." I shine my phone torch at the tent roof; it's sunken further since my last check. Outside I use a branch to sweep the snow off the tent roof and leave the door ajar. Once the sun's up, it will be the warmest spot for Bear to sleep while I'm with Libby helping with the ball stuff.

The day drags; Libby wasn't in art. After school I ride against the wind up Main Street, careful not to slip in the snow. As I walk into the café, I'm greeted by a wall of warm air and Libby making coffee over the heavy hum of afternoon chatter.

"You look frozen! What would ya like?"

You, as my girlfriend. Luka kissed Katie.

I'm assuming she's talking about coffee. "Flat white, thanks." I don't know what they taste like, but I've heard other people order them.

Libby pours three coffees in keep cups and passes one to the lady named Jill, apparently, and one to me. Then she picks up a bunch of food in paper bags. I place both my hands around the cup and soak in the heat.

"Come this way." Libby leads me to the red door. She's wearing a long, oversized knitted cardigan.

We walk up a steep staircase to her apartment, where Libby unlocks another red door.

The back wall of the lounge and kitchen is a canvas of giant windows with a view over the snow-covered city. Plants hang everywhere. There's no TV; a brown leather sofa covered in cushions faces a wall jammed with vibrant artwork and a messy, tightly packed bookshelf. It reeks of home.

I follow Libby down the hall, the walls covered in mismatched family photos, the window at the end giving a view of overhanging trees dusted in white, and the ocean in the distance.

We go into Libby's room.

"Take a seat." She points to the bed. My nerves twist, but I'm made better by her room looking how I imagined – art everywhere, pinned to the wall, a giant poster of Frida Kahlo, intricate detailed anatomical portraits in overlapping shades of popping colours.

I sit on the edge of Libby's unmade bed. Her desk in the corner is jammed with jars of black pens, coloured pencils, and stacks of paper. Pinned to a corkboard are detailed drawings of organs, of a skeleton. Front and centre, the card I gave her is tacked next to a photo of her and Luka. And I'm reminded of what I need to tell her.

Tell her.

Libby opens her wardrobe and throws me a top. "Yours – thanks heaps for letting me borrow it." I can smell the washing powder.

"No worries." I stick it in my bag.

With Libby, there's never any awkward quiet spots; she chatters about how the ball plans are coming along, how it's hard to find people who have enough time, especially since Katie and Luka have so much study and after-school commitments.

I nod. I have feelings on that topic.

"So, we are waiting for the others, and then we can start our official ball meeting."

I'm gutted. I hadn't figured there would be others.

Libby taps the iPad on her desk, and the room fills with music. She sits next to me, effortlessly, casually, like she's not nervous at all. I sip my coffee; the warm frothy milk calms my stomach, which is screaming at me for food.

I glance at her artwork on the wall. "You know you could go to art school."

Libby beams. "I thought about it, but I've wanted to be a doctor since forever."

Tell her. Just say it.

She hums to the song and holds up her phone, showing me the playlist labelled *Ball*.

"What do ya think?"

A knock comes from downstairs; she disappears for a second and comes back with Luka and Katie. My insides scream. I could tell her now, get it over and done with.

There's a round of awkward "heys." I stare at Luka, back at Katie. Libby blissfully chats about the ball, unaware of what two of her most important people are doing.

We follow Libby into one of the smaller galleries. "This is the paint and the canvas that Mum said is ours."

I inspect the sprays and paint: they're all used – open cans and pots – but they're the best quality.

"It's great you can do it for us," Katie says.

I can't even look at her. I focus on the art supplies and imagine how big the rolled canvas pushed up against the wall is. The length of it alone would cover the back wall of the school hall.

Libby stands next to me. "Mum said you can have any of the leftover supplies." It's hundreds if not thousands of dollars' worth of paint.

"Thank you, that's incredible."

She hands me a box of test pots. "This is a subset of all the colours."

Luka playfully pokes her side, and I'm not sure how much of that I can take before I knock him over. Libby ignores him, and he pouts. I almost feel sorry for Katie, who's by the door, eyes on her phone.

I pull out the graph tab, flick to my drawings of the banner, and unroll the massive canvas.

"That's perfect." Libby breaks away from Luka, pulls the gold, black, silver, and bronze from the box and stands next to me, pointing to where each colour could go. "Gold here, what do you think?"

As Luka drapes his arm over Libby's back something animalistic roars inside me, a caveman urge to protect her, rip her away from being touched by him.

Katie's one foot out the door. "You guys have got this. I'm going to head off."

Luka drops his arm off Libby like a boulder off a cliff.

I should say it now. I'm stuck with the thought that Libby might not believe me. Who's she going to believe? Her best friend since primary school and boyfriend, or some homeless dude with criminal convictions?

Libby hugs Katie. "You okay?"

Katie shrugs. "Just tired." She gathers the heart-shaped locket that hangs from Libby's neck. "Is this new? It's so pretty." She opens the locket. "Oh, it's a picture of you and Luka." She smiles, but her eyes say *broken.*

"Luka gave it to me this morning."

Katie steps out the door. "Oh, nice. I've got a headache, so ..." And she's gone, leaving Luka silent in the corner, his focus at the door, and I swear by his downcast frown that he wants to go after Katie.

Libby points to the areas on the banner where she's written in pencil what colour could go where. "I hope that's okay, Dylan – just ideas."

"Epic." I agree with all her colour decisions, especially the gold that rims all the letters of the *Gatsby.*

Luka stands behind us. "I could have done that without Dylan." Like I'm not in the room. My insides snarl.

Libby grins. "Trust me, it'll be awesome; it'll blow everyone away."

"Whatever, actually, who cares? Are we going to this movie or what, Libs?"

Luka wraps his arms around Libby, and I'm near ready to pounce on him. I can't hold it in any longer.

"Think I saw you at the beach the other day." It's directed at Luka, and his jaw falls to the ground. *Yeah, buddy, you heard right.*

He clutches Libby tighter. "Let's go. We'll miss the movie, and I already got us tickets." He drags her by the hand towards the door.

She turns to face me. "I'm so sorry, I completely forgot."

"It's all good. I can stay and paint if you like, tick one of those things off ya list."

She grabs my hand, takes the pen from the top pocket of her dungarees and writes six numbers. "For the security system." Our eyes connect for a second longer than necessary, and boom, electricity surges between us.

"I can't thank you enough. Are you free the same time tomorrow? We can finish what you start." And I don't know who lets go first, but our hands drop, and Luka tugs her out the door.

As they walk down the hall, I hear Luka say, "Should you really trust him with the alarm code?"

At first, I can't concentrate, but eventually I find my groove and finish the pencil outlines. I'm alone in her gallery. She trusted me with the lock to the whole place. As I work, I hear the café staff leave, and Francesca yell, "Going to the shop, see you for dinner upstairs."

Francesca walks past, and I hold my breath, but she doesn't look in the room. She thinks Libby's in here. I've got nothing to hide, I'm just a hard-core avoider of all things awkward. What will she say if she learns Libby has entrusted me with the password to the entire café?

The van engine starts and fades.

I continue to work, turn the radio on, and find the SOFA radio station. Chill beats sing from the tinny radio. I finish the outline of *Gatsby*; it takes me ages to get the font style consistent across all the letters.

I flip open the white paint and block in the basecoat for each letter. As it dries, I eat the leftover food that Libby brought in. Like a king, I place the food on a plate at the table stacked with boxes of spray paint, eat half the vegetarian filo pie and apple cake and save the rest for Dad, on the miniscule chance he'll show up.

I text him: *I have food, where are you? Please come back.* I know it's pointless.

I watch the snowfall through the window. It looks idyllic from the inside, but outside is another story. I should get going soon. Bear will need my warmth in the sleeping bag.

After I've eaten, I wash the cup and plate and stack them on the kitchenette. But instead of leaving, I walk around the gallery, soak in the art like I haven't seen it before.

Libby probably would expect me to be gone by now.

I lay the next layer of basecoat, gliding the paintbrush slow and steady, avoiding the inevitable – that I will have to leave and face the frigid cold.

The announcer on the radio says, *"Hope you're hunkered down. It's cold out."*

At the far end of the gallery, a bunch of woollen blankets are draped between canvases stacked against each other. Warm blankets. In a warm place, out of the snow. I can't believe I'm stupid enough to contemplate sleeping here. If Libby found out, it would break her trust.

I think of Bear and how I can't stand the thought of another sleepless night frozen, and before I know it, I text Marv: *Mind babysitting Bear for the night?* And I send him directions to the tent.

He replies immediately: *Yeah, man, I'll pick her up on my break, she can hang with me at work and I'll take her home after. You alright bro?*

I can't believe I'm doing this. Every part of me screams this is a dumb idea, but I can't bring myself to leave. I've seen café lights on here as early as five a.m. I'll be gone before then.

I set my alarm and turn off the light. *What am I doing?* No matter how much I want to make the right decision and leave, the warmth wins. I slide the blankets off the canvases. In the corner out of sight from the door, I fold them in half and form a mattress, roll another into a pillow, and lay on top, pulling three blankets over me. Zero worry the roof will cave in, or that I'll freeze to death, or that someone will steal my stuff while a party rages around me. I'm safe. And like all the tiredness and cold has caught up with me, I can't keep my eyes open any longer.

Seventeen

I jolt awake in a warm, dark room, at first with no idea where I am. I search the bottom of my blankets for my phone. A message from Marv at 12.35: *We're slammed man, you'll have to get Bear, and anyway I think the road is closed. Yal be better to get her on ya bike*

Fuck. Guilt consumes me, followed by panic. She's old, it would have been well below zero, and if the tent collapsed, she'd have been buried, scared to death.

I bolt out of my makeshift bed. In Libby's apartment above, there are footsteps and muffled voices. I can make out Libby's voice but not the exact words. A soft glow of light shines through the glass door, voices chat and then the coffee machine starts up from the direction of the café.

I hear the back door open and squeaky footsteps. I duck flat under the covers as café staff arrive to start their shift. Libby could come down any moment. I shouldn't have done this. If she finds me, I've blown it with her, ruined her trust. She'd never trust me again. And how stupid was I to leave Bear?

The hallway light flicks on, and quick steps walk past. I lay silent; in the door window I see the reflection of someone walking past carrying a tray. They yell, "Vee Street Café van will be here in five minutes to collect their order."

How am I going to get out of here without being seen? I picture Bear frozen; I'm in panic mode.

I wait for the hall to go quiet, pissed at myself for being so incredibly dumb. Footsteps head towards the gallery. I dive behind a pile of stacked canvases as Libby races past, then back again carrying milk crates. I peek over the canvases, and she whizzes past again. I'm paranoid that at any moment she'll pop in the gallery to check out my work.

"That's it," a guy yells from the back door.

Libby hollers, "Thanks, man, see you tomorrow."

Time to leave.

I grab my stuff, my heart disordered as I open the gallery door and gap out the back. The milk truck is still there. I slide down the side and jump the fence into the alleyway, and a rush of relief slows my heart back to a regular beat, but I can't relax. I have to check on Bear.

In Central Garden Square, a snow sweeper clears the snow from the footpaths. I unlock my bike, glad I didn't park it in direct view of the café window. Pausing at the bench where me and Libby sat, something bright and colourful grabs my attention. I glance over at the statue and the wall, and see that the black outline of a deflated heart balloon I painted, that I left empty, is filled with intricately detailed flowers in reds, purples, and pinks. Underneath, someone has written, *Never Give Up on Love*. It's perfect and beautiful, and I'm so taken back that Libby sees art how I do, and I'm gushing for her hard.

I speed home, drop my bike, and call out to Bear, scanning for her as I make my way to the tent. It's invisible – it's fully collapsed, buried under snow. On my hands and knees, I manically plough snow with my hands. I call, "Bear, Bear!" until my voice cracks and squeaks and tears roll. If I find her dead, it's my fault. I can't lose her, too.

I find my sleeping bag, where Bear would usually sleep, and search the tent floor; she's not here.

I race to the toilet block and jump the gate. The smell's intense; I cover my nose and find her curled in a tight ball in the corner of the toilet cubicle. I scoop her up, push her under my shirt. She wheezes and coughs. "I'm so sorry, girl." I wrap my jacket around her and do up the zip.

She pops her head out the top, sneezes, and licks my face. My shoulders drop. She must have slipped under the gate, and as I peer towards the door, I see the gap is just Bear-sized enough for her to fit under.

The bathroom smell makes me dry retch, but it has four walls and a roof. Why did we not use this before? I open the utility cupboard and wade through the box of cleaning supplies, rolls of cloth, hand towels, litres of hand soap, toilet and hand cleaner, cleaning brushes. I empty the container, stuff it with my puffer jacket and the towels, and gently lower Bear in. Using the mop and cleaning supplies, I strip the bathroom clean. It's still polar in here, my breath escapes as streams of smoke, but it's the best we've got. Using the hand soap, I wash my uniform and hang my shirt and pants on the fence rails outside to dry. There's no heat in the sun, but they're clean. I leave the gate open so Bear can come and go, and bike to school.

At four, I stand outside the Red Gallery door and wait for Libby, hoping she's remembered she invited me to help with the banner. No one else is here; please let it just be us.

The café door opens, and Libby's head pokes out. "You know you can come inside, right?" She grins, a coffee cup in each hand while she uses her elbow to hold the café door open.

"For you." She grins again. "A flat white." She leads me through the café to the gallery space, where the large canvas is unrolled. I glance at the stack of blankets, still set up as a bed, heat inching up my neck and into my face. While she checks out the banner and the work I completed last night, I gather the blankets in a bunch and dump them in a pile by the canvases. Better that than a makeshift bed lying there as evidence.

She inspects the banner. I watch her smile, and it's contagious.

"Your work is amazing."

Butterflies fill my stomach; she runs her finger over the G of *Gatsby*. "It's dry enough for a second coat." The insides of the letters are empty, waiting to be filled.

A plate of food rests on a stool.

"For us."

Filled buns. My stomach growls. I'm more than hungry, but I ignore them. Nothing says homeless more than a dude wearing the same clothes from yesterday, charging for the free food.

She inspects the table of paints. "You know your work is amazing, right?"

My palms instantly sweat, and my cheeks warm. "Happy to help." A technicolour explosion replaces the butterflies. "We just need to fill in the letters."

She starts at one end, and I start at the other; my motivation is to meet in the middle.

She plugs her phone into the sound system; chill summer beats fill the gallery. I'm not sure if it's the music or the way Libby's constant conversation makes sure there's never any awkward silence, but a calmness washes through me as we chat and laugh while we paint. It's easy to be around her, like my battery is set to recharge.

As we block in colour, Libby chats about how hard it is to get good grades in chemistry, how her dad has moved out, and her mum is *not* coping. We talk about favourite bands and artists, and it feels like there's so much to talk about and not enough time. One conversation effortlessly leads to another. Part of me is guarded, careful not to say too much. No one can be fully trusted.

"I love this song." Libby turns it up and hums along.

"What *is* this?" I laugh. She's cute.

Libby sings louder and more dramatic. I shoot her an exaggerated eye roll; I'm happy she finds it funny.

The song finishes. She giggles and holds up her phone. "You choose something."

I stroll over until she's right in front of me, dungarees with a big pocket, and a cropped white t-shirt, which shows her stomach at the sides, not that I'm looking. Face to face, my heart drums, faster and faster. She passes me her phone, and I scroll through her song choices, feeling her watch until I press *Play*. Happy, chill beats fill the gallery. She's still in front of me, so close I smell her shampoo.

"Perfect." And we're beaming at each other.

"Yeah, it really is." I search her face, and she beams smiles, agreeing with the song choice.

We go back to painting, opposite each other, the banner between us.

She dips her brush in the paint pot and glides it over the pencil outline. "Are you going to the ball with anyone?"

I pick up a pot of the silver paint and search through the box of brushes. "Not my thing." Which, before all this ball stuff with Libby, was the truth. Now I wish I could go with her.

I carry the paint and brush to the banner, pop the paint top off and dip my brush. I begin to fill the G of *Gatsby*. Even if I wanted to go, I don't have the gear, and who wants to turn up to a ball in the clothes they wear to school?

"I'm assuming you're going with Luka?" Saying his name lights a fire and reminds me what I should tell her.

"He's got a limo for us, and there's a before party at his house. You should come?" She's gushing. I'm dying. "He's more into the party than the ball. He's refusing to dance with me." Her smile fades.

He's a loser. I don't care that I have zero rhythm. I'd set all shame aside to dance with her.

It's the perfect opportunity to tell her, *Luka is cheating on you*. She kneels next to me, swipes behind her and grabs an iced bun. She's so close, my stomach bubbles, fizzes. It's nerve-racking as hell. Painting is the only thing that contains my moxie.

Would she believe me if I told her the truth? If I was her, I'd be pissed I didn't tell her ASAP.

Libby picks up a paintbrush, wobbles as she crouches down, balanced on her toes. She takes a bite of her bun, and at the same time leans to dip her brush in the pot. She slips forward, and before she faceplants, I grab her arm to try and steady her, which makes things worse. She swings back, and her butt knocks over two pails. Pools of paint are now all over the carpet, and we both land our arses in the paint like we're painting butt prints, hers gold, mine silver.

Libby scrambles to her feet, leaving a perfect stamp of her left and right butt cheeks on the carpet and on her jeans. I can't contain the laughter, it bursts out beyond my control, and I'm glad she finds it just as funny. Libby giggles so hard she snorts, and we're hysterical; my cheeks hurt from smiling and my stomach aches from happiness. As she tries to wipe the paint from her face, she only makes it worse. Paint streaks her hair, her cheeks, and the tip of her nose.

She leans down and rests a hand on my arm. "Are you okay?"

"Better than ever." A grin spreads across her face, and the imprint of the hand spreads sparkles throughout my body.

She pulls her phone from her front pocket. "You've got paint on your nose." She takes a picture, and turns it around to show me. She giggles. "You look like a rabbit."

"Oh, yeah?" I twitch my nose and motion for her to hand the phone over. "Smile, Thumper." I snap a picture and extend it towards her; her face is even more rabbit-like.

She chuckles. "That's what I get for making fun of you." She takes her phone back, then holds out her hand. It's covered in paint, but I'm not going to *not* take it. I grab it and she nearly pulls me up, but the paint is too slippery; I can't grip. I slip back, pulling her with me back into the same puddle of paint.

We lie on our backs next to each other in hysterics; it's the best and funniest moment of my life.

She turns towards me. "You know, you're a lot of fun, Dylan Marshall."

I turn to face her. Our noses are centimetres apart; she has a faint scar on the top of her forehead and the longest eyelashes. I don't know what to say. She's a lot to take in. I pull out my phone and, shielding the screen from her view, message her the emoji that sends hearts floating up the screen.

I should tell her about Luka. She deserves to know, but I'm selfish and I don't want to ruin this moment.

My heart is pounding through my chest. "You're a lot of fun yourself, Libby soon-to-be Doctor Green."

Right now, being with her is filling me up, like a missing part of me I didn't know was lost has been found. I watch her check her message, and her mouth forms a smile as she turns back to face me. Every cell in my body is electrified; my laughter stops, replaced with an inability to stop smiling at her. It would help if she wasn't smiling back. Our eyes feel locked. I could look away, but I can't; a magnetic force wants to bring our heads together.

"Oh, right – um, yeah." And her smile snaps. "We'd, er, better get cleaned up." She jumps to her feet, pulled out of whatever moment we had.

I wish we could go back.

She extends her arm and helps me up. This time the paint on her hand has dried a little, and as I get to my feet, that magnetic feeling is replaced with awkwardness. And I regret sending the heart emoji, worried she thinks it's too intense, and dodgy, because she's got a boyfriend.

"I'll get some stuff to clean up," Libby says, more serious, almost robot-like.

We rinse our hands, taking turns at the sink; there are no towels that aren't covered in paint. Libby fumbles trying to open the gallery door.

I push the door open and let her out.

"Thanks," she says – orderly, like she's on a mission.

She returns almost immediately with a scrubbing brush, bucket, and soap.

We scrape as much paint off the ground as we can with the paint scrapers, tap it into the bucket, and spray the paint-covered area with paint remover. We lay clean towels on top and stand on them, soaking up the water and the paint, and repeat the process.

As we pick up the towels for the last time, Libby's hand brushes mine. Tingles surge up my arm and burst across my chest. I want to grab her hand and pull her close. *She's with someone.* She's not the kind of girl to cheat. I'm not that kind of guy. Well, maybe I would be. Let's face it, if she kissed me, I wouldn't stop it.

Her phone beeps. I watch her intently as she takes it from her front pocket. "Luka." But she doesn't text back, and I'm reminded of what I should tell her.

"Come up to the apartment; I'm sure there are some of my dad's clothes hanging around that would fit you."

I'm so taken aback, I don't say anything.

We put all the lids back on the paint tins, which rubs more paint onto our hands.

I follow her up the steps to her apartment; a laugh slips out at the perfect bum- and handprints on the back of her dungarees.

"Are you laughing at my butt?" She twists around, attempting to get a better look at her backside.

"Yep."

She spins me round. "The same thing is on your arse, too."

Libby points me in the direction of her shower. She opens the wardrobe opposite and passes me a complete change of her dad's clothes. "These will work. I chose them for Dad."

She drops a towel on top of the pile. "Use whatever you like in the bathroom. I'll shower in Mum's."

Libby heads down the hall and into her mum's room.

I flick the shower on, and the warm water cascades down my back. I can hear the sputter of water from the shower in the other room. It's odd knowing that right through that wall, Libby is naked.

I turn up the heat, wash my body and hair. I can't remember the last time I had a shower like this, in a family bathroom with warm fluffy towels. A dressing gown hangs off a hook on the door; there are plants and seashells arranged on the windowsill.

I make sure to click off the shower before Libby does. I don't want to drain all the hot water or to come across like I've been in there too long. I pull on the boxers, slightly amused at wearing Libby Green's dad's undies. The black jeans are loose, but pass, even the length, and I slip on the t-shirt, navy blue with a pocket on the top right-hand corner. It's mint. I look at myself in the mirror and tame the mop of messy waves. I look … not homeless. A massive improvement. It's the best I've looked and smelled in ages.

Using the squeegee in the shower, I do my best to clean up the paint, rinsing away any traces. Before I exit, I make sure the bathroom is in the same order as I found it and hang my towel on the towel rail.

I gather up the dirty, paint-covered clothes and open the bathroom door, holding the pile away from my clean, dry clothes so not to get them covered in paint. Outside the door is a plastic bag. Libby whizzes past me, wrapped in a towel. I can't help but notice her bare shoulders with a lingering tan line.

I fill the bag with my clothes, then, awkward about where to wait, wander through the lounge and into the kitchen. On the fridge is a photo of Libby, Luka and Francesca from the gallery opening. Libby faces Luka with a lovesick grin.

I gotta tell her.

The longer I leave it, the longer she's fed a lie, and I can't handle that.

Libby's bedroom door opens, and as we walk down the stairs and back into the gallery, Libby turns the conversation to serious ball talk. "Let's finish painting this banner."

We set out the paints, this time on a tray with a lip around it, so as not to repeat the same bum-print situation. I'd be lying if I said I wasn't disappointed to know that option is off the table.

We begin blocking in the gold, Libby on one side of the canvas, me on the other.

I'm not sure *how* to begin or push the words out. I figure the best way is to just say it. Things are good between us, and maybe she'll be so grateful, things will get even better?

Libby carefully glides her brush around the edge of the B.

And since she's not looking at me, I spew the words out. "Libby ... I saw Luka and Katie kiss at the beach."

Her brush jerks and paints over the edge of the letter. She looks up, her eyes wide with disbelief. "What? Sorry, back up. What did you say?" She shakes her head. "No."

She stares at me, and as I predicted, I spot the second her world shifts, from happy to broken.

"What, how, when ..." Her voice catches, and the look on her face is the same as when I picked her up off the steps at school, after she found out her dad was leaving. All the sunlight has faded.

I tell her about the white car, how it was the same one we saw when we thought it was Mr Campbell's. "It was Luka with Katie, not Mr Campbell."

"What the hell? When?" She bats tears away.

Do I hug her, put my arm around her? She looks broken when she cries. I'm not an ideal emotional-support person; I never know the right thing to do or say, for fear I'll do something stupid that makes it worse.

"A few days ago." I step forward, ready to wrap my arm around her shoulders.

She snaps, "You've known for a few days? You've been here hours, and you tell me *now*?"

And I step back. "I didn't know how to tell you. I didn't want to hurt you. Oh, shit, I'm sorry."

"You should leave." She turns her head.

I grab my bag.

She doesn't look back. "Go." This time her voice turns harsh, and my heart falls off a cliff.

"I'm sorry." I close the door behind me.

I walk down the hall. Every step further away makes me want to turn back. I reach the back entrance to the café and sulk through; Francesca fills a water jug from a tap next to a table stacked with glasses.

My voice cracks. "Libby really needs you."

She doesn't look up and continues to stack cups. "I'll be there in a second."

"Probably best you go now."

When she faces me, it must be written on my face that I'm cut up as hell and that Libby needs her help ASAP. She leaves immediately.

At least Libby will have the person who loves her more than anything with her. I walk back to my bike, which is covered in snow, and look up at the window of Libby's apartment.

I yank my phone from my pocket. It's stupid to imagine she'd have sent a GIF; even more ridiculous that I want to send her one. I search for one that says I'm sorry, and that I never realised I wanted to be with someone until I started hanging with her, that she brightens my insides and makes me feel alive. I write *Sorry*, and press *Send*.

I ride towards the tent through mounds of white; it's slow going. The howling wind drives snow sideways into my face. If it weren't for the lit snowplough clearing the main road, I wouldn't know where the footpath ended and the road began. When I reach the toilet block, I push away the snow piled against the door. Bear isn't in her box bed or anywhere inside. It's barely warmer inside than out.

Using my phone torch, I call outside, imagining her frozen, lifeless body. "Bear! Bear!" I manically search through the old tent site and under the trees; she's not there. What if I can't find her?

I'm desperate; she's old and small and wouldn't survive the night outside. I can't lose her, too; she's all I've got left. She was Mum's dog.

A sneeze and cough come from under the toilet block. I shine my light towards the back wall where the pipes and drain come out, and there she is.

I drop down and scoop her out; her body shivers uncontrollably, and with every breath in, her chest wheezes. Inside the toilet block, I slide down the wall, sit on the ground, and offer her food. The water in her bowl is frozen solid, and she can barely stand, let alone lift her head. I pull her under my top, wrap my arms around her and hold her close.

My hands and feet sting, and I legit see my breath freeze on its way out. It's too cold for Bear. What if she doesn't last the night?

Bear doesn't stop shivering for the next half hour, and no matter how close I hold her, her breathing doesn't get better. There's a break in the wind, and I know what I'm contemplating is the stupidest idea on the planet. But it could save Bear's life.

I wrap her in a jersey, a towel over the top, stick her back under my jacket, tuck it into my jeans and zip it up. Bear's wheeze vibrates through my chest as I ride towards the Red Gallery Café, hoping I've remembered the door code correctly and that the gallery is closed.

The café is blacked out; the lights are on upstairs. I cut into the alleyway, tie my bike to the lamppost, and haul me and Bear up and over the fence into the café car park. I'm an idiot, but I don't know where else to go that's warm and that has food. If I'm caught, there's zero chance for Libby and me to be friends again.

I bolt to the back door; the security lights flick on, and my heart drums. Libby's bedroom light is on; one look out the window and I'm snapped. I push the combination and the door lock releases. As I gently close the door behind me, the warmth is tropical. Using my phone torch, I sneak into the kitchen, grab a bowl, fill it with cubes of cut cheese from the fridge, and a wedge of chicken and vegetable pie. I pour a cup of milk and contemplate heating it in the microwave, but the hum of the microwave could be heard from upstairs. Footsteps travel in Libby's apartment above, moving from one room to the other, followed by voices.

I carry the food back to the gallery and offer it to Bear. She laps up a little milk but doesn't touch anything else. It's better than nothing; at least it's warm and dry, and it's gotta help her lungs.

I make up the bed like last night. Bear curls into me under the covers and falls asleep, still wheezing, but better. I watch her chest rise and fall until my eyes can't stay open any longer.

Eighteen

"What the actual hell?"

My eyes flick open.

"Is that Dylan?"

Libby's and Francesca's faces appear over me, scowling. I bolt to my bag, pull on my jeans – correction, Libby's dad's jeans. I swoop up Bear and run for the door, avoiding all eye contact, my focus firmly on the way outta here, my heart panic-beating.

Both Francesca and Libby yell, "Dylan!"

I bolt through the back door and glide over the fence to my bike. Adrenaline rushes in my ears as they call after me. I'm too wired, too ashamed. I just want to be alone.

My phone rings and rings again. Then it beeps with messages I don't want to see.

I ride to the beach, and me and Bear sit in the public toilets protected from the snowstorm still raging outside. I slide down the wall and sit on the ground, now understanding Dad's compulsion to get off-his-face drunk, a perfect way to forget the world and everyone in it.

I pull out my phone. Three missed calls and texts from Libby. I can't face them.

Bear wheezes and struggles to breathe, and this time it's enough to shake me out of my sorry-for-myself coma. We stay in the toilet block; it's too polar outside. The next safe, warm place is school – the last place I want to be, but we have nowhere else to go.

I take Bear with me, hidden in my school bag. As I walk down the corridor, she pokes her head out the top of my bag, making it impossible to go unnoticed. She lets out a wheeze followed by a sneeze, and a group of juniors stop in front of me. "Aww, she's soooo cute."

I pass Libby's locker; my insides twist, and by the time I reach art class, my body is a mass of frazzled livewires. Katie and Luka will know it's me who narked on them, and Libby won't ever trust me again. Our friendship is ruined.

I open the art-room door and focus on my seat by the window, rather than on Libby, who's at the bench seat on the opposite side of the room. Bear sneezes, and half the class crowds around. Luka sits alone upfront, his attention out the window, quiet; it's completely unlike him.

I take Bear out of the bag and everyone pets her; she laps it up. I glance at Libby. She's wearing headphones, but I know she can hear – they're not plugged into her phone.

Katie arrives and takes the seat closest to the door.

Libby bats tears away from her cheeks, trying her best to hide it, and it kills me; the Libby spark has gone out.

I pull out my phone, my heart techno-style, and text: *I'm really sorry, I shouldn't have stayed in your gallery. Bear is sick and I was worried. I don't expect you to forgive me, but I am really sorry.*

I watch her check her phone and will her to reply. Nothing.

Mr Campbell walks in, just as Bear is mid-sneezing fit.

"Mr Marshall, get rid of the dog."

My focus is on Libby.

Luka pipes up, "Yeah, Dylan, you need to leave."

And that's it. "Really? You think it's *me* who should be leaving? Wanna inform the class what a shit storm you caused?"

I don't care that everyone is watching. I've got nothing left to care about; what more could go wrong? I've got nothing to lose.

"Whatever." And he sulks into his seat and looks out the window.

Mr Campbell snaps, "Both of you, shut up or leave."

Bear wheezes, which turns into a coughing fit. It's getting worse. She needs the vet, and I have zero money.

"Leave the dog outside," he says, as he writes a list on the board.

1 Grades for essay

2 Written references for art schools

Outside, snow falls sideways, pushed by the wind.

Half the class yells out, "Come on, sir, it's freezing out."

Bear wheezes and repeats the sneeze.

Mr Campbell draws an oval and writes: *Add your name here if you need a written reference.* "Don't forget to add the name of the school or scholarship you are applying for so I can start working on them," he says.

He turns to me. "That dog needs the vet."

"Yes, sir."

He ignores me and disappears into the art resource room.

I continue louder, "I'll take her to the vet after class." Not sure how I'll find the money.

Mr Campbell comes back with a cardboard box and two old towels, sets the box next to me, folds the towels and places them in the box.

"Thank you so much, sir." And I mean it, taken back at his kindness after the shit I've put him through. "I promise it won't happen again."

I slip Bear into the box and cover her in the towel; she shivers. I take my hoody off and lay it on top of her.

Every minute that passes, I find myself peering over at Libby, willing her to look. I check my phone to see if she's replied to my message. Nothing.

Mr Campbell announces, "Your applications for SOFA, including your referee statement and complete portfolio, must be submitted by the twenty-sixth of next month."

We're given time to work on our portfolios. I move the pen around the paper, the class a buzz of activity. My mind is fuzzy; unable to concentrate.

The bell rings. Libby packs her things and is the first to leave.

I put Bear back down my top, zip up my jacket over her and return the box and towels to the resource room. Mr Campbell is at his desk; he flicks through a pile of student artwork. Under the sentence *Put your name here if you need a reference for art school* written on the whiteboard, I add my name, and SOFA in brackets, thinking about the mess I caused him. It's a ballsy move. I figure I've got nothing to lose.

Mr Campbell clears his throat. "I'm sorry, I can't be a referee for you, so you'll have to find someone else. Given what's happened, it's for the best."

I can't bring myself to rub the letters of my name off; it's admitting defeat.

"I'm sorry for the mess I caused." I hate how it sounds like I'm apologising only to get the reference; I'm not. I *am* sorry. Like the black outline of the empty heart I bombed at Central Garden Square, see-through, empty, devoid of life and colour and fully deflated.

As I walk out of class, I spot Libby at the end of the corridor, ignoring Luka as she unloads a book from her locker and places it into her bag.

I slow my pace; Luka's pleading. "I'm sorry. Please, say something. Let me come over, and we can talk."

Bear sneezes as we edge past, and Libby looks my way.

"Dylan, I'll give you a lift to the vet; it'll have to be quick." She abandons Luka mid-sentence, and we walk together down the hall. Heart-popping colours fill my insides.

"That'd be so great, thank you."

Luka yells loud enough that people on distant planets could hear, "You know Dylan Marshall is homeless? He's Xavier – the dumb-arse artist." He belly laughs. "Caught him stealing deodorant, and he's got newspaper curtains in the car he's living in." He's hysterical. He waltzes over to Libby and stands in her way; he moves side to side, not letting her pass.

"Leave. Me. Alone. Like – forever." She shouts it, but he's too stupid to get it. He tries to grab her hand; Libby snatches it away. He tries again.

I pass my bag to Libby, grab a handful of Luka's shirt, slam him hard into the lockers, drive my arm back and stop just before my fist slams into his guts. "She said leave her alone."

His face drops.

I could carry on; I want to pummel the shit out of him, but he drops to the ground in a heap, and I can't push it too far – oh, I want too. I could, but I'd waste precious time with Libby, and the way I see it, at least she's talking to me.

I grab the bag off Libby, and we walk in silence to her van. Libby starts the engine.

"I'm so sorry, I shouldn't have stayed in the gallery; really, it was wrong and creepy, and I shouldn't have." I look right at her.

Bear coughs and wheezes, and Libby ruffles the fur on her head. "Y'all be alright, girl, we'll get ya all fixed up." Bear wiggles her way out of my bag and onto Libby's lap. It's adorable; Mum always said Bear was the best judge of character, and she wasn't wrong.

Libby giggles. "She's adorable." She looks up at me for a split second before turning her focus to the windscreen. "Right, the vet."

As we make it into town, Libby responds, "It *was* a bit creepy, but I understand why you did it." No smile, dry and robotic.

I couldn't wipe the smile if I tried. She's talking to me; it's a start.

I don't have money for the vet. I figure Libby will drop me off, I'll get up the guts to ask for free vet care, they'll say no, and I'll take Bear home and google what I can do, which will possibly involve a break-in at a chemist.

Outside the vet, Libby turns off the engine.

"I can't thank you enough. I'm sorry, and I'll finish the banner – all the ball stuff, if you still want help." I realise I'm rambling, but I'm not sure when or if she'll talk to me again.

I step out of the van and close the door, expecting her to drive off, but she gets out and follows me into the vet. I dread seeing her face when she realises she drove me here for nothing, that I could have told her at school, before she wasted petrol getting me here, that I have no intention of seeing the vet because I have zero money.

Inside, Libby greets the vet nurse. "Hey, Morag."

"Libby, what can I do ya for?"

"Got any free consults left for the street dogs' programme?"

Morag has the pinkest hair I've ever seen. "Not entirely sure, hold on. Take a seat, and I'll get back to you."

Libby and I sit next to each other in the waiting area. She gazes at Bear, sitting upright on my lap. I can tell she wants to hold her. I lift her onto Libby's lap, and she wraps her arms around her as Bear licks her cheek.

"Aww. I never knew you had her. She's the sweetest."

Morag comes back. "We don't, but Todd will do it anyway. It's on the house."

"I've got to get back to bio," says Libby. "You know you're intense, right?"

I'm processing the words, confused by what she means, and I want to question her when the vet nurse interrupts: "Come this way."

Libby hands Bear to Morag, and I follow the nurse as Libby leaves, without a goodbye.

Libby was right; the vet doesn't charge me, and it turns out Bear has mites up her nose, nothing serious. They let her stay there while I go back to school and fetch my bike so I can take her home.

By the time I haul food from the supermarket – no easy feat with every second person coming up to pat Bear – and ride back to the toilet block, it's a freezer inside.

I unearth the tent from under the snow and shake it clean. It's ripped, but I figure if I can set it up in the toilet block, it'll be like an igloo – maybe a few degrees warmer. I clean the tent and lay it in the sun, and once it's dry, drag it inside and set it up the best I can, tying the rips together, securing the string at the window locks to hold everything upright and in place. We climb in, and I tie the ripped door shut, plug gaps with random stuff to stop cool air coming in; it is warmer.

I call Dad. No answer. I text him: *Dad, do you think you can come back? I miss you.* No reply.

I text Libby: *Thank you, and sorry,* and I attach a pic of Bear.

She replies: *I'm glad Bear is better, and it's probably best we keep our distance. My head is a bit weird right now.*

I was stupid to take Libby's kindness with Bear to mean we were going to be okay. I know we were never together so it's not a break-up. It just feels like one, and my soul is crumbling.

I email Mr Campbell: *I am really sorry, is there anything I can do to help you reconsider being my referee for SOFA?*

I get an immediate response: *No, sorry.*

And I feel as if the ground collapses and my insides freefall into a dark empty ocean; I don't have the energy anymore to tread water and keep my head from sinking.

I climb out of the tent in search of food for Bear. As my light flicks to the wall, I notice a brick sticking out a bit from the rest. There's something behind it. I pull the brick out and find, concealed in the gap, an entire bottle of rum and a baggy of weed.

I twist the top off and skull, and smoke Dad's weed, until my eyes glaze over, and it's knocked me out to perfection. The world is paused, my mind numb.

Nineteen

My headache screams, *Coffee!* and my guts tell me never to touch Dad's booze again. I'm on the border between wanting to spew and needing to spew – the epically worst way to feel when you're about to board a bus for a school trip.

At school I push my bike into the rack.

Mr Campbell stands outside the school bus. "You're late." He ticks my name off a list he's compiled on his phone. "Where is Katie?" he huffs.

Only the two seats at the front are empty. I scan the bus and spot Libby in the back row, her focus out the window. Luka sits next to her, talking at her.

Katie gets on the bus. I spot the moment she sees them sitting together, her gaze dropping, the small breath in. She slumps next to me.

Mr Campbell clears his throat. "I have an announcement. As of the end of next week, I will no longer be your art teacher. I have handed in my letter of resignation, and my last day is next Friday. You will have a relief teacher until a suitable replacement is found."

The class fires a bunch of questions at once, the bus a commotion of "There's no way they'll find a teacher this close to the end of term." "Where are you working?" "What's happened?"

"For those applying to SOFA, you have the option of being your own referee. It's a new system SOFA is trialling. The entry requirements remain the same; for some of you, that is the best option. Most of you should have received your references from me by now, those I said I was happy to do."

Being your own referee ... that's never going to work.

We pull into the SOFA car park, the doors swish open, and everyone piles out. I freeze as Libby walks past, Luka close behind. She looks at me for a nanosecond, ignoring Katie.

Katie waits until they're out of earshot, then faces me. "He said he'll do anything to get her back." She holds up her phone and plays a video from Luka's Facebook page; he's playing guitar and singing a song called "I Want You Back, Libby."

"Libby wouldn't get back with him." I'm not sure I believe my own words. "Not after everything." And definitely not with that song.

Katie shrugs.

The SOFA auditorium is crammed with stalls, each representing a different discipline. Busloads of students are packed inside, and street artists spray the back wall in a live demo. These are my people, and this is my home.

I wade through the hordes of people to the SOFA admissions stall. At the opposite end of the hall, Libby stands in line at the pop-up café, Luka still at her side. She hands over her debit card to the café guy. Luka pushes in front and swipes his card first.

"How can I help?" asks a guy in black-rimmed glasses, standing at an admin desk, a laptop in front of him.

I ask, "Is it true that you can be your own referee when applying for the undergraduate scholarship programme?"

The guy chuckles, then grimaces. "Technically, yes, but I wouldn't. It's admission suicide." He passes me a pamphlet: *How to Maximise Your Chances of Admission.*

"They only allow the self-reference thing because the school got done for not being inclusive enough – people complained." He rolls his eyes. "SOFA's way to deal with the bad publicity, stupid if you ask me."

I open the pamphlet. *Complete portfolio. Nail interview. Provide a written reference from someone who can vouch for your work and work ethic (recommended). Alternatively, you can provide a self-written reference.* And it lists some helpful hints and tips.

"You've got a month." He points to the date. "Application's due four weeks from today." He speaks in a monotone, and something tells me he's been asked that question a million times.

"Here." He passes me two free coffee vouchers and holds out a jar of lollipops, and I take two yellow ones with smiley faces.

I crane my neck towards the pop-up café. Luka and Libby wait by the cart for their coffee, deep in conversation. Libby's arms are folded, and neither of them are smiling. Luka holds his hands together, like he's praying or begging, when Libby yells something at him. I wish I could hear. She paces out of the hall without her coffee, leaving Luka alone.

It's a dumb idea, but I follow her outside, past the administration block, an almost entirely glass building with a café attached. Taking up the entire side of the café window are the words *School of Fine Arts* in black, and a tropical forest of colourful vinyl-cut flowers. The rich aroma of coffee fills the courtyard next to the café.

I spot Libby by herself, sitting on the grass knoll; she blends in with the other students. Some chat in groups, others draw. I go inside and order two coffees.

I stand in front of her and hold out the takeaway cup.

"For me?"

I nod and turn to leave; she did tell me she wants space, and I don't want to annoy her.

"Thank you."

I'm a few paces away, wishing I could sit next to her and hang, when she says, "Dylan," and I turn. "How's Bear?" She pats the ground next to her, and my chest tingles.

I sit next to her. "She's heaps better. Thanks again for your help."

"No problem." Her tone is downcast, the Libbyness drained.

She passes me one side of her earphones, and we lean against the café wall and listen to her terrible selection of sappy love jams and sip coffee with the winter sun all up in our faces. Hanging with her at SOFA, it's living the dream right here.

Every now and then I look at her, and she half smiles – the fake kind, to mask how all the glow inside has gone, and she needs some space from the world right now. And I get it; it blows my mind that she's happy to sit in silence with me.

The good vibes are broken when Mr Campbell yells at us that the bus is ready to move, and we're herded back onto it. Libby bumps into an old friend and hangs back.

As soon as I take my seat, Katie sits next to me again. "How can I get her to be friends with me again? She hates me."

How about not hooking up with her boyfriend? Instead, I say, "Apologise." It's lame, but it's a good start.

Libby walks past to her seat and ignores us.

"She won't return my texts or calls; she won't even look at me. If I go into the gallery, she leaves."

"*Show* her how sorry you are."

"How?" She peers at me, a shell of someone who's lost the most loyal best friend they ever had. I can see she regrets what she's done.

"Don't give up, and try harder."

She glances over her shoulder at Luka. "I hate that I still love him. He's gonna get her back." Her voice cracks, and she bats tears from her cheek. Crying girls are awkward, and I never know what to do in these situations. I pass her a lollipop. It's lame, but it's all I got.

"Even if he chose me, I'd give it all up to have my best friend back."

"Tell her that."

I've dished out some stellar advice, but I'm a complete hypocrite. I have no idea how to execute anything like that myself. I squash thoughts of Dad, of how I shouldn't have said the things I did.

"You know it's just her on the ball committee now? She kicked us out."

With the ball in four days, I bet she's under the pump to pull it off. I'm gonna find a way to help her, if she lets me – not that I'll tell Katie that.

As soon as the bus stops, Libby races past Katie and me, ignoring us, and runs towards the science block.

I hang out in the library and charge my phone; I call Dad and get an automated message: *This number is no longer connected to our provider.*

The only connection I had with him is gone.

Twenty

First thing in the morning, I re-check all of Dad's spots, then I call Ginge.

"Sorry, haven't seen 'im. I'll let ya know if I do."

I lean back against the toilet block wall; the clouds are black, heavy. I'm sick of snow. Bear climbs on my lap as I type a text to Libby; I delete it, then rewrite it a billion times, before settling on: *Would you like help to finish the ball stuff?*

I hit *Send*. I can see she's online by the green dot by her name. No matter how much I will the little dots to show she's typing back, they don't appear.

It's Monday tomorrow, and the ball is Wednesday. Am I going to be *that* person who goes alone without the excuse of being part of the ball committee? Surely she wouldn't turn down help on the day if she really needed it. I should go just in case. I bury my head in my knees and wrap my arms around my head; what the hell has happened to me? I used to think balls were dumb and stupid, and here I am stressing about one.

Mum's birthday is the day before the ball. It's a hard day for Dad; at least he's consistent and predictable, and he'll go on a bender. For how long, I never really know. And then I realise there's one spot I haven't looked for him.

Before I leave, I check my phone again. Libby is offline and hasn't read my message. On the ball Facebook page, Libby has posted a list of all the best second-hand shops to get Gatsby-themed costumes.

I ride up the road to the cemetery, and a chill runs down my back. I haven't been here since we buried her. Graves line either side of the sweeping drive; I lean my bike against the crematorium building, and memories flood back, watching her coffin being lowered into the grave, propping up Dad, who was too drunk to speak.

The good times – the art missions.

The bad times – always Dad related.

I weave my way through the graves till I reach Mum's tree at the top, her grave underneath. I drop to my knees and frantically pick grass until her name shows, brush her plaque clean. My body shudders as if it's been turned inside out, raw and exposed.

"I'm sorry, I'm trying." I gasp in a breath. "I miss you." I swallow hard; she's too close, the missing is too heavy to fight, and for once I let the tears flow.

I look around for flowers; there are none, only mounds of snow.

Behind the tree is a bench seat with empty booze boxes scattered underneath. Hidden under the seat, I notice a black rubbish bag. I pull it out and untie the handles; inside are a sleeping bag, a pillow and an old jersey – definitely Dad's. My chest tightens, and I want to swing my arm back and punch the tree. But Mum would hate that. I breathe out hard, force myself to stop.

I pick up all the rubbish and bottles, take them to the skip bin behind the crematorium and slam each bottle in. It does nothing to calm the rage at Dad. I hate him. I can't believe he'd drink here.

The bare sidewall of the crematorium is begging to be bombed. I spray the outline of me and Bear looking up at the indigo sky bursting with silver stars, and along the top in loopy white handwriting, *You are the brightest star we see.* I don't add Dad. I'm taking a picture when my phone beeps.

It's Libby, and I boxer-punch the air.

You can help on Tuesday? Lots to do. Meet at the gallery after school. 1. Finish painting banner. 2. Help shift it from the gallery to the school hall and hang it. No one else is free to help. Dad is out of town, and Mum has a massive catering event the same night.

I reply: *I can definitely help* and attach a GIF of a fluffy baby penguin wearing a top hat and cane that says, *Help is on the way.*

And wait for her to reply with another GIF, but nothing comes.

I ride into town and spot heaps of seniors up Main Street. I slot my card into the ATM; there is twelve dollars available. In the dairy next door, I buy gum and get ten dollars cash out. I find Recycling Boutique – the shop Libby recommended on her Facebook post as the cheapest and best place for second-hand suits, shoes and shirts. A buzzer goes as I walk in. An older lady sits at the front desk, unpicking the cuff of a pair of trousers. She smiles.

I search down the back, and there are people from school in every aisle. A guy I recognise stands in front of the mirror and holds up braces, clips the clasps to his jeans and yanks them over his shoulder. I want some, and grab the only pair left, which are hanging off the corner of the mirror. Given how many people are in here, I don't bother trying them on. Behind me are rows of neatly hung and perfectly pressed white shirts. It doesn't smell like a second-hand shop; it smells like Mum's just done the washing. I flick through the shirts till I find one my size, and hold it up against me in the mirror.

"Lovely," the lady at the front says. "Perfect size." She comes out from behind the desk. "For the ball?" And she flicks through a rack of trousers.

"Yes."

She pulls out three pairs: one pinstriped with thick cuffs at the bottom, the other two plain black. "These would look fabulous on you." She holds out the pinstripes and passes me three pants on hangers. "Try them all, and this." She pushes another shirt onto the pile. The shape is more fitted, better suited to the Gatsby style.

I've never had help shopping before, possibly because I never buy new things. Store clerks tend not to be helpful when I uplift things, and there's never an option of trying on for the best fit. It's more a "grab and run" kind of deal.

Mum would love it in here, and they'd love her.

I survey the line of shoes on the rack, unsure if I'm allowed to try them on or if it's more of a "good luck if they fit" kind of thing.

"These would be perfect," the lady says and holds up a pair of black patent shoes with white tips on the toes. Possibly a smidge too big, but worth it.

"You will look *wonderful*." She spins me towards the changing room.

I pick up the price tags that dangle from the collar and sleeves. "I don't have enough for all of this, sorry."

"Try them on." She repeats it, turning to help a girl pin the bottom of her dress.

Inside the changing room, I pull on the pinstripe pants and white shirt with a fine white stripe that you can only see if you look closely. I push my feet into the shoes.

"And this." The lady's voice comes from behind the door, and she drops a waistcoat over. "Really, I don't have enough ... money." I whisper the last word, aware that everyone in the changing room would be able to hear.

Is she waiting for me outside? Her feet are still there – immaculate, polished leather; old woman's shoes. Not a single scuff.

I tuck in the shirt, pull the braces over my shoulders and slip the waist-coat on. I stare into the mirror. *Damn.* I turn slowly, admire each side of me. I've never seen myself in anything this tidy. I like it. I can only afford one of these items, and I can't decide. I deflate, sure Luka will laugh at my mismatched suit.

I open the door, take off the jacket and hang it on its hanger.

"Oh, that's absolutely spot-on," says the woman. "But the waistcoat's too big. Take it off. I'll bring the seam in. Are you uptown long?"

I look at all the price tags, adding them together. Thirty-seven dollars. I'm twenty-seven short.

"Sorry, I don't want to waste your time. I don't have enough money." I can't steal from her; she's too lovely.

"What's your budget?" she asks, walking up to the front desk and immediately starting to unpick the back of the waistcoat.

I check no one is close. "I'm sorry, this is all I have." I unfold the ten-dollar bill and place it on her desk. "So sorry, I didn't mean to waste your time."

"Consider it a 'fill a bag for ten dollars.'" She lowers her voice. "Grab the entire outfit, and pop it here." She winks and passes me a plastic bag. "Don't tell anyone."

Gratitude swells within me. "Thank you so much."

She bags all the stuff, throws in one of those bow ties on elastic, and takes the ten dollars. "Come back on your way home, and this will be ready."

I don't have a home, but I'm up to be adopted as her grandson, if she's keen.

Twenty-One

It's the day before the ball. I walk down the school hall, which is buzzing with ball talk. A banner hangs on the back wall: *Get Your Gatsby On, One Day To Go.*

Energy lingers in the hallway. As I walk into class and take my seat, something's different. Music's playing, and the walls are plastered in student artwork – everybody's, not just the good stuff. Totally *not* Mr Campbell's style.

A lady with grey hair waltzes out of the resource room, carrying a plate of muffins. "Help yourself," she says, extending the plate to me. She reeks of kindness.

"Thank you." I scoff the muffin; it's still warm in the middle.

"I'm Mrs Gibbs. Nice to meet you, Dylan." And she places two more muffins in front of me "for later."

Libby slips in, and butterflies engulf my chest. She takes her seat on the other side of the room, alone, and plugs in her earphones. When Luka arrives, he sits next to her, and I can't take my eyes away, watching for anything that gives me a hint of how she feels about him. Katie plops in the seat next to me and blocks my view.

Mrs Gibbs reintroduces herself to the class, and she's immediately asked a ton of questions.

"The marking of portfolios will be done in conjunction with Mr Campbell, as it wouldn't be fair considering he's seen your progress and knows your portfolio projects."

Dammit. I thought this could have worked in my favour.

Mrs Gibbs gives the class time to work on our portfolios. I glance over at Libby; she walks into the resource room with her bag and shuts the door. Luka bangs his head gently on the desk; he's not winning. Not gonna lie; feels pretty good.

Katie turns to me. "Think you can convince Libby to speak to me?" Her voice is crumbly.

"I'm not sure I can convince her of anything."

I spend the rest of class sketching on the new artist pad that Mrs Gibbs has kindly given me, and force myself to focus on coming up with ideas for the last three art pieces I need to complete my portfolio for SOFA.

When the bell rings, I keep working until the resource room door pops open and Libby walks out of class, without a glance or smile.

I catch up to her down the hall. "So, what time would you like me to come to the gallery and help?"

Luka is right behind us. Libby briefly looks at him, then back to me. "How long does it take for the paint to dry enough to move the banner?"

"A few hours at least, probably best to move it to school and paint it here."

She avoids eye contact and continues to walk; Luka lags behind.

We reach the door to the science block, and she finally faces me. Electricity tingles my insides.

"Meet me at the gallery at lunch; that should give us time."

"Done." I grip the straps of my bag and smile, hoping she returns it. She does, but like she's been wrung of energy, it's faded, dull. I can't tell if it's because she doesn't want to be around me, or it's everything that's gone on, or it's Luka being annoying.

"Thanks, I really appreciate it," she says.

For a second, we stare at each other. People pass; the background noise is blurred.

"Oh so, okay, I'll be seeing you then," I say, and she heads outside towards the science tower.

Luka follows her, and I look back to see if there's any hint she's warmed to him, but they disappear out of view.

I race back to the toilet block, let Bear out for a pee, and make sure she's set up for the night. In the utility cupboard, I pull the suit off the hanger and roll up the pants, shirt, and jacket and place them into a plastic bag, then into my bag. I've got two hours till I need to be at the gallery.

I turn my attention to my portfolio for SOFA. I sit on the floor next to Bear, count the bombs good enough to be used for my application, and check the SOFA requirements: a minimum of ten pieces needed. I have seven. I pull out my sketchpad and force my focus on moving the pen around the paper, finishing the sketch I started in class.

It's finally time to leave and I bike towards town. Balls are lame, but not gonna lie, I'm amped. As I ride, I dream up ridiculous hypothetical and unrealistic ways this ball will play out. Me and Libby dancing, her happy ... to be with me ... What the hell has happened to me?

One block away from the Red Gallery Café, my path is blocked by a flower delivery truck. I wait as it backs into the drive of a florist shop. The truck stops, and a guy pulls open the side, lifts buckets of flowers in every colour onto the ground and begins ferrying them inside. Libby would love these. Would a bunch of stolen blooms be considered cute and thoughtful, or stupid? I grab a random selection and slide them in my bag; the flowers poke out the top and I ride through town.

My phone rings; I stop in Central Garden Square.

"Hello?"

"This is Dr Kali from the ER department at Saint Clements Hospital."

Twenty-Two

Dad is dead.

My body shakes and shivers, my ears ring, the sounds of the city blur. *Dad is dead* shouts, on repeat. I ride hard, gulp air in uncoordinated breaths, out of time with my techno heartbeat. Cars beep as I cut the intersection, gripping the handlebars tight, my fingernails piercing the skin on the palm of my hand. The pain does nothing to release the pressure in my chest.

Down Main Street cars speed past me. One intentional wrong twitch of my handlebars and I'd be free, the crushing weight gone. I wouldn't have to face his lifeless body, like I had to with Mum. The images is cemented forever – her taking her last breath, her eyes that rolled, her grey, lifeless face that would never speak and which I'd never see again; it'll torment me till the end of my days.

The hospital looms in front. I can't do it again. I carry on past.

I bike along the beach track, further out of town than I've ever biked before, until the track ends and the main road turns away from the coast and winds up a forested hill. I turn down Boulder Bank Beach Road. My chest heaves; it takes three gasped, forced breaths to inflate my lungs. The tears catch the wind and sting my eyes. I should have tried harder to get him help, to find him, to say sorry.

On one side of the road, houses sprinkle the grassy hills. On the other, paddocks with sheep and cows extend to the beach line. At the end of the road, I stop at a fish-and-chip shop slash dairy. Inside I pick up three bottles of wine and walk out unnoticed. I need to detach from reality. Right now, I'm teetering on crumbling ground above a black hole. What will happen when I fall is too unpredictable, too uncertain, the aftermath un-survivable.

Across the road, I lock my bike to a children's slide, wind the top off the bottle of red wine and skull the alcohol, which flows, warm and tingly. I pace around the kids' basketball court, pull my fist back and slam it into the concrete wall below the basketball hoop.

Searing pain radiates through my fingers and up my shoulder. Blood drips from the gashes onto the concrete as I gulp more wine till the bottle is empty and I crack open the next.

"I get it, Dad!" I yell. "You needed a break from your own brain."

I stumble down a track and through a thick hedge to the beach. Instead of sand, there are smooth stones, all different sizes. Waves rush in and crash on the shore, raking the pebbles, grinding them against each other.

Down the beach is a tepee made from long, weathered pieces of driftwood. I sit inside and skull till the bottle's empty; the view out to sea is perfectly out of focus, and reality is nearly on hold.

My phone beeps. And rings. Beeps and rings. I check my emails, but the words and their meaning are a blur.

This text is to confirm that your interview with SOFA is tomorrow at nine. Please check your confirmation email for further details as we have been unable to reach you at the previous address.

I'm probably hallucinating.

I stumble along the rocks back to the playground and drop the wine bottle in the empty rubbish bin. The glass shatters into a thousand pieces.

"We're all a bit broken, aren't we?" I can't tell if it's night or day, or remember where I am. Once the wine fully hits, I won't be able to walk.

I crawl under the hedge and lie down, using my bag as a pillow. The trees and stars wobble out of focus, and I pass out.

I bolt awake. Beams of first light stream through the tree canopy; the children's playground is dusted in white.

Dad is dead.

I'm flooded with memories. Every Sunday after footy practice, me and Dad would order hot chips if we had the cash, and eat them on this beach. We'd collect rocks and stack them in mounds, largest to smallest, Dad always with a beer in hand. It was just him and me while Mum worked. That was ten years ago, and there have been no moments like that since.

I crawl out from under the trees, wander the beach, pick up a rock and skim it into the ocean, though I use too much force and instead of bouncing it plops dead, lost at sea. I let the tears fall, let it all out, don't hold back, not because I'll miss him but because I'll never be able to change the fact that things didn't end right with us. I failed Mum.

I check my phone and ignore the missed calls and messages.

I re-read the SOFA interview message and see that my phone will run out of power at any second.

Dad was uncomplicated. He never spoke of having big dreams, or maybe he did. I never asked, and I'll never know. He seemed content with his life – to just exist. The polar opposite of me. At my core, I won't be satisfied if I don't at least fight for better.

I change into my ball clothes. My phone is flat.

I ride along the beach track, still drunk from last night. Bumper-to-bumper cars on the main road toot their horns as they hustle into a single lane; whoever is on the interview panel, I hope they're stuck in traffic.

SOFA Enrolments is etched on the giant frosted windows of the gallery where, inside, dreams happen. I wish I'd dragged Dad here, told him about SOFA. But the fact is, he wouldn't have come, or got it.

I open the heavy glass door to enrolments. My head pounds and my stomach churns, turning queasy somersaults.

"Dylan Marshall, here for the SOFA interview," I say to the receptionist, my voice cracking. The room is packed with interviewees and their support people; I suck in a purposeful breath and swallow hard.

The receptionist peers at me with kind eyes. "Take a seat; they'll come get you."

I take the seat furthest from anyone else. It looks out over the car park.

A car skids into a car park and lurches to a stop. Miss Reed bursts through the doors. How'd she know about the interview ... and, by her screwed up face, about Dad, too?

"Dylan," she gasps, sitting down next to me. "I'm so sorry about –"

Dad's dead, Dad's dead. I shake my head. "Shhh. Don't."

She eyes me up and down. "Right." I've never seen more pity in a look. "Have you been drinking?"

I don't answer. I can't. If she asks how I am, it's all over.

"You know you don't have to do –"

"Don't."

A lady with thick, black-rimmed glasses, wearing a mustard-coloured floaty skirt and white shirt walks down the glass corridor. Noticing these small details helps – the wood grain in the clipboard she's holding, her skirt swishing side to side with each step. The twelve different-coloured pencils in a mug on the receptionist's desk.

I'm about to go into a room to be judged by strangers, to see if I'm good enough. I'm not sure I can speak without my voice quivering, my outsides cracking and what's left spilling out.

"Dylan Marshall," the lady says to Miss Reed, as if they recognise each other.

"I'm Pam." The lady reaches out to shake my hand all formal-like.

Miss Reed stands. "I'll come? Be your support person." They stare, waiting for me to follow.

"No ... thanks." After the thing with Mr Campbell, I don't need another person judging me.

I follow Pam up a long, glass hall. The silence suffocating, the walk too long. *Dead. Dad is dead.* We turn into the last classroom.

A desk sits in front of a black brick wall with the words *SOFA is Art* in gold cut vinyl. The colours and the vinyl remind me of Libby and the ball. I park that for later. Sitting behind the desk is Mr Campbell. I do a double take. I'm at capacity, zero room left for more. My mind numbs like I'm watching a bird's-eye view of someone else's life about to fall apart.

"This way." Pam motions for me to take a seat in front of the interview panel.

I'm never going to see Dad ever again; he's dead, gone.

"Nerves can be mean, can't they?" Pam says.

I say nothing, avoid eye contact with Mr Campbell.

Pam grins. "Let me introduce you to the team. This is Mr Campbell; he will be taking over when I retire in a few weeks."

Mr Campbell holds out his hand, I shake it.

"Michael. He tutors our first-year programme," Pam says.

I shake his hand.

Pam looks down at the piece of paper in front of her. "Tell us about yourself."

Dad is dead, Dad is dead. I gulp tiny quivery breaths to inflate my lungs.

"Do you need a minute – a glass of water?" Pam passes me one.

Don't ask me if I'm okay. Don't ask.

"I'm a homeless street artist."

Surprise and confusion etch their faces. I could lie, be embarrassed, or tell the truth. But I'm done living a lie.

The silence isn't unexpected; it's more confronting for them than for me.

"Art is my life. It's not what I do; it's who I am." I know I'm being deep; they're lucky I'm not a blubbering mess, lucky I haven't mentioned Dad yet.

Pam looks directly at me. "I see. It must be extraordinarily tough. Is homelessness what motivates your art?"

"My work reflects my world, but to me, art motivates me to fight for a better life, to inspire others to do the same." I pause. "Sorry, I'm rambling."

"It's okay," Pam says. "Go on."

My voice quivers. "My point is, my art is a voice for those who don't have one."

Michael flicks through pages of my work, his face expressionless.

"I like to capture raw emotion and challenge people's misconceptions about homelessness to show we're imperfect beings with hopes and dreams, like everybody else."

Pam flicks through the folder. "Your art clearly reflects empathy."

Dad lived up to the stereotype. He wasted his life; I can't be what everyone believes homeless people to be.

Mr Campbell passes me tissues; I ignore the welling tears and push the box away. *I can be sad later.*

"I admire your passion for your work," Pam says.

Mr Campbell clears his throat. "Street art is often sprayed in illegal places; does that bother you?"

I can't pick his tone; he speaks as if we've never met before, and I appreciate that.

"I choose walls based on having the greatest emotional impact, not because that location is illegal to bomb."

Mr Campbell continues, "Being homeless would certainly be a barrier to studying with SOFA, especially storing and carrying out assignments. How would you get around this?"

"Being homeless hasn't stopped me from handing in all my schoolwork to you. I'm two pieces from completing the portfolio for school and the SOFA competition."

Mr Campbell shifts in his seat. "How will you cover fees if you're unsuccessful with the competition?"

"Find a full-time job; it's my only option."

"Managing a job and full-time study is quite a challenge for many of our students who don't have the added challenge of homelessness."

"I'm aware. I'm not unfamiliar with challenges; most of my life has been one challenge after another." I can't tell if Mr Campbell will make this harder or easier – he's in a privileged position; he could easily turn them off me.

After a round of questions about what majors I'll consider, they wrap up the interview. Shorter than I would have thought if they were *actually* considering me.

Pam escorts me down the glass corridor that overlooks the grass courtyard where me and Libby had coffee. "Once your portfolio and referee report is in, and we've had a chance to go over them, we'll let you know the outcome."

Back in the waiting room, Pam announces the name of the next person.

Miss Reed ushers me towards her car; I beeline for my bike. "I know it's god-awful," she says, "but you need to come to the hospital."

I ignore her, put my helmet on. Dad's grey, dead body lies in a chiller.

She rests her hand on my forearm. "You're in shock, and grief is a scary thing. Let me drive you. We can pick up some things; we can call whoever you like. It's going to be okay," Miss Reed says.

I can't stand it any longer. I jump on my bike and ride; it's all I know that makes sense.

Miss Reed yells, "Please let me help."

I ride towards the library, my lungs bordering on collapse. I dump my bike behind the bush and climb the fire escape. All my work has been painted over in black – the portraits of Mum, Bear, Dad. My life, gone, empty. I peer down at the library car park, at the spot the Mitsi was towed, me red hot and fuming, him drinking his life away. It must have been hard knowing it was his fault Mum died, the burden too suffocating. He gave up on life, and I never once asked how he was. We ignored it; that was our deal. I could have done more.

I look for details in the view from the rooftop – the swirling clouds over the sea. I count the buildings around Central Garden Square, and stop at Libby's apartment, where we fell in paint and Libby snort-laughed. I spot the seat in Central Garden Square we sat at when Libby was drunk, and remember the moment she filled me with technicolour.

A van parks below and the driver steadies an elderly lady out and onto the footpath.

I lean over and shout, "I love you, Libby Green." Weight rises from my shoulders, the weight of the universe lifts from my chest, and I'm feather-light, and for the first time all day, I can breathe with the full capacity of my lungs.

The elderly lady looks up. "Isn't that lovely? Grab that girl and never let her go." And she fists-pumps the air.

A man pokes his head out the van window. "Never stop telling her, that's the key."

THE ART OF LOVING LIBBY GREEN

It's dark by the time I climb down the fire escape and ride to the servo to charge my phone. I ignore all messages; all she knows is I let her down, left her to manage alone with the ball stuff. I flick through her messages, the photo I sent of Bear. She's all I've got left.

I dial Miss Reed's number. I don't have to say anything.

"Where are you? I'll pick you up."

"The library. Can you pick up Bear from here?" And I attach directions to the old stadium, the closest listed address to the tent.

"Sure, on my way."

Her car pulls up, she gets out and launches her arms around me. "I was so worried about you."

I let myself sink into the hug. Bear pops her head out the window, and I can't hold it together any longer.

"Dad's dead."

She releases the hug, grips my shoulders, face to face. "Yes, sweets. But I'm going to be here always, every step of the way."

And I can't hold it in any longer and gushes of tears let go. I grip onto Bear and take the front seat.

"For you," she says, motioning to the bag on the back seat.

Inside are clothes and tissues, dog food.

"So, I've told the school you'll be away the next few days while we make arrangements, and that brings you to exam week, so officially, you have no classes."

"Thanks." I barely have the energy to speak.

We pull up to a white weatherboard house; there's a veranda with five hanging flower baskets.

"I thought a sleep ..." She pauses. "And tomorrow we go to the hospital."

I nod and follow her inside, to her spare room. Dinner sits on the desk, covered with a plate; a clean towel rests on the corner of the made-up bed.

A bunch of street-art mags and books are on the bed. Miss Reed picks them up. "For you." Out of the wardrobe, she pulls a plush dog bed, and Bear immediately climbs in.

"You're welcome to stay as long as you need."

Mr Campbell appears in PJs dotted with surfboards. "Really, bud, it's all good." Easy-going, genuine. Like he's a different person.

Why are they so lovely? I don't get it; they don't have to. I've bombed about people having empathy for street people for so long. Is this what it feels like? Is this it?

Twenty-Three

I sit on the edge of Miss Reed's spare bed; it's my third morning here. Today, I bury Dad next to Mum.

At the hospital, when it came time to view his body, to say goodbye, I couldn't force myself to step into the room. I'm not sure if I'll regret it or not. I'd rather my last memory was of him alive.

Miss Reed knocks at the door. "You ready?"

I don't say anything. I'll never be ready for this.

Mr Campbell and Miss Reed never push me to talk, never crowd me, but there's always someone here checking in.

Miss Reed organised a grant from the government to cover Dad's burial. I know people will be there, but I don't know who or how many. I study the painting of the Buddha on Miss Reed's wall, the purposeful peeling gold paint.

"It's time to go?" I focus on the wallpaper, its intricate texture, a train-track pattern of eggshell white, only noticeable if you look closely.

Miss Reed sits next to me. She doesn't say anything – she doesn't have to. I know Dad's body is on its way to the gravesite, and we need to be there before all the people arrive, before Dad. My core shivers; none of this feels real and I can't bring myself to move.

We drive along Beach Highway. The sea's flat; seagulls circle a boat – I count eleven, I wish there were thousands.

Mr Campbell turns off towards the cemetery. I count the trees along the passenger side, weeping willows like upturned umbrellas, thirty-six.

Like in a horror film, that moment before someone is stabbed and you know it's about to happen. It's horrific, but the worst is yet to come.

We stop next to the hearse; Miss Reed's face says it all.

Out of the car, my focus firmly on the ground, we walk past the hearse, its fat, black, shiny tyres. I fixate on Bear, matching her prancing pace, blissfully unaware of who she's lost, till the path ends and there are legs and feet, and the voices silence. The path is made of crushed white stones, and I want to count every single one till everyone leaves.

Black basketball boots – Marv. Gumboots – Jack. Steel caps – Ginge. Black suede heels – unidentified. And white Chucks – Libby is here.

I look up at her and she waves gently, mouths, *Hey*.

Everyone stares, all the same downcast, sombre faces.

Marv leans in for a hug. "So sorry, bro."

Ginge squeezes my shoulder. "Thought we'd pay our respects."

I have no words, the coffin right there, the dug hole, my legs jelly, my mind too, ready to pass out, I *want* to pass out.

Francesca wraps her arms around me in a warm, all-encompassing hug. I sink in, not because it feels right; it's awkward, but I've got no energy to fight.

Francesca pulls away. And there's Libby, right there.

She wraps her arms around me; we sink into each other, melded together. "I'm so sorry."

"Thanks for coming."

She smiles, then stands back with Francesca.

Miss Reed hangs close as the funeral dude takes his place. He makes a short speech. As they lower Dad in the hole, I dig the nails of my forefingers into the side of my thumb, the sting a relief. I swallow hard as the coffin hits the ground, then the dam breaks and tears roll down my cheeks. The funeral guy asks if anyone wants to say a few words; there's silence, uncomfortable and testifying to Dad's uselessness. I want to step forward and say something good about him, to let people know he wasn't all bad, but my feet are frozen to the ground, my tongue stuck.

The funeral dude clears his throat and thanks everyone for coming. I pick up a handful of earth and throw it onto his coffin.

I have no one.

I wasn't aware that everyone would meet at the tent after the funeral. I turn behind Miss Reed's car to see Francesca and Marv following behind, in the same car.

"Do they have to come to the tent, too?"

"It's going to be okay; there's a wee thing that everyone's pitched in for, you'll see."

It's kind of them, but everyone, including Libby, will see where and how I've been living. Does Miss Reed know how crazy that is? Dad would hate it.

We pull up into the car park, where Dad would usually park, next to the toilet block. The Mitsi sits there, abandoned and lonely, full of beer bottles – all that's left of Dad. The word *Home* is bombed on the wall.

"I can tell them to go if you want me to."

But everyone has already parked and is out of their cars.

"It's okay." It's really not okay.

On the grass, next to the toilet block, all of Dad's empty bottles are gone. Fairy lights hang in the trees, and three picnic tables are laid out with tablecloths, plates of food and pitchers of lemonade with real lemon pieces. Mr Campbell loads things from a chilly bin onto the table. After everything I've done to him, he's here helping me.

"Dylan," Miss Reed whispers, "I can tell them to go."

"It's okay." I swallow hard, blown away by their kindness, embarrassed they know this is how I live, in a toilet block.

Miss Reed opens the car door, nods, and we climb out.

Marv plays some music through his mini speaker, some chill beats that do a good job of brightening the mood. Mr Campbell passes me a plate. Everyone sits around the table, Libby opposite me. I know this is food from Francesca's café, and Marv has brought the tables from the souvlaki hut. I can't bring myself to eat as I look at each face, here to support me.

I can feel Libby watching me; everyone else is deep in conversation. I don't look up. She glances towards the bathroom; the door's open, revealing part of the tent. *Yes, that's where I live.*

After everyone has eaten, Francesca and Libby pack the leftover food into the chilly bin. Libby carries it over to me. "For you – it should keep you going a while. Where should I put it?"

I know she's nice. And it's sweet, but now that she knows the true me, the person who lives in an abandoned public toilet, I'm exposed, inside out, naked, like she can see right through me. Where does she expect me to put the food?

I take it into the toilet block and stick it in the corner of the tent. As I turn, I see her face. She stands at the door, looks in. She can't even step inside.

For a second, as I pass her on my way out the door, there's this "who goes first" thing. She leans back into the side of the door rather than stepping out, and we're face to face, jammed in the door. Electricity fires every cell.

"Oh, cool. So hey, um ... yeah ... okay," she says.

Isn't that how I'm supposed to feel?

"Err so, yeah, hey, um, well ..." she repeats, not moving. We're both frozen. "We're heading off, so I guess I'll see you at graduation." And she steps out from the doorway.

Since there are no more classes left, and seniors are officially on study leave, there's no occasion to bring us together, no reason to be at school, no excuse to see her.

"Yeah, I guess."

And there's a look from her I can't read. Our eyes do that held-connected look; I'm flooded with all the gushy feels for her, and it doesn't feel finished between us, for me at least. Hell, things didn't even get started.

Francesca joins us, breaking Libby's gaze. Her attention drifts back to the toilet block.

"Bye." Francesca gives me a giant hug, which is a tad awkward considering I know her the least out of everyone here.

"Thanks, both of you." I look up at Libby. "For the food and for coming."

Libby smiles briefly and heads to the car.

It takes me half an hour to convince Miss Reed that I'm okay to be alone, that I want – need – to be alone. After she checks that my phone has enough battery power and texts me to make sure I have her number, even though I've had it for years, she leaves.

Everyone is gone, apart from Miss Reed and Mr Campbell, who are camped out in their car just down the road. It's cute how they think I don't know. I can make out their headlights, which flick on and off every now and then to check what I'm doing.

I go through Dad's box of stuff: clothes, dirty washing, his lighter and an empty packet of tobacco; that's what his whole life amounted to. He's been gone four days. In some ways, it feels like four seconds, in others it's like he was never really here – he died when Mum did. I don't know how long I'll stay here; it's my way to say goodbye. I've no clue where I'll end up or how I'll get there, but anything is better than here.

I spend the night thinking of ways to apologise to Mr Campbell. For so long I've been bombing about empathy, and it turns out I could show some. Before the sun rises, I bike to his shop.

Behind me is a massive blank advertising board in front of a construction site – the new arts wing. Part of SOFA dwarfs Mr Campbell's art shop. I have an idea that hopefully will reek of me being sorry and show my thanks.

I drop my bag in front of the sign, take the pre-cut stencils and tape them in position. The spray fills in the gaps. I use black to overlay details of a bold, brightly coloured forest, the words *Mr Campbell's Art Supplies* set in flowers. I'm pumped with how it's turned out. I stand in his car park; the sign pops and it's a shame about his shabby shop front. *EVERYTHING MUST GO, CLOSING DOWN* is written on cardboard and taped to the window. I'm going to bring the love back. I repeat the same bomb on his shop front window. It looks mint, eye-catching, like a new shop that an artist would want to enter. I hope he likes it, that he takes it for the apology it's supposed to be.

Twenty-Four

Monday rolls around, the deadline for my portfolio. Prize-giving is on Friday. This is my last week of school ever. I need to edit my images and write a five-hundred-word essay to go with the application. The worst bit is, I gotta be my own referee.

I park outside the school library. Inside, I spot zero seniors; most go home to study, only coming to school if they have to.

Using the school computer, I collate all the photographs of my work into one file and log onto the SOFA portal, checking I have everything I need for my application.

The library fills with juniors, the class a hum of noise in the background. I tap my pen as I think of the two hundred words explaining why I should get into SOFA.

I don't deserve a place at SOFA any more than anyone else. I'm not going to tell you a sob story or preach about my inflated talent. But I can say, if given a place, it wouldn't be wasted. I'm eager to grow as an artist. Most people want

221

to get into SOFA so more people can see their art. That's up there for me, but I'd instead use my art to make people feel. In a harsh and critical world, I want to challenge the critics to feel empathy and let those being judged feel seen and heard.

I check and re-check what I've written, re-count the images and hover over the green *Submit Application* button, hoping it's enough, that I'm enough, that the impossible might be possible. I use the school address for the home address; I could mention that accepting me into SOFA would mean I'd no longer be homeless, but who wants to get in with pity? I've been honest with my work and my words, so the rest is up to them. I attach all the required documents and hit *Submit.*

There's nothing more I can do but wait. I tap my pen on the desk, re-log into the SOFA portal, application status: *Pending approval.*

All the hype of creating works and meeting the deadline gave me a target. Being productive fuelled hope that each new piece I added to my portfolio was taking me a step closer. Now it's done, there's nothing left but to wait. It's anticlimactic. My application is one of thousands and getting in is a long shot; now it feels like I'm waiting for the inevitable, crushing let down.

Katie turns up, guitar case in one hand. "Hey." With her foot she pushes the loose carpet by my chair.

"Hi." I look behind her, not expecting to see Libby since they no longer seem to be friends. It's more wishful thinking.

"She still won't talk to me."

"Sorry." It's awkward. It was her fault, and I'm not sure what to say to make her feel better.

Katie looks at the computer screen. "Great, you applied." She smiles, and I feel like it's genuine. "Libby always said your work was amazing."

"She did?" My voice is a tad more upbeat than I intended, my nerves tingling.

"You know she organised all the ball setup, then left ten minutes after it started? Her mum came and picked her up; she got all dressed up for nothing."

"That sucks." She'd been so excited about going, had planned the ball for months. She had playlists and mood boards; her words, *it was going to be the best night ever.* I'm partly responsible for killing her ball dream, and she'll never get that night back. There are no do-overs when it comes to senior balls.

"You've just given me the best idea."

Katie looks confused.

"Hey, I've got to go, but are you around later? I might need your help with something. It's Libby related."

"Yeah, sure."

Twenty-Five

It's the evening of prize-giving, and I race through town. A truck passes me, street cones on the back, neon orange signs with *EVENT* written in black. I cut through Garden Square; a crane has lifted a massive skull on top of the clock tower. Yellow, red, blue, purple and pink flowers cover its head. Sparkling diamantes circle its eyes. A banner with *Día De Los Muertos* – the Day of the Dead festival – hangs from the skull.

At graduation, they'll announce the winners of the SOFA comp. *The Day of the Dead* is fitting. It all comes down to tonight. I have no other plan. I'll get into SOFA and live the dream, or I won't, and I'll do something else. What, I have zero clue.

At the bottom of the clock tower is a band of guys in Mexican hats, white shirts tucked in, silver discs sown down the sides of their black pants. The guy playing the guitar leans into the microphone – "Testing, testing" – and plays a crazy-fast riff.

I bike down Main Street, congested with people dressed for the Day of the Dead festival and students from school heading to prize-giving.

I push the buzzer at the crossing; across the road, the event centre is lit up like a beehive. My gut rumbles, from both hunger and nerves.

When I reach Miss Reed, who's wearing a vest with *USHER*, she engulfs me in a hug while directing the swarm through the door, beyond which is a sea of uniforms.

"You're at the back." She points to the far back row. "Once everyone's in, I'll come sit with you." Since the whole Dad thing, she checks in a lot, brings me food, and it's okay.

As I walk down the centre of the hall, gossip and laughter echo off the walls. I search the crowd for Libby. No sign of her. I take my seat, the entire school in front of me. The seat next to me is empty.

Miss Reed shuts the doors to the hall and, as far as I can see, Libby isn't here yet. I check my watch. It's already five minutes past when prize-giving was supposed to start.

A whoop of excitement rises from the other seniors; cheers, the excitement thick.

More whoops and hollers. I get it – the last day of school – for them a whole new adventure awaits, they have only good options to choose from.

Katie is two rows in front. I pull out my phone.

"Put that away." Miss Reed takes the seat next to me.

I turn my back to her and text Katie: *Libby?*

I watch her, but she's too busy chatting and the hall is too loud to hear her phone.

The stage lights flick on, and the lights over the audience dim.

"Good luck," Miss Reed whispers. "Exciting!" She says it like she's twelve, silently clapping her hands.

Mr Anderson takes the stage as the seniors and teachers in their gowns and hats fill the back-row seats. Cheers erupt from the rows in front. I spot Luka and crane my neck to see if Libby is with him; she's not, but there's an empty seat next to him.

Mr Anderson steps up to the microphone. "Good evening, students and families. Welcome to our awards ceremony and final assembly for this school year." His voice booms through the hall, followed by hoots, cheers and whistles.

I fiddle with the two middle buttons on my shirt and straighten the folds of my cuffs. I look to Katie, but her focus is on the stage. I avert my attention to the double doors – the only entry to the prize-giving – now shut. My stomach churns.

Mr Anderson goes on about the year ending and the start of new beginnings. He welcomes the juniors on stage to perform a song from *The Sound of Music*: "The Hills are Alive," butchered to death.

It finally ends, and the juniors line up and bow. Parents hold up their phones and click photos. I look at the door, willing Libby to walk in.

Mr Anderson takes the stage and hands out the junior awards.

My phone beeps, and nearly the entire row in front turns and glares.

"Turn it off," Miss Reed whispers.

Why is she not here?

Mr Anderson announces the last junior award. As the recipient takes to the stage, there's a crack of light from the hall door opening, and I spot Libby and Francesca. They duck down and sit with the juniors at the front. I'm relieved.

"And now we move on to the senior awards." Mr Anderson goes through history and art history, geography ... "And that brings us to the sciences."

The microphone squeals. I look to where I think Libby and her mum are sitting, but there are too many people to see.

"Top in chemistry ..."

Luka accepts his award. I can't bring myself to clap, and I wonder if Libby is. But as I watch him receive his award, proud, I realise I'm being shallow. Maybe his douchebag-ness is a cover. Everyone's battling something. I mean, he earned it. So I clap for Luka.

Miss Reed gives me a "what?" look.

"And the next three awards remarkably go to the same person." I'm nervous for Libby; I know this means so much to her. "Top in biology, statistics, and physics ..." My leg jiggles, and I move to the edge of my seat. It takes an eternity for him to speak. I roll my fists down onto my thighs. "Top in biology, statistics, and physics is ... Libby Green."

I let out, "Woohoo!" and clap furiously.

Francesca jumps up, pulls Libby up by the hand, and hugs her tight. As the crowd claps, I stand, woohoo for a second before too many faces stare, and sit back on my seat, pulled down by Miss Reed.

"She did it," I say. "I knew she would."

Libby walks on stage as Katie and I clap like idiots. Luka sits with slumped shoulders and glances back, giving me the stink eye. I brush it off.

"And Libby is off to medical school next year," Mr Anderson announces. Libby takes the three certificates and returns to her seat.

"And now for the senior art awards."

I dig my thumbnail into my thumb and try to break the skin.

Miss Reed turns to me and beams. "Good luck; I so want this for you."

I want this for me. It could change everything. My heart races, my leg jiggles, faster and faster.

Mr Anderson says, "I'd like to introduce Pam from the SOFA."

The words ring through me, vibrate every cell. Pam takes the stage and talks about how there were five hundred entries from all over the country submitted to the SOFA competition.

"First and third prizes have been awarded to students at your school. We'll start with third prize."

I ball my fists, scrunch my face, keep one eye closed, the other on the stage.

She opens an envelope and pulls out a card. Someone sniffs, someone else coughs. I peek out of the corner of my eye and catch Miss Reed watching me.

Silence. Third wouldn't get the halls of residence, so it wouldn't help me be un-homeless, but it's still a place. Pam fumbles with opening the envelope. I wanna jump up and tear that thing open.

Pam puts her mouth to the speaker. "Winner of the third prize and a scholarship place, fees covered for a fine arts degree at SOFA, is ... Marie Wilson."

My heart sinks. I look at my legs. I can't look at Miss Reed or tilt my head in Libby's direction. The chance of me winning third is higher than first. The hall is filled with clapping and cheers as Marie walks onstage and collects her prize. As she smiles, her proud parents click their phones, snapping pictures to mark the start of her new incredible life, photos they'll proudly pull out later to show off their daughter's not-sucking-at-life-ness. At least with no family here, there are fewer people for me to disappoint.

Marie walks off stage after thanking her supportive family. As she says "family," the word vibrates me into reality. I'd love for Dad to have been here, but I know he'd never have shown up.

"And now for the first-place winner."

Pam goes on about how the winner had exceeded expectations and is the first of his kind of talent to be awarded, that the skill and attention to detail are what blew them away.

"The winner of first prize, and a three-year scholarship including one year in the halls of residence is ..."

Miss Reed grabs my hand, holds it tight. I squeeze my eyes shut, waiting for this bit to be over, jealous already of who has won, and I'm not even sure who that person is.

"And the winner is …" Paper rustles. "Dylan Marshall."

Miss Reed squeals; someone up front squeals. Miss Reed wraps her arms around me. I'm not sure why I'm not dancing around in circles, clapping furiously like everyone else. My heart pounds through my ears. I look towards the front and see Francesca and Libby standing up, clapping. I make eye contact with Libby, all the noise in the background a hum, and we smile at each other. And the electricity, the light, the colour is raging.

I'm genuinely lost for words. Instead of flustered excitement, I'm overcome with relief, like a hurricane has passed through, and now the sea is calm, flat, warm.

"Go, go – they're waiting for you." Miss Reed pushes me forward.

"… and we'd like Dylan to come up and say a few words, wherever you are."

I walk down the aisle with a vibe of how I imagine those chilled-out Buddhist statues feel, zoned out, content.

I pass Katie. She mouths, *Go you.*

Even with a million eyes on me, right now, for the first time, I'm sure of what I want to do with my life, where I'm heading and what I need to do to get there: Art, and Libby. I walk up the steps on stage as images from my portfolio appear on the back wall. I know Libby's watching. As I take the last step to Pam, the bomb appears of Libby at the train station with hearts floating out her mouth and down the side wall. I avoid looking at her. Part of me can't wait to see her reaction; the other doesn't want to ruin the moment, in case she's not feeling it for me.

Pam whispers, "Love your work, Dylan. You deserve this; you're a true artist."

She hands me the certificate, and I can't believe the words written on it: *Winner of the SOFA Scholarship Competition, including one year in the halls of residence.* Wherever Dad is, he'd have to be proud; at least I pretend he would have been. I know Mum would be.

Pam reads from her notes. "Dylan's work was chosen because it showed excellent technique and mastery of his chosen medium, street art, but he does it with such honesty, integrity, and the professional care and skill of a true artist. And now, Dylan will say a few words."

On the one hand, I know exactly what to say; on the other, there's too many to thank. With too much to say, I don't know where to begin. The school has uncovered my life, my true identity. I look back at another of my bombs projected on the wall – the tent, the toilet, *Home* bombed on the toilet block wall. My life lived homeless. They know the truth, and I don't care. In a way, accepting my truth has set me free.

"I'd like to thank Miss Reed, Mr Campbell, and Libby. Without your help, it wouldn't have been possible. Libby, thank you for everything." I can't believe I just said that in front of the entire school. There's a second of silence, maybe two, and a whole bunch of "awwws."

I look out to Libby. But the light shining onto the stage is too blinding, and I'm unable to see her face.

I end it there, and step off the stage, carrying my certificate. As I walk down the middle of the hall back to my seat, I pass where Libby and Francesca were sitting – their seats are empty. Miss Reed stands at the end of the row, and she swings her arms around me. Mr Anderson takes the stage, and the hall is back to quiet.

I slide into my seat, next to Miss Reed's empty one. There's a bunch of whispered "awwws" from down the hall, and I see Libby edging her way down the aisle as half the school turns to face us.

"We'll wait till everybody is seated," says Mr Anderson.

And there she is.

Libby sits next to me in Miss Reed's seat. My heart motors. We've not yet looked at each other; both of us stare at the front stage, aware that people keep turning to look at us.

I watch the stage. She leans close. "So happy for you. Congrats." She leans down to her bag and pulls out the crown and moustache on a stick that we made for the ball, and passes me the crown. The hall is silent. I hold the crown above my head. Libby grins, giggles, her spare hand over her mouth. She lifts the moustache above her lip, and my grin turns to laughter.

My phone vibrates, a message from Katie. *You two are ridiculous; you know we can hear you down here, right?*

I don't care.

PS are we still on for the plan tonight?

I reply *most definitely, I hope she likes it.*

Katie: *only one way to find out.*

"And that concludes our ceremony." Mr Anderson steps off the stage, followed by the teachers in single file, the school song playing. The hall lights flick on. There's officially no more school, no reason for us to hang out, apart from the thing I've planned with Katie's help, which could go wrong. I'm not sure if it's winning the competition, but confidence might be my new thing.

I turn to Libby. "I was going to ask if –"

But Francesca interrupts. "Libby," she says, "we've got to go, we have to pack." She puts her phone to her ear. I realise she looks different – no makeup. "Sorry to interrupt, Dylan. Massive congrats, so deserved. But we have a flight to catch," she finishes, her voice subdued.

Libby raises her hand in a half-hearted wave. "So … I'll be seeing ya then."

And I watch them walk away.

Mr Campbell jumps in and shakes my hand, blocking my view of Libby.

"Thank you. I couldn't have done it without all of you," I say, my focus on Libby and Francesca.

Mr Campbell pats me on the back. "I think Francesca's mum passed away last night, they're bound for London tomorrow morning."

"Oh."

"So," Mr Campbell says, "about that spare room of ours." He looks at Miss Reed. "It's yours if you want it, till the halls of residence open, but I'll need some help in the shop to pay for your board. Turns out we're swamped after someone redecorated."

A grin spreads from one side of my face to the other.

"Deal." A home and a scholarship in one night – whoop whoop.

"We're heading back now; you want a lift?" He digs into his pocket and pulls out a door key. Hands it to me. A freaking key to a house, as if this night could get better.

"Wow, thank you."

He searches my face. "You're all right, mate. Congratulations."

I look over at Libby and Francesca as they walk out of the hall. "Mind if I come later? I've got something I need to do."

Mr Campbell looks at me, then at Libby and back at me. "Righty, yes, I see, of course. You go celebrate." He smiles and pats me on the back. "Not too late, okay?" He expects me to stay with them. That last comment might piss off some people, but he wants me to stay; he expects me back.

"Definitely."

We follow the crowd out.

Up ahead, Libby stands at the lights with her arm around her mum. I want to call her back, tell her to come with me. But as the buzzer goes, I don't follow them across. There's a family crisis going on; Francesca's upset. It's not the right time.

I text Katie and Marv: *It's go time.*

Marv: *On it.*

Katie: *Fingers crossed, it's the sweetest surprise, she's gonna love it if I can get her there.*

There's always an *if.*

Twenty-Six

I walk my bike through crowds of people, the festival raging, faces painted as skulls, jewels dotting their eyes. I head towards the library.

From out of the car, I grab my paints, ball costume, and a bunch of other supplies.

It's nine p.m. and I've got a lot to do. I climb the fire escape to the rooftop; I wish Dad could be here. On the stairwell wall, the first thing you see as you climb the fire escape, I spray an outline of me and Libby, comic-book style, a close-up of our faces, my lips pressed to hers, our eyes closed.

From the roof I can see the packed Garden Square, the city lights and the beach in the distance. Music from the band vibrates in the air. The stars are out in force. I unroll the blanket from my bag. I unlock the padlocked door to the stairwell, and I'm stoked to see some of my stuff is still there – the fairy lights, a small beat-up table. I wind the fairy lights around the edge of the blanket and set up the table to one side, resting my speaker on it.

I change into my ball costume, cleaned, thankfully, by Miss Reed: the shirt, the waistcoat, the jacket, even the shoes. From the 7-Eleven next door, I'd bought grape juice, plastic wineglasses, and chocolate. Mum would approve. I set the grape juice and glasses out on the table.

I check my phone. No message from Katie to tell me how things are going.

A message from Marv: *We're slammed at the mo, will get there as soon as.*

With my bag of sprays, I climb back down the fire escape. On the wall, someone has left a bunch of unfinished noughts and crosses games. I look at the time on my phone: 9.50. It's a big ask for Libby to come out tonight; an even bigger question is if Katie will be able to get her here.

I stare up at the wall and spray across one of the squares, finishing the game off. She probably can't make it. What was I thinking? The hype of winning the competition has carried me this far. Doubt sinks in – I mean, her grandmother died, and she's about to jump on a long-haul flight to the other side of the world. It's unlikely she'd show, even if she is keen to come, and it's a legit excuse if she's not.

If Libby doesn't show, I won't know for sure how she feels. If it's me or she just can't make it.

I finish two more noughts and crosses games, spraying an X in one and nought in the other, and a line through the row, finishing both. And really, it's a distraction. At 10.46 I check Facebook and see she's online; she's awake, looking at her phone. I told Katie ten-ish, if possible. She's forty-six minutes late, and there's no text to say she will or won't come.

I respray some grids, the black can hissing its last few drops as I force it on the wall.

And then, from behind, "Can I play?"

I drop my spray can; it rolls towards Libby's feet.

She's dressed in a gold sequin dress, plunging back and front, and a necklace drops down her chest. Katie managed to get her here in her ball gear – I'm not sure how, but our plan worked.

My chest swells. "You are so beautiful." The words float out like I'm worried she'll go before I get a chance to say them. My body tingles; all I can focus on is her, like nothing else exists.

She swishes side to side, and the tassels from the knee down swish with her. Her hair is loose, parted at one side, the light-pink waves hanging over her shoulders.

She scans her eyes over me from top to bottom. "You look handsome."

I can't take my eyes off her. Her smile, it glows.

She's in bare feet with a toe ring, which makes me love her even more.

"My shoes hurt my feet."

I'm so filled up right now, warm with love, I desperately want to grab her hand, pull her towards me.

"Sorry about your gran. I didn't think you'd be able to make it."

"Mum's finally getting some sleep. Gran died last night. We leave first thing tomorrow to sort the funeral arrangements." Libby folds her arms; they're covered in goosebumps.

I take off my jacket and hold it out for her. She comes close, turns around and slips in each arm.

"Why are we here?" She picks up a spray can and sprays a cross inside the last game, puts a line through it.

"You'll see."

Marv turns up, carrying a bag of food. He hands it to me. "Thanks, man."

As I take it, he's already turning around. "Gotta go, bro; nice to see you, Libby."

"And you." She cranes her neck to see where he's gone, but he's disappeared.

"Follow me." I climb the fire escape.

Libby looks around. "Are we allowed up there?"

I pause on the first rung of the ladder. "No."

She follows me anyway.

At the top, the first thing we see is the wall with us kissing. It's not immediately obvious it's us.

She stares at the wall, then takes a closer look. "It looks like yours, but there's no *Xavier* sprayed in the corner. Very similar to your style though – crazy, aye."

I grab the can out of her hand and spray *Xavier*. I laugh.

She looks down at the bag of spray paint resting by the blanket. I set out the food on the table and she watches me, looking back to the bomb, to the table, the picnic I'm setting up. Either she's figured it out and isn't saying anything, or she doesn't want to be here.

"I'm sorry about your dad."

We kneel, leaning over the edge, looking at the view.

I pass her my phone. "You choose the music."

I watch her face turn to a grin. "Did you copy my ball folder?"

"The ones I could remember that were on the list." I laugh. "All of them are terrible, so they're easy to remember."

She laughs. "Really? Well, you're in for a doozy." And she hits *Play*.

A cheesy love ballad plays, and it's perfect. I open the boxes of food.

"I know you like these, but I didn't know what kind." I open the mixed takeaway platters of shaved meat, salads, rice, hummus, pieces of pita bread. Marv's put in a bag of baklava.

Her eyes bulge, and she immediately digs a fork in. "You're the best; I'm starving. I've barely eaten all day."

As I pass her a drink, there's that eye thing, where it's like we're magnets, energy gravitating to each other. I grab a blanket from my bag, shake it out, and lay it over our legs. We sit next to each other, eating, laughing, the conversation easy. I'm as close as I can be without touching. As she looks down at the car park, words bubble up – so many things I want to say; that she makes me feel alive, happy.

We finish our food, and her hand rests on her lap. I want to grab it, pull her close.

A car toots in the car park below.

"Hurry up, Libs! It's past my curfew," Katie screams out her mum's car window.

Libby laughs. "Didn't take long for her to get annoying again."

I'm assuming things are okay between them; it feels good to be part of that.

"Not sure I've forgiven her, but this makes it easier." She gives me a look and glances down at Katie.

"Would you hurry up already!" Katie yells, beeping the car horn in one long blast.

At the same time, Libby and I laugh and call, "Shut up, Katie!"

"I can't be grounded," she shouts. "I'm going to hold the horn down and not let go till you get in the car." The horn continues its long beep.

"Oh my god, you're annoying," Libby yells over the edge.

The horn stops.

She looks at me. "I can't stay too long. I don't want Mum to be alone if she wakes upset."

I'm unsure where the confidence comes from, but I grab her hand.

"Go," Libby yells. She links her fingers with mine.

I pull her up. For a second, we stare at each other. Then I tow her in, and our bodies press against each other, my arms gliding around her waist. Our bodies fit together perfectly. An instinctive thing takes over. My eyes close and I kiss her, our lips soft together, and she kisses me back. Standing on the roof, the music, the entire sky, and stars out in force watching from above. All the energy powering the universe flows in and around, igniting us with every colour imaginable.

Twenty-Seven

"When was the last time you wore shorts?" Libby asks, smirking and staring down at my legs. Then she goes back to inspecting the photos of Miss Reed and her family on the wall of my bedroom.

"Woo, there's a lot of reflection in here." Miss Reed stands in the doorway, covering her eyes. "Blinding." When Libby's here, Miss Reed and Mr Campbell have an open-door policy. "You two ready?" She holds a picnic blanket under her arm and a chilly bin in the other.

"You guys are quite the comedians, ha ha." I pretend to be angry, doing my best sarcastic look. The truth is, I can't remember the last time I wore shorts; I haven't owned a pair in years.

Libby pulls down her sunnies. "It's just so bright." Dimples pop, one in each cheek. She's adorable.

We pull up to the SOFA car park. People in shorts, carrying picnic chairs and chilly bins, flow into the main entrance. Music blares from speakers. The arts festival is held every year before the first semester begins; SOFA opens

240

its galleries to the public and provides a band and food trucks. And every year, I've avoided it. But this year, I'm part of it; Libby, too.

I grab Libby's hand, and we all walk past the administration block, the green space between the café and galleries set with picnic hampers and blankets. A tiny lady with a big voice sings.

Libby sits next to me, her folded legs leaning on mine as we listen to the music.

"Show me around." Libby holds out one hand.

"You've been here a hundred times."

She shushes me and whispers, "I want an excuse to kiss you in private."

We walk hand in hand; I pull her into a gap between two galleries and plant a kiss on her lips. When we part, I swing my arm around her shoulders.

The public gallery is grand, with SOFA alumni displayed on the walls. I stop at a colourful oil abstract; up close, its dots and brush strokes are amassed in colour. From afar, it's a portrait.

"Susan Marshall" – I lean in and kiss Libby's cheek – "meet Libby Green, my girlfriend."

Libby's brows lower. "Who are you talking to?"

"Mum. That's her self-portrait, right there."

Libby steps up to the painting, peering at the image. "It's amazing."

A sense of pride overwhelms me. "Yep, my mum's work."

"Aww, she'd be so proud of you."

"Yeah, she would be."

About the Author

BELLEBIRD JAMES is the author of *The Art of Loving Libby Green* and *Bloom*. She lives in Nelson, New Zealand, with her husband, two children, and an excessively hairy dog named Sir Fluffy Pants. Coffee enthusiast, sun chaser, and recovering chocolate fish addict. When Bellebird's not reading or writing, she can be found hurtling down a mountain bike trail (badly).

bellebirdjames.com
Instagram: @bellebirdjames

If you liked The Art of Loving Libby Green, you'll love Bloom!